"He ran after m_____
catwalk—Gar_____

Stevie went on, in spite of Allister's efforts to stop her. "I remember thinking that if I could beat him outside and get into my car, I'd be safe. But then he was right behind me."

"Stevie, you don't have to—"

"Allister! Allister, wait! I remember...when I fell, just before I blacked out, I saw him again. He was leaning over me. The catwalk...it was dark, and his face was in shadow. But I remember him coming closer.... And then I saw a scar."

"A scar?" Allister couldn't breathe. He pulled away from Stevie, needing space. This couldn't be happening. A kind of excitement lit up her expression now—excitement at her newfound memory.

"On the man's face." She drew a finger along her left temple, and as he watched her, it felt as though an invisible icy finger touched his own temple where the ragged scar indelibly marked him.

ABOUT THE AUTHOR

Although Morgan Hayes has never suffered temporary blindness, she suspects that blindness, whether temporary or not, is a condition that many people have pondered at least once in their lives. And she thought it would be a fascinating challenge to experience it through one of her characters, especially a photographer whose livelihood is dependent on sight.

Morgan loves to hear from readers, and invites you to write her c/o:
Harlequin Superromance
Harlequin Enterprises
225 Duncan Mill Road
Don Mills, Ontario M3B 3K9
Canada

Books by Morgan Hayes

HARLEQUIN SUPERROMANCE
591—TWILIGHT WHISPERS
632—PREMONITIONS

SEE NO EVIL
Morgan Hayes

Harlequin Books

TORONTO • NEW YORK • LONDON
AMSTERDAM • PARIS • SYDNEY • HAMBURG
STOCKHOLM • ATHENS • TOKYO • MILAN
MADRID • WARSAW • BUDAPEST • AUCKLAND

ISBN 0-373-70722-3

SEE NO EVIL

For Dennis and Sandi Jones—the truest partners in crime a gal could ask for

And for Pat Skinner, who is always there between all the chapters...taking breaths

Heartfelt thanks go out to Dr. Jeff and Brenda Freeman, who gave graciously of their time and medical advice

PROLOGUE

THE DARK CLOUD that had been hanging over Vince Fenton's head all day had just gotten darker. From the moment he'd awoken this morning to a godawful hangover and a phone call from Edward Bainbridge, he should have known that things could only get worse. In retrospect, he never should have answered the phone. He should have figured it was Bainbridge calling about Gary Palmer and the shipment.

Then again, Vince thought as he followed the catwalk above the loading area of Palmer Storage and Shipping, if he played his cards right and this deal went through, he stood to gain more than the measly pittance Bainbridge had been paying him. Bainbridge was so uneasy about his package that he'd now offered Vince a handsome bonus if he could get it back from Palmer.

Vince wasn't surprised that Palmer had called Bainbridge the night before requesting a meeting. The shipper had seemed suspicious from the moment his services were requested. The fact that the overseas shipment should have left days ago without a hitch was proof that Palmer was on to Bainbridge. It was clear he'd discovered the package's contents and now hoped to cash in on what promised to be Bainbridge's most lucrative venture yet.

With a collection of rare Spanish coins at stake, Bainbridge should have been more discriminating when selecting a shipper. He should have anticipated that someone like

Palmer might see the opportunity for blackmail. If he had, this entire mess wouldn't be happening. And Vince would not have had to come out here to Palmer Shipping this afternoon.

Well, he'd tried his best. He'd talked to Palmer like Bainbridge had asked him to. In the closed confines of the man's office, Vince had pressed Palmer as far as he'd dared. He'd reined himself in when he'd been more than ready to take a piece out of Palmer just for wasting his time. And still the shipper refused to hand over the coins. As far as Vince was concerned it was time to take care of Gary Palmer once and for all. In fact, he'd call Bainbridge and offer to do it himself tonight. It had been a while since he'd had the pleasure.

But first, he needed to get out of here. He needed a drink.

A sudden resounding crash, followed by the shatter of glass brought Vince to an abrupt halt. Voices cursed in unison.

Only twenty minutes ago, when he'd come in the side entrance, he'd assumed the place was empty. It was Friday. Palmer's crew had kicked off early for the weekend. Palmer was supposed to have been alone.

Vince looked down from the catwalk. Immediately he squinted against a brilliant glare of lights.

"Dammit, Ralph!" a woman's voice echoed through the building.

Vince's quick gaze caught sight of her. Wearing faded jeans and a white shirt with the sleeves rolled to the elbows, the woman stood in the middle of the loading area. She shook her head and turned on the heel of her boot, swiping one hand through cropped black hair as she gripped a camera in the other.

A photo session?

Vince's fingers tightened on the handrail as he assessed the situation.

Around the photographer, a half-dozen crew members snapped to attention. They scrambled to arrange lamps and panels as several long-legged models strutted casually in stiletto heels and scanty outfits that mocked the frigid January temperatures. No doubt this was some sort of fashion shoot.

"Sorry, Stevie," one of the men called out.

"It's all right, Ralph." Curbed frustration marked her voice as she waved her hand toward the set. "But look, apologies aren't going to get this job done. Just be careful with what lamps we've got left, okay? And can we get a broom to sweep that up before someone gets hurt?"

She glanced down at the camera in her hands, adjusting something before she looked up again.

"Now, let's get this going, folks. We've got another... two hours here, and I'd like to take *something* home besides broken lamps. Paige, we need more light from the left. Yes, that's it. All right. We're looking good now."

And in seconds her camera was up and snapping. The shutter whirred rapidly as she called out encouraging directions to the models.

He should have left right then, Vince realized a moment too late. He should have slunk away before anyone saw him, before the photographer brought her camera up on enough of an angle that he was certain the lens had caught him at the railing.

Vince darted back into the maze of lockers behind him and saw the woman lower her camera. She'd seen him. He was sure of it. Why else would she have stopped? And why was she gazing up at the catwalk, at the very spot where he'd stood only moments ago?

Hidden in the shadow now, Vince looked down again. The photographer was back at work, kneeling by a bag on the floor. "No, Paige, we don't have time to fix it right now," he heard her say. "Can you bring me the Pentax? We'll use it, instead."

Vince took a deep breath. He had to relax. There was no way of knowing if she'd actually seen him. And even if she had, who was to say she'd caught him on film?

He could hear the distant whir of the shutter again.

Still, he couldn't afford to be placed at the warehouse. He made his way to the back stairs. If things went sour, as he suspected they were about to, no one could know he'd been anywhere near Palmer Storage and Shipping.

The entire situation with Gary Palmer was getting too risky. Something was going to happen and soon. And with his criminal record, Vince couldn't afford to have any-thing—especially some damn photographer's film—con-nect him to Palmer and that shipment.

No, he'd have to assume the worst. He'd have to get the camera and the film. Cover his tracks. Look out for him-self. But right now he had to call Bainbridge. First the coins, then Gary Palmer.

After that, he'd take care of the photographer and her film.

CHAPTER ONE

THE EVENING NEWS had forecast only the possibility of snow. "A mild disturbance from the north," the weatherman had warned, "bringing with it lower-than-seasonal temperatures and a twenty percent chance of precipitation." That was three hours ago.

Now, as Allister Quaid grasped the handrail of the warehouse door with gloved hands, he wrenched it closed against the tornado of blinding snow. He dusted off his leather bomber jacket and jeans, and knocked the snow from his runners.

He'd driven his Explorer around to the back of Palmer Storage and Shipping before remembering that Gary had given him keys for the side entrance only. It had been a short run through the mounting storm; even so, his hair was wet and he shivered with chill as he headed to the cavernous loading area.

The dimmed lighting far overhead did little to dispel the shadows in the labyrinth of corridors, and for a moment Allister was reminded of a carnival funhouse. At the mouth of the loading area, he stopped and reached into the pocket in the thin lining of his jacket. From it, he withdrew a crumpled shipping order—the order he'd found on Gary's desk just this morning.

He unfolded the carbon and tilted it to catch the light. If it hadn't been for the company name at the top, Allister wouldn't have looked twice at the form. And the vehement argument that followed between him and his best friend wouldn't have happened.

At ten this morning Allister had gone up to Gary's office to ask about a late delivery. His friend had been on the phone. He'd waved Allister in and given him one of his boyish grins, and it was while he waited that Allister saw the shipping order with "Raven Antiques" scribbled at the top in Gary's left-handed scrawl.

Allister could still picture the look on Gary's face when he'd hung up the phone and met his gaze.

"You weren't supposed to see that," Gary had admitted, reaching across the desk for the pink form.

But Allister snatched it up first.

"Al, come on. I can explain if you'd just—"

"Explain what? You know who this is, don't you?" The thin paper had crumpled in the fierceness of Allister's grip.

"Yeah, yeah. So I'm taking care of a shipment for Edward Bainbridge. It's what I *do,* Allister. I *ship* things."

"It's Edward Bainbridge, Gary. Dammit, you *know* what that man did to me. What he did to my business. How can you even consider getting involved with him knowing what he's capable of?"

"I can handle it."

"Meaning I couldn't?"

"I didn't say that, Al."

"No, but you're thinking it. Otherwise you wouldn't have accepted this shipment."

Gary, his face sagging with exhaustion, stood up and began to pace behind his desk. He looked like a caged animal, Allister thought, an animal that had been trapped with no way out.

"What's in the shipment, Gary?"

"I don't know. I don't *check* the packages. I just *ship* them."

"What's in the package?" Allister demanded again, knowing by the way his friend chewed the corner of his lip that he was lying. It was a nervous habit Allister had come to recognize even before they'd taken the training wheels off their matching CCM bikes all those years ago.

"I told you, I don't *know*. So just drop it, Al, okay?"

But it wasn't that easy. The topic of Edward Bainbridge could not just be dropped. Not for Allister. With the shipping order in his hands, with the mere mention of the antiquity collector's name, everything Allister had fought so hard to leave behind came flooding back. Standing in Gary's office, knowing what his friend might be getting into, Allister had used every ounce of restraint he had to bite down the anger and resentment he still felt toward Edward Bainbridge—the man who, in one fell swoop, had taken everything Allister had loved and worked for. The man who would do the same to Gary without thinking twice.

It had been six years ago that Allister had experienced firsthand the extent of Bainbridge's corruption. At that time, Allister had owned a shipping company much like the one he helped Gary manage now. He'd spent eight years salvaging his family's business and turning it into the most reputable in Danby.

But it had taken only one shipment, one seemingly innocent package from Edward Bainbridge, to destroy it all. Destined for a collector in Buenos Aires, the shipment had contained several pieces of near-priceless antique jewelry and a number of rare gems. Allister had handled Bainbridge's exporting needs in the past; he'd had no reason to believe that the package bound for Buenos Aires was any different from the others.

But when Allister's company was burgled the night before the shipment was scheduled to go out, the bricks had begun to fall one by one. First there'd been Bainbridge to deal with, then the insurance company and finally the police when they came with a search warrant four days later and confiscated three of the stolen gems, wrapped in an old T-shirt of Allister's, from under the spare tire in the trunk of his car.

The gems had obviously been planted there by one of Bainbridge's goons. Or, quite possibly, by the police themselves, Allister later suspected. It was obvious, too, that Bainbridge must have been paying someone off—someone on the force—to see the million-dollar scam through. The whole setup had been too easy, too slick.

The rest of the gems were never recovered; Bainbridge collected a tidy sum from the insurance company, and no doubt turned around and sold the other "stolen" items to the intended buyer with no more a glitch than a two-month delay. Allister's business folded, and after a grim and incontestable trial, he was convicted of grand theft.

Four years in prison was a long time. But not long enough to forget who had put him there, Allister thought as he looked at the name of Bainbridge's company on the Palmer shipping form. Below "Raven Antiques," Gary had scrawled the aisle and bin numbers. That was why Allister was here tonight. With the building empty, Allister intended to search for Bainbridge's package and check its contents himself. If there was even the slimmest chance that Bainbridge was up to his old tricks, Allister couldn't stand idly by. He wouldn't let it happen again, not to Gary, not to his closest friend.

Across the main loading area were aisles ten to fifteen. From the shadowed corridors, Allister could almost feel Bainbridge's shipment beckoning him. But when he stepped out into the open area, he saw the light from Gary's office upstairs spilling out the doorway onto the steel catwalk.

With a muttered curse, Allister tucked the slip of paper back into his pocket. He couldn't check for the package now. Gary would be sure to hear him, if he hadn't already.

"Gary?" His voice boomed through the old converted mill. "Hey, Gary!" he shouted again, but there was no response.

Letting out a long breath, Allister headed to the stairs. It was as good a time as any to apologize for the harsh words he hadn't managed to swallow before he'd stormed out of the office this morning. And maybe there was still a chance of talking some sense into Gary about Bainbridge.

Taking the steps two at a time, Allister felt the catwalk vibrate beneath his runners. An apology was already forming on his lips as he stepped across the threshold of Gary's office, but instantly the words froze.

The room had been torn apart. Papers were strewn everywhere, spilling from filing cabinets and thrown from the desk that, despite its weight, had been shoved across the room a good five feet. The cheap vinyl chairs had been hurled in several directions, and the cooler that had stood in the corner still glugged softly as water washed across the tiled floor.

But it was the sight of blood that made Allister's heart stop. Not much of it at first. Nothing more than a few red smears. But then Allister saw the crimson pool behind the desk and—

"Gary!" He fought his panic as he rushed forward. "Oh, my God! Gary?"

STEVIE FALCIONI pulled the key from the Volvo's ignition and switched off the headlights. Leaning forward against the steering wheel, she gazed up through the blurred windshield at Palmer Storage and Shipping. In the sallow light from the sodium vapor lamp mounted above the side door of the building, the snow seemed to be driving horizontally through the night. The full force of the sudden winter storm whistled around the old station wagon, rocking it gently. Stevie searched one deep pocket of her lined trench coat for the key Gary had given her, preparing herself for the freezing dash to the warehouse.

Crossing the city of Danby had proved to be a small miracle in itself. The storm had been a complete surprise, and in the fifty-minute drive that normally took her twenty, Stevie had seen more accidents than she'd been able to count. Each time she'd passed another fender bender or an abandoned vehicle at the side of the road, its hazards blinking through gusts of snow, she had silently thanked her father for persuading her to buy the ten-year-old tank of a Volvo.

Regardless, it had been a stupid idea to head out on a night like this—driving all the way to Gary Palmer's warehouse for a forgotten camera. The Nikon had jammed only minutes into their shoot this afternoon, when she'd been momentarily distracted by the man on the catwalk. With no time to deal with the faulty camera, Stevie had shoved it into the closest bag, a black duffel, and when she'd glanced back up, the stranger was gone.

Just before seven, with the shoot complete and the models weary, Stevie's assistant, Paige Carpenter, and the rest of the crew had cleared up, collecting the equipment and all the bags except Stevie's. And after Stevie had finished thanking Gary for the use of his building and left, she'd realized she'd forgotten the bag—and the camera.

Right now Paige was back at the studio madly printing contacts for another job so that they could begin work on today's. Whatever film was in the Nikon, if it was salvageable, needed to be developed tonight along with the rest. Brian Armatrading, the man behind the contract, was due at the studio at ten tomorrow morning to check the work they'd done for his summer line of clothing.

He wanted something innovative, something young and fresh, he'd told Stevie within minutes of breezing into Images, Stevie's studio-apartment, two weeks ago. She and Paige had been booked solid with other jobs, but they'd have been fools not to shelve everything in favor of Armatrading's offer. This one was big. This was the contract that could quite conceivably boost Stevie's career to a level she'd hardly dared imagine.

When she'd signed her first free-lance photography contract ten years ago for a meager $135, Stevie hadn't imagined it could lead to anything like a full-time career, let alone something as potentially lucrative as shooting an entire line of Armatrading fashions.

Ever since her father had given her that old Leica camera for her tenth birthday, photography had been her absolute passion. She'd lived her life through the dingy viewfinder of that battered camera and the many others that followed. Over the past few years, Stevie's reputation soared with the phenomenal success of Images, and she considered herself truly blessed to be doing what she loved most in life.

Battling a winter storm for the sake of some jammed film in an aging Nikon, *this* she could have lived without. Stevie groped for the Volvo's door handle. As she stepped from the car, a gust of frigid air sucked the breath from her lungs, and sharp pellets of snow stabbed her exposed skin. Stevie pulled up the collar of her coat and raced for the warehouse door.

"GARY? GARY!"

In his frantic dash across the ransacked office, Allister stumbled once, banging his shin on the chrome leg of a toppled chair. He ignored the pain as he forced his way behind the desk to where Gary lay in a crumpled heap amidst scattered file folders.

"Gary!"

He heard a quiet moan, and one shaky hand reached toward him from behind the desk. Fear seizing him, Allister shoved the office chair aside. When he looked down into the bloodied face that gazed up at him, he hardly recognized his friend.

"Oh, God, Gary." He knelt beside him. "What the hell happened?"

Gary tried to push himself up, but the effort was futile and he moaned weakly. Going against what little first aid he knew, Allister grasped Gary's shoulders and eased his head onto his lap.

He hadn't imagined that one person could bleed so much. The front of Gary's denim shirt was soaked, and his blond hair was matted to his head. But it was his face that appeared to have taken the most abuse. A two-inch gash above his right eye still flowed freely, and Allister couldn't tell if the blood that Gary choked on came from the split in his lip or from internal injuries. Fear coiling in his stomach, he suspected the latter.

Allister scanned the debris for the phone. But it, too, had been smashed into shards.

"Gary, I have to get you an ambulance. I'm—"

"No." Gary's head wobbled to one side in feeble protest. "No," he muttered again, his voice a strained whisper between weak coughs.

"Gary, you're bleeding."

"No, Al...listen. You have to listen...to me." His hand shook as he reached past Allister's open jacket and clutched his shirt with bloodied fingers.

He was dying. He knew it and Allister knew it. He could feel the life slipping from Gary's battered body as he cradled his friend's head in his lap and held his weakening gaze.

"You...you were right, Al," Gary said, each word, each syllable, wrenched with pain. "I should...have listened to you. You...warned me."

It wasn't supposed to happen like this, Allister kept thinking even as Gary struggled for breath. This kind of brutality—it wasn't the way it was supposed to end.

"Al, listen to me. I—"

"It's Bainbridge, isn't it, Gary? It's Bainbridge who's done this."

Gary gave a single nod, swallowed hard, then coughed again. His hand sought Allister's. His grip was weak through the thin leather of Allister's glove.

"It's the shipment, right, Gary? Bainbridge's shipment. What's in the package? What's he dealing?"

"Coins. It's...coins."

Allister shook his head. "Coins? I don't understand."

"From the museum...the collection...remember?"

Allister was still shaking his head, trying to put the pieces together. "The burglary? Back in May? That was Bainbridge?"

Gary nodded feebly, and then his eyes closed.

"Gary, no! Stay with me, you hear?" Allister's fear rose again, and finally his friend's eyes flickered open.

"Where are the coins now, Gary?"

Allister wondered if his friend even heard the question through his pain.

"Where are the coins? Does Bainbridge have the coins?"

Gary shook his head. "No..."

"Where is the package?"

"Safe..."

"Where, Gary? Where is it safe?"

"Stevie."

"Stevie who?"

"Fal...Falcioni."

"The photographer? Your friend the photographer?"

Gary nodded.

"She has them? She has the coins?"

This time when Gary shook his head, it was followed by a rattling gasp. "You have...to...to get...Stevie, Al. And tell...Barb...I love her. Tell her...for me, will you?"

And then, with one final shuddering breath, he was gone. Allister felt his body slacken. His eyes, suddenly vacant, gazed upward. In the silence of the warehouse, Allister held the man who had been his dearest friend, the man who had always been there for him. And yet, when Gary had needed Allister...

No, he thought, as he gently eased Gary to the floor again. No, he couldn't think about the way things might have been. How if he'd forced Gary to hand over Bainbridge's package, or if he'd gone to check the shipment this morning, instead of waiting until tonight, his friend might still be alive. There were other factors to consider now. Like Edward Bainbridge.

From what Allister remembered, the coin collection, with an estimated value in the seven figures, had been stolen from a touring exhibit hosted by the Danby Museum in the spring. Definitely the kind of job that had Bainbridge written all over it. No doubt the collector had a buyer in mind and had hoped to use Gary to ship the stolen goods for him.

But why kill Gary? It didn't make sense. Not unless Bainbridge had found out that Gary knew the shipment's contents. Not unless Gary had tried to blackmail Bainbridge.

Allister stood, his gaze surveying the destruction of the office. There wasn't time to sift through it for clues. Six years ago Bainbridge had successfully framed him. Allister couldn't take any chances. He had to assume that this time, too, the collector had something similar in mind.

But *this* time it was murder.

He had to get out. If, as he'd always suspected, Bainbridge had connections on the Danby police force, Allister had to get as far away from the warehouse as possible. Until he knew what Bainbridge was up to, he couldn't risk being placed at the scene. Gary was dead because of the stolen coins. Once the police put the pieces together, with Allister's record, he was sure to be their prime suspect.

Allister stumbled toward the door. He'd get back in the Explorer and drive to his apartment. He would tell the police that he'd spent the night in front of the TV. It would be easy enough to check the local listings and make up an alibi.

But halfway to the door, Allister stopped.

He couldn't do it. He lowered his head and closed his eyes, imagining that when he opened them, none of this had happened. But when he did, all he saw was Gary's blood. On his shirt. On his gloves.

No, he couldn't just leave his friend lying there on the floor. And what about Barb? What on earth was he going to tell Barb?

Then above his own hammering heart, Allister heard a distant footfall—boots against the concrete of the main floor, slow and assured. As he stood in the middle of the office listening, he could think of only one person who would be lurking in the warehouse this late at night—the man who had killed Gary. Maybe he was searching for the package now, checking the aisles and the bins. Maybe he'd heard Allister come in.

And maybe he was coming back up to the office.

There was no time to think. Allister moved on instinct now, instinct and adrenaline. He scanned the office until he saw the heavy fire extinguisher mounted by the door. Certainly not his weapon of choice, he thought as he grappled with the clips, but it would have to do.

STEVIE WALKED through the warehouse toward the area she'd been shooting in earlier, searching for her bag. The old building creaked and groaned under the force of the storm outside.

In the main loading area, the rough stonework and massive timbers attested to the original function of the structure. The building had serviced Danby for decades as a mill before it had been shut down. Years later, after Gary had bought and converted it, some of its authentic charm remained. And it was that charm that had been the deciding factor in choosing it as the backdrop for the Armatrading shoot.

Luckily, when Stevie had arranged to meet with Gary for coffee only two weeks ago to ask him, he'd been more than willing to grant her access to the building. It had been the first time she and Gary had seen each other in months. She'd apologized for that, and also for the fact that it took a photo shoot to bring them together again.

She'd first met Gary at college when he'd briefly dated her roommate. But for some reason, Stevie had clicked better with him than her roommate had, and they'd been fast friends ever since. After obtaining their respective degrees, Gary had moved upstate to his hometown of Danby. And then, a few months later, Nick, the graduate student Stevie had been dating for the last two years of college, had accepted a position with a Danby-based engineering firm. She'd moved with him and landed a job at a local photography studio.

It seemed so long ago that she'd had the time for social-izing with Gary and Barb. That was before Nick had been transferred and Stevie had decided to stay in Danby, before she'd left the studio to start one of her own, before the suc-cess of Images put greater demands on her time and en-ergy. She hadn't sat still since. And, regrettably, she hadn't seen much of Gary and Barb, either.

Gary had changed over the past couple of years, Stevie had thought earlier this evening when she'd spoken to him in his office after the shoot. He'd aged. He'd looked tired and strung out, almost nervous in a way.

She'd suggested he take a holiday, but he'd attempted to assure her that he was fine. She hadn't met Gary's friend Allister, but she knew he'd been helping with the company over the past few months. Gary could have Allister take care of things for a couple of weeks, she'd said. When Gary told her he would consider it, Stevie knew he only said so to pla-cate her.

Maybe she'd try talking to him again, Stevie thought when at last she found the black duffel bag and shouldered it. Bracing herself to face the winter storm, she was about to leave when she saw the light upstairs. Gary's office door was open, and the overhead fluorescents from inside glared coldly against the subdued night-lighting throughout the rest of the building.

Stevie shook her head as she checked her watch. That was Gary. Almost ten o'clock, and he was still at his desk. She was smiling to herself as she took the stairs to the upper-level catwalk and headed toward the office. Gary had always bragged about being able to outdo even a diehard worka-holic like Stevie.

Well, if she had her way tonight, she'd convince him to take some time off. Maybe she'd even speak to his friend Allister herself, get him to side with her.

Stevie's smile dissolved the moment she reached the office doorway. Gary's name caught in her throat and the room seemed to tilt in slow motion as shock and disbelief washed over her. She saw the devastation of the office. She saw the smears of blood. And then she saw Gary.

He lay in a crumpled heap amongst blood-soaked files and papers; his face was turned away from her. One tentative step was as far as she got before her peripheral vision caught a sudden flash of red. It came from just inside the door to her right. She gasped and spun around, dropping her bag.

In an instant she registered the man's bloodied hands, gloved fingers gripping the neck of a fire extinguisher. *Gary's blood,* she knew. There was more of it on the man's shirt, and a crimson streak along one high cheekbone. She saw the dark hair, the tanned face and raging black eyes.

He'd killed Gary. And he was going to kill her, too.

Stevie ran.

He yelled something after her, but she couldn't make it out over the slamming of her hard-soled boots on the steel grating.

And then she felt the vibrations of the catwalk. He was coming after her.

She couldn't afford to look back. She had to focus on the stairs. Get to the stairs, then through the main loading area and to the side door. She wouldn't need the keys; pushing the handrail would unlock it. Then the car, and she'd be home free.

Frantically she slid one hand into her coat pocket and grabbed the Volvo's keys.

Only another five yards to the stairs. She could make it.

Her heart slammed against her ribs. Her lungs screamed for air. And all the time, the walkway shook beneath her feet.

He had to be right behind her now.

Without slowing, Stevie readied her keys between her fingers. She'd be prepared if she couldn't outrun him.

But the thought had barely formed in her mind when she felt his hand on her shoulder. The vicelike grip stopped her dead in her tracks.

She heard him say something. It sounded like "Wait," but she couldn't be sure. It was now or never. She had to defend herself. She had to swing at him before he had the opportunity to overpower her.

She brought the fistful of keys up—but he was too fast. With one forceful jerk, he spun her in the opposite direction. The smooth leather soles of her boots were useless against the hard surface of the catwalk. And in that critical moment, they slid out from under her.

She pitched backward, flailing for anything to stop her fall. For an instant she imagined herself plunging to her death on the concrete floor two stories below. That was before the pain, blinding excruciating pain that pierced through her head from the base of her skull. She slumped to the steel grating.

The shadows around her reeled and blurred. She heard the distant whir of the industrial ceiling fans spinning lazily farther up in the rafters, coupled with an intensifying buzz in her head, and then his voice.

"Oh, God. Stay with me now. Do you hear me? Stay with me."

He was kneeling over her. A pallid finger of light from the dimmed lamps high above touched one side of his face as he came closer. And in that split second, through a semiconscious haze, Stevie saw the scar, a jagged scar, along the man's left temple, twisting down from the corner of his eyebrow to the top of his chiseled cheekbone.

She didn't think about death then. Nor did her life flash before her eyes as she'd always expected it would. Instead, it was the man's scar. Absurdly, in that last shred of consciousness, Stevie wondered what might have caused such a scar.

And then, finally, the blackness swallowed her.

CHAPTER TWO

BENEATH HIS FINGERTIPS, the woman's pulse fluttered rhythmically. Her breathing was shallow but steady. Allister withdrew his hand from the silken smoothness of her neck and eased her head to one side. Fearing the worst, he feathered his fingers back through her sleek, jet black hair, searching for injuries.

There was a small gash, hardly worthy of stitches, and a rapidly swelling lump. It would be pretty painful, he guessed, given the force with which she'd struck the railing when she'd lost her balance.

Lost her balance. Allister shook his head. No, her fall had had more to do with his manhandling than any action of her own. He'd been so determined to stop her, to explain why he was in Gary's office and why he'd appeared poised to swing a fire extinguisher down on her head, that Allister had grabbed for her without any thought beyond self-preservation.

Now she lay on the shadowed catwalk, unconscious, and most likely concussed. She needed medical attention. Even in his own panicked state, he recognized that.

It was one thing to leave Gary at the warehouse and remove himself from the crime scene for fear of being framed by Bainbridge; there was nothing he could do for Gary. But it was quite another to leave this woman here. He couldn't do that.

Allister paced the distance between her and the office door, uncertain of his next move but knowing he had to do something. Finally he saw the black duffel bag. He picked it up. Giving her another sidelong glance, he unzipped it. He wasn't sure what he was searching for, but when he brushed aside the nylon flap, Allister saw the Nikon.

This woman, no doubt, was Stevie Falcioni.

Allister looked at her again. Her right arm was stretched out toward him, her slender fingers partially curled. It was as if she was reaching for him. And the way her delicate face was angled, the tenuous light from the overhead lamps lending a warmth to her unconscious expression, only served to increase that impression.

No, he couldn't leave her here, even if he placed an anonymous call to the police. Whoever had beaten the life out of Gary could still be on the premises. Gary had said Bainbridge didn't have the coins. And when Allister had asked about the shipment's whereabouts, Gary had mentioned Stevie. Chances were good that Gary's killer would be back to look for the package—if he wasn't still here.

Allister slung the duffel bag over one shoulder and knelt beside Stevie. Slipping his gloves on again, he realized the risk he was about to take. Yes, there was the very real threat of being framed by Bainbridge. And in all likelihood, the police would not believe his story once they'd placed him at the scene of Gary's murder. Then there was Stevie Falcioni; it was going to take some pretty creative explaining to convince her that he hadn't been trying to kill her when, mistaking her for Gary's assailant, he'd come at her with the fire extinguisher. But given the circumstances, he thought as he lifted her limp body from the catwalk and shifted her weight against his chest, he would have to run those risks.

The stairs were the trickiest. After Allister maneuvered them, he found carrying Stevie through the warehouse to the side door relatively easy. Outside, the storm had risen to its full force; the wind howled and the snow had turned to biting pellets of ice. After struggling briefly with the passenger door of the Explorer, Allister eased Stevie onto the seat. He reclined it, then fumbled with the seat-belt clip until he heard it catch.

In another moment he was behind the wheel, and the engine rumbled to life. Above the thrashing wipers and the noise of the fan, he heard the radio announcer on the local station advise people to stay indoors and caution drivers about the hazardous conditions.

"...and you can certainly expect to wake up to a few more inches of the white stuff tomorrow," the announcer said, "after that green Christmas, it looks like winter's finally settling in..."

Allister steered past Stevie's Volvo, out of the warehouse lot and onto the deserted street. Five blocks later, he brought the big vehicle to a sliding stop at a red light and restlessly drummed his fingers against the steering wheel as cars crawled through the intersection.

In the close quarters of the Explorer, Allister detected a faint trace of her perfume. He looked over and saw how the yellow glow of a street lamp through the windshield cast gentle shadows across her striking features: high cheekbones, a square yet delicate jawline, a small straight nose, and lips that looked as though they'd been carefully sculpted into an enticing curve. Allister didn't doubt that Stevie Falcioni had seduced countless men with little more than a smile.

"...and remember, drive carefully if you have to be out tonight," the radio announcer cautioned again. "Police are reporting numerous accidents in and around the city, and we've just received word of a multicar pile-up along the north branch of the Harriston Expressway near the Jefferson exit. We'll have more details on the ten-o'clock news coming up in seven minutes. For now, though, here's something that should brighten things up a bit for all you storm-bound listeners. The golden oldie 'I Can See Clearly Now'—''

Allister switched off the radio and eased the Explorer past the intersection. The rest of the drive to Danby General Hospital was a white-knuckled ordeal. Throughout, he snatched quick side glances at the woman next to him whenever the driving permitted. Her small frame rocked with each bump and swerve.

He had no idea what he would have done had she regained consciousness in the car—would she have believed he was actually trying to help? And by the time he pulled into the hospital lot, Allister was grateful she hadn't come around. He turned off the ignition and in the welcome silence looked at the emergency entrance.

Three ambulances were parked out front, one with its lights still strobing. Beyond the wide sliding doors in the bright glare of the ER, he could see a blur of activity.

This was it, he thought, taking a deep breath. As soon as he carried Stevie Falcioni through those doors, there would be no turning back. He'd have to give his name, address, phone number. And shortly after that, the police would be knocking on his door, if they hadn't already picked him up at the hospital.

Allister glanced at Stevie again. So how *was* he going to explain his apparent attack? Who would believe him? And what made this any different from six years ago?

But right now there wasn't time to debate these questions and fears. What mattered was Stevie and getting her the medical attention she needed. He owed her that much.

When the emergency-room doors swung open at his approach, Allister shifted Stevie's weight in his arms, careful not to drop the duffel bag, which he also held. Her head rested on his shoulder, her face only inches from his, and again he detected a subtle hint of her perfume. Dodging two attendants wheeling an empty gurney back to the ambulances, Allister stepped through the second set of doors.

He stopped abruptly.

The ER had more than activity; it reeled in utter chaos. The waiting room was jammed; people without seats paced or leaned against walls, while another dozen waited impatiently to give information to the harassed desk nurse. Orderlies flew from one station to the next, their crisscrossing paths seeming more like a well-choreographed dance than the frantic scramblings of an ER staff beleaguered by a sudden string of accident victims. Behind him, Allister could hear the approaching siren of yet another ambulance.

"All right, people, we've got another two coming in!"

A woman in green scrubs moved past Allister at full tilt. "Let's make some room out here. Jerry, use the halls if you have to. Karen, Dr. Stowe needs you in number four. And, Alex, get another crash cart down here."

"Excuse me?" Allister hurried after her, twisting his way through the crowded corridor.

The woman briskly signed two charts thrust at her by interns, before starting down the hall.

"Excuse me!" This time he shouted, slowing his awkward pursuit only when she spun around on one sneakered foot.

Even then, she didn't look at him. Her attention was riveted on the woman in his arms.

"I need some help here," he said. "Are you a doctor?"

The woman nodded. "Dr. Delaney. Is this one of the expressway-pileup victims?"

"No. She fell," he explained, shifting Stevie's weight, his arms beginning to feel the strain. "She hit her head."

"Carol, find a gurney," Dr. Delaney called to a nurse, her eyes never leaving Stevie. "How long has she been unconscious, sir?"

The doctor reached up and lifted Stevie's eyelids to examine her pupils.

"I don't know. Fifteen ... twenty minutes, I guess."

"Where did she hit her head?"

"The back. She fell backward."

The doctor was already probing Stevie's skull when the gurney arrived, and Allister lowered Stevie onto the crisp sheets. Dr. Delaney pulled open Stevie's coat, as well as the shirt beneath, and grappled with her stethoscope. When he saw the edge of a white lace bra against olive-colored skin, Allister redirected his gaze. He waited, shifting his weight from one foot to the other, as the doctor looked Stevie over and finally muttered something to the nurse.

And then the emergency doors slammed open.

"Here they come!" someone shouted.

All available hospital staff, including Dr. Delaney, raced to the doors as attendants rushed in with the next accident victims.

"We need these forms filled out, sir," the nurse said, shoving a clipboard at Allister. "Dr. Delaney will be with you as soon as she can," she added as she scrambled to the speeding gurneys and was swallowed up in the frantic flow of medical staff down the main hall.

Allister looked at the form and then at Stevie. He moved to the side of the gurney, which had been pushed up against the corridor wall, and lowered the black duffel from his shoulder onto the sheets beside her. She appeared paler now under the harsh unforgiving fluorescents, her face framed by the short gleaming black hair.

Her beige trench coat was splayed open, and the edges of her white cotton shirt were still brushed aside. Gingerly Allister reached out to pull it closed over the delicate lace bra. And then he noticed the red smear on her jeans.

For the first time, Allister looked at his gloved hands. There were traces of blood—Gary's blood. And there was more on his shirt, his jacket, and his jeans.

Panic rose again. He *had* to get out of here. Four years in prison. There was no way he was going back. He was not about to be framed by Bainbridge a second time, and that was exactly what was going to happen if the police found out he'd been at the warehouse tonight, if they matched the blood on his clothes to Gary's.

He needed to think this through, away from the clamor and confusion of the ER. He needed a plan. Some way to get to Bainbridge before Stevie Falcioni had a chance to identify him.

As the rest of the ER whirled in confusion, Allister recognized his one and only opportunity. If he left now, before the doctor returned, he'd be able to slip out without anyone noticing. And with the frenzy caused by the expressway pileup, chances were no one would even remember him later when the police came around to question Stevie and the rest of the hospital staff.

He'd have to leave her.

She'd be all right though, he tried to convince himself, or else the doctor wouldn't have left them here unattended in the middle of a corridor. Stevie was in good hands now. He'd done all he could. There had to be identification in the fanny pouch she wore around her slim hips; the attendants could get any information they needed. They'd call her family or a friend. She wouldn't be alone.

Allister took one more look at Stevie, but somehow suspected it wouldn't be his last. She was a part of this—part of Gary's murder and Bainbridge and the coins. How she was connected, Allister didn't know yet. But why else had Gary whispered her name?

He could only hope to have the answers soon. For now he had to get out.

And, leaving Stevie there on the gurney, running off into the night like some fugitive, for the first time in his life Allister felt like a criminal.

"YOU WEREN'T SUPPOSED to *kill* him, dammit!" Edward Bainbridge yelled into the phone. "You were meant to get the coins, Vince. Remember? The coins? Without them, we don't have a deal. You were supposed to go over there last night to get them from that weasel, Palmer. After that, I didn't care what you did with the son of a bitch."

Gary Palmer's murder had been on the front page of the *Danby Sun* and the first story Edward Bainbridge had read with his morning coffee. He'd gotten as far as "...police speculate the murder was a result of a random break-in." Seconds later he had Vince Fenton on the phone.

"He didn't have the damned coins," Vince was saying.

"What the hell do you mean, he didn't have them?"

"Like I said, I went over there, roughed him up a bit—"

"He's *dead,* Vince."

"Okay, I roughed him up a lot. The point is, he didn't have the coins. I searched the office. They weren't there. If you ask me, Allister Quaid's probably got 'em."

Edward Bainbridge's grip tightened on the cordless phone. He squinted against the glare of the sun and gazed past his stables to the snow-covered paddocks marking the north end of his property.

This couldn't be happening, he thought. It couldn't be falling apart like this. First, he'd lost almost everything when the building-development project in London had fallen through, then his offshore-oil company had gone into receivership, and finally, after pooling his remaining resources into this last attempt to see himself out of his financial hole, everything was coming apart at the seams.

It was Vince Fenton's fault.

No, it was his own fault for hiring a moron like Vince in the first place. He should have known better. And he should have put Vince to work on Palmer the second he'd found out about Allister Quaid a couple of days ago. He should have pulled up stakes right then, knowing that the ex-shipper would almost certainly mean trouble.

There could be only one reason Allister Quaid was hanging around Palmer Storage and Shipping, and no doubt, it had to do with him and his shipment. Vince was right. If anyone had the coins, it had to be Quaid.

And if that was the case, Allister Quaid would have a lot more to deal with this time than a prison term.

"I'D LIKE YOU to deliver the eulogy, Allister."

Allister's back was turned to Barb as he stared out the patio doors. It had stopped snowing finally, and the late-afternoon sun filtered through the bare trees that bordered the Palmers' backyard.

Allister closed his eyes. He was thinking of Gary.

Last night, after he'd left Stevie in the hospital corridor and slipped out unnoticed, he'd initially driven toward home. The sanders had been out, and the snow had begun to taper off. But two blocks from his apartment building, Allister had turned around and headed back to the warehouse. Thoughts of Gary lying there alone in the ransacked office haunted him.

He had no idea what he intended to do even as he pulled onto the quiet industrial street at ten-forty-five. Part of him—a very small part that hadn't been crushed by four years in prison—had wanted to believe that the truth was best. He'd wanted to believe that he could call the police, that he could tell them everything he knew and they would actually believe him.

In retrospect, he was glad that by the time he got to the warehouse the police were already there. He'd seen the blue strobes of the patrol cars as he neared the building. And then he'd spotted the white van next to Stevie's Volvo. The cleaning crew had been late because of the storm, but they'd still showed up. And obviously found Gary's body.

Allister had kept driving, back to his apartment.

Barb had called almost four hours later, long after he'd gotten home and washed up. She was at home. Two detectives were there with her waiting to take her to identify Gary's body; she asked Allister to meet her at the morgue. She sounded amazingly calm and in control. Allister arrived at the morgue right behind her, and after they'd confirmed Gary's identity, the two detectives had mounted their preliminary questions.

Eventually they'd asked about Stevie Falcioni. The detectives told Barb and Allister that shortly after arriving at the scene, a phone call came through to Gary's business. It had been Stevie Falcioni's partner, the older detective explained; she'd become concerned when Stevie hadn't returned. With the Volvo still parked at the warehouse, the police had called around and located her at Danby General. They told Barb how they suspected Stevie may have stumbled onto Gary's killer and consequently been attacked herself. It was only when they stated that Stevie was still unconscious in the intensive-care unit that the cumulative shock of the night's events had begun to show on Barb's face.

Allister had been able to persuade the detectives to postpone their questioning until the next day and had driven

Barb home. Except for this morning, when he'd managed to slip away for an hour, he'd been with her ever since.

"Allister," Barb tried again, exhaustion dragging at her voice, "I think you should deliver the eulogy."

He shook his head, still unable to face her or her request. "Barb, I—"

"You have to, Al. Please. You were Gary's best friend."

Best friend. Somehow, that title didn't seem exactly appropriate after last night. What kind of best friend left a man lying dead on the floor of his office? What kind of best friend lied to the man's wife about his knowledge of her husband's murder?

"Allister?" She came up behind him now and laid a hand on his shoulder. "You must."

When he turned to her finally, he was surprised by the firm set of her mouth and the determination in her pale blue eyes. Barb Palmer was a strong woman. From the moment they had stood together looking at Gary's body on the stainless-steel table at the city morgue in the wee hours of morning, she had been holding up unbelievably well.

And ever since that moment in the morgue, Allister had wanted to tell Barb the truth—that he'd been in the warehouse last night, had held Gary in his arms and that Gary hadn't been alone when he died. Most of all, he wanted to tell Barb how her name and Gary's love for her had been the last words from Gary's lips. But Allister couldn't. *No* one could know he'd been at the warehouse last night.

"I know what you're thinking," Barb said. "I know the two of you had grown apart while you were..." She shook her head, unable to say the words. Both she and Gary had always made a painful habit of trying to deny what Allister had gone through, where he'd been those four years and how it had altered his life. "But still, Allister, no matter what you think, you were closer to Gary than anyone. You knew him best.''

Allister looked out across the soft blanket of snow that covered the backyard.

She was wrong. He didn't... hadn't known Gary anymore. They *had* grown apart—on that point, Barb was right. But there was much more about Gary now that Allister didn't know or understand.

Like his failing marriage, for one. Barb had shocked him this morning with the news of their plans for a divorce. Gary had never even let on that there were problems, and here Barb was, already planning to sell the house and leave Danby for a new life.

Even more disturbing than that, Allister couldn't understand what had possessed Gary to try to double-cross a man like Edward Bainbridge, especially after what Gary knew about him, after Allister had warned him.

Was it for money? Because of the divorce? No. Barb wasn't the type of woman to take more than her share when she left the marriage. As a family counselor with a successful practice, she had her own money.

It just didn't make sense. The Gary he had known and grown up with wouldn't take those kinds of life-threatening risks. Then again, maybe that was it. With Barb leaving, maybe Gary figured he had nothing to lose by taking on the likes of Edward Bainbridge. Maybe he figured he could make some extra money.

Or maybe he'd just gotten restless. Gary had always been restless, even as a kid. Always wanting to move on, try new things. Allister had never pegged him as the settling-down type, never believed he could put work aside long enough to maintain a relationship, let alone a marriage.

But he and Gary had still been friends. Gary had stuck by him during those hard years, believed in his innocence when everyone else had harbored doubts about what had gone on and how Bainbridge's gems had come to be in the trunk of his car.

Even Michelle hadn't believed him. Out of everyone, Allister had thought he could count on his fiancée the most. Three years together—he thought he knew her. But before the trial had even finished, the day before the verdict was to be handed down, Michelle had returned his engagement ring.

Only Gary had believed in Allister throughout. And only Gary had come to see him in prison. Then, eight months ago, it was Gary who'd been waiting for him upon his release. It was Gary who'd calmed Allister down, taken him for a beer when all he'd wanted to do that afternoon was drive to Bainbridge's estate and strangle the smug bastard with his bare hands.

Gary had tried to convince him that the revenge Allister was seething to exact on Bainbridge was only a product of the ordeal he'd just suffered, and not a reflection of the man Allister really was. He'd told Allister to put it behind him, to start again, start fresh.

But to forget those four years, to forget how Bainbridge had taken the life he'd known and worked for, these were impossible. He could never put them behind him.

Allister brushed a hand through his hair, and as he did, his finger grazed the jagged scar that curled up from his cheekbone to the top of his eyebrow. He traced the gnarled ridge of skin with his fingertip, recalling the brawl with another inmate and the resounding crack when his head had struck the metal bars of the cell-block gate. But now, four years later, he couldn't even recall the name of the man who had initiated the fight. As far as Allister was concerned, it was Edward Bainbridge who had put the scar there.

"So can I count on you, Allister?" Barb asked once again.

He nodded. "Of course, Barb. I'll give the eulogy." Now all he had to do was figure out a way to speak at Gary's funeral without Stevie Falcioni seeing him. He wondered if there was any chance she'd still be in the hospital by then, because if she wasn't, he was definitely going to have to let Barb down.

He couldn't risk coming into contact with the photographer and having her identify him. Not unless he managed to speak with her before the police did, not unless he could convince her that he had not been trying to attack her, had not been the one who'd killed Gary. If only he could see her before the cops got to her.

But there was little chance of that. Allister had already tried.

That was where he'd gone this morning, before Barb had woken up. He'd left her a note, telling her he was running a few errands, and he'd headed to the hospital. In the car, outside the main entrance, Allister had tried to prepare what he could possibly say to convince Stevie he was telling the truth. He would try to explain how he'd arrived only minutes before she had, how when he heard her in the warehouse, he'd mistaken her for the killer returning, and when he'd run after her, he'd only been trying to stop her.

And then he wanted to ask her about the coins. He wanted to know why Gary had whispered her name on his dying breath.

It had been barely 6:00 a.m. when Allister slipped past the front desk and checked the hospital directory board. He took the elevator to the tenth floor. But when he rounded the corner of the wing that housed the ICU, he pulled up short. One uniformed officer paced the width of the corridor, a plastic-foam cup in hand and a paper tucked under his arm. Obviously the police recognized Stevie's potential as a witness and weren't taking any chances.

During the drive back to Barb's through the early-morning streets, he'd thought about Stevie Falcioni, and he'd begun to doubt whether she really *would* have believed him if he had managed to see her.

No, it was probably better this way, Allister thought now, holding his empty mug and gazing out at the snow. He couldn't trust anyone.

When Stevie Falcioni did regain consciousness, the police would talk to her. All Allister could do was pray that she hadn't gotten a good look at him. And maybe, with any luck at all, she might not even remember whatever she'd seen.

Then again, luck hadn't made a habit out of knocking on Allister's door in the past.

"Want more coffee, Al?" Barb asked.

"Sure, thanks." He left the patio doors and followed her into the kitchen. "Have you heard from the hospital yet?" he asked, handing her his empty mug.

She shook her head and poured his coffee. "I called a couple hours ago and spoke to Stevie's assistant, Paige. There's still no change, but Paige promised to call if there was any news. The doctor told her this morning that they won't know much more until Stevie comes around. It must be serious if they're keeping her in the ICU."

Allister only nodded, remembering how pale Stevie had looked, lying on the gurney last night in that bustling corridor.

Barb's empty cup slipped from her hands, clattering against the countertop but not breaking, and when she reached for it, her hands were shaking. "I just thank God Stevie wasn't killed, too," she stated, and then looked straight at Allister. "To think she might have been there. She might have...seen Gary's killer..."

But Allister didn't have to respond. The doorbell rang, and Barb almost dropped her mug again.

"It's all right," he assured her. "I'll get it."

Through the frosted-glass panel of the front door, Allister saw two blurred figures, and when he opened it, he was not surprised. He'd been expecting them.

"Detective Devane, good afternoon," he greeted the older of the two homicide detectives with whom he and Barb had spoken last night.

"Mr. Quaid. Well, this is convenient," the man drawled caustically, a sour grin turning up one corner of his crooked mouth. "I was hoping to talk to you, as well as Mrs. Palmer. Is she home?"

"As a matter of fact, she is. I'll see if she's up to—"

"It's all right, Allister." Barb stood at the end of the hall, her cup clutched in both hands now. "Let them in. I want this over with."

SHE'D BEEN DREAMING about being in the kitchen of the old house on Cicero Avenue. Her mother was baking bread and bottling tomato sauce the way she always did on Sunday afternoons. Stevie had almost been able to smell the sweet aroma of spices and the yeast from the rising dough, when a voice broke the spell.

"I think she's finally coming to." It was a female voice—distant, as though it traveled down a long hollow tunnel. "Stay with her. I'll get Dr. Sterling." The voice was closer now. It sounded as thick and heavy as the pain that throbbed in her head.

And then she heard the door. It slapped in its frame, just like the two-way door that separated her mother's kitchen from the family room. It swung a couple of times, and in between, she could make out other sounds: ringing phones and buzzers, and something that sounded like the chime of an elevator.

Then there was silence again. Silence and the stringent odor of antiseptic. This was not her mother's kitchen.

"Stevie?" A different voice this time, but familiar.

There was a hand on hers. She tried to pull away. She didn't want to be dragged from this warm place. She wanted to stay in the kitchen. It was safe there. Her father was in the family room, listening to the Sunday opera on the radio. The final act of *Tosca* was playing, and he'd promised that as soon as it was over, he'd show her how to develop the film from her camera.

"Stevie? Honey? Can you hear me?"

Perhaps if she kept her eyes closed, she'd be able to go back to the kitchen, to linger in its warm memories. Her head—it hurt so much. It hadn't hurt when she was in the kitchen.

"Stevie, come on. I know you can hear me. You've got to snap out of this. Please."

And then there was another voice. A man's this time.

"Stephanie?"

Her father? No, it couldn't be. He was dead. He died three years ago, the day after her twenty-seventh birthday. She'd gone home to Chicago for a visit. It had rained the whole weekend. A cold late-September drizzle that hadn't let up until after the funeral.

"Stephanie? Can you hear me? I'm Dr. Sterling. Can you open your eyes, Stephanie?"

"Her name's Stevie."

Now she recognized the quiet soothing voice. It was Paige.

"Stevie, you're at Danby General Hospital. You've had us all pretty worried. Stevie? Can you hear me?" he asked again.

She tried to nod, but pain hammered through her head. She wanted to answer him, but her mouth felt dry, her tongue swollen.

"Yeah." The word rasped in her throat.

"I knew you'd come around sooner or later," the man said, a smile in his voice. "Paige here tells me you can develop quite the appetite when you miss meals. I figured you'd be getting pretty hungry by now."

She attempted a smile, surprised that the effort didn't hurt as much as she'd anticipated.

"Can you open your eyes, Stevie?"

She licked her lips and finally opened her eyes a crack, expecting shards of light to pierce her already throbbing headache. There was only darkness. She opened them farther. Still darkness. And then there was Paige's voice again.

"Hey, Stevie. How're you feeling, honey?"

"Paige?"

She felt a hand take hers. "I'm right here."

"Where?"

"Right . . . right beside you."

Stevie squeezed the hand. She blinked several times. Or at least, she thought she did. But all she saw was darkness.

"Man, this is one strange dream." She let out a weak laugh.

"Stevie?" The hand tightened around hers. "Honey, it's . . . it's not a dream."

She blinked again and was met by the same chasm of utter blackness—a dizzying abyss.

"Paige, what are you saying?"

"Stevie, listen to me . . ."

She tried to sit up. Instantly there were hands on her shoulders, on her chest, holding her down, forcing her back into the pillows. And she felt something sharp pull on her arm.

Then there was Paige's voice again. "Stevie, just take it easy. You're going to be all right. Dr. Sterling's here, and—"

"I can't see!" Panic coursed through her, and another wave of nauseating pain knifed along the back of her head. "Paige, what's going on? I can't *see* you!"

CHAPTER THREE

DETECTIVE JACKSON was a man of few words, Allister decided as Jackson perused Gary's collection of bottled ships on the mantel of the flagstone fireplace. It was Detective Devane, the older of the pair, who was the lead man in the investigation into Gary's murder and who had taken an almost immediate dislike to Allister. Last night after they'd identified Gary's body, the gruff detective had undoubtedly recognized Allister from six years ago. When he'd asked Allister his whereabouts at the time of Gary's death, Devane had shot him a look of distrust across the corridor outside the morgue. And later, as Allister ushered Barb out the door and to the car, Devane had said good-night with a definite ''don't leave town'' tone in his voice.

Today, the detectives had asked to speak with Barb alone. But she'd remained firm in her demand that Allister be present, and Devane had had no choice. He eased his broad muscular frame farther back into the striped wing chair across from the couch where Allister and Barb sat. Her hand hadn't left Allister's the whole time.

''And you were home in your apartment last night, is that correct, Mr. Quaid?'' Devane turned his questions to Allister now.

''That's what I said, Detective. I already told you, the last time I saw Gary was yesterday morning. We spoke in his office about a couple of late shipments. I ran a number of errands for the company in the afternoon, and then I went home.''

''But there's nobody who can confirm you were there?''

Allister shook his head. ''No, I don't suppose there is. It's a big building. The neighbors pretty much keep to themselves.''

''Did you receive any phone calls last night?''

''Phone calls?''

''Yeah, you know, did anyone call when you were home? Anyone who can vouch for you?''

''No. No one called. Not until Barb rang me around three.''

Devane nodded wordlessly, but continued to squint distrustfully at Allister. No doubt, if Barb wasn't present, Devane would not be holding back the accusations Allister sensed beneath the detective's reserved composure.

Barb, however, was quite aware of what was going on.

She squeezed his hand. ''What is this all about, Detective?'' she asked, disbelief lifting her tone slightly. ''Is...is Allister a suspect here?''

''At this point, Mrs. Palmer, everyone is a suspect. And quite frankly, considering Mr. Quaid's record—''

''Oh, my God!'' Barb bolted from the couch. She stalked to the other side of the room, and when she turned again, even Allister was surprised at the fury that had flared across her previous calm. ''I don't believe this! You've really got some nerve, you know that, Detective? Coming in here and accusing Allister after everything you people have already put him through.''

''Barb.'' Allister went to her. He felt her tremble when he placed his hands on her shoulders, and when she looked up at him, he wondered if she was going to cry. ''Barb, it's all right,'' he whispered.

"It's wrong, Allister. What they're doing, what they're implying, it's wrong."

"Barb, trust me, it'll be all right," he said again, wishing he had faith in his own words. "Don't worry."

She relaxed somewhat, and in time she followed him back to the couch.

Detective Jackson paced behind them before stopping to gaze out the patio doors.

Devane was loosening the tie around the yellowed collar of his shirt. He scratched at a day's growth of stubble on his chin, and then ran a hand over his silver-flecked hair. Last night, when the early-morning hour and the harsh lights of the morgue had been unkind to everyone's appearance, Allister had pegged the senior detective in his early fifties. Still, he was a commanding presence—muscular and fit, almost a full head taller than his younger and slighter partner.

"Right now, Mrs. Palmer," Devane said at last, "we're working on the assumption that last night may have been a random break-in. We've had a couple other burglaries up there in the Dumphries area. We've got the warehouse closed off and my men are going over every square inch of the place. Your husband's secretary, Mrs. Dorsey, is helping us out with the inventory of the office, and we should know soon if anything was stolen. Until then, you have to understand, we can't rule out any possibility."

Barb only nodded.

"And there's still Ms. Falcioni. With her car parked outside the warehouse, we figure she might have interrupted the offender. We're hoping she got a good look at the guy, and that could be all we need. I have an officer posted at her hospital door, and we'll question her as soon as she regains consciousness."

"And what about the man who brought her in?" Barb took Allister's hand again. "Do you know anything more about him?"

Devane shook his head. "No one on staff at the hospital last night was able to give us a description beyond what we got from the nurse who actually spoke to the guy—tall, average build, with dark brown or possibly black hair. Beyond that, he could be anyone. Although we're almost certain he was at the warehouse, too."

Barb shook her head. "But last night you suggested that Stevie might have wandered out of the warehouse. That she may have even been picked up along the road somewhere."

"We found traces of blood on Ms. Falcioni's clothing. On her jeans and coat. Since she wasn't bleeding herself, we can only assume that it was your husband's. And considering the way it was distributed on the clothing, it would appear that it was put there by whoever carried her into the ER last night. We'll know better in a few days, but I'm willing to bet it'll match your husband's blood type, Mrs. Palmer."

"So what are you saying, Detective? That whoever this mystery man is, whoever brought Stevie to the hospital, he could be the same man who killed my husband?"

Devane made a noncommittal shrug. "Given the immediate evidence, I'd say it's one possibility."

"That's absolutely insane. You can't honestly believe that—"

"Mrs. Palmer, it doesn't matter whether or not I believe that your husband's killer may be the man who took Ms. Falcioni to the hospital. It's still a possibility we have to investigate. There are a lot of unanswered questions right now, but I'm certain that we'll be getting some answers soon— when Ms. Falcioni regains consciousness."

Barb stood up again, letting out a frustrated sigh as she moved to the fireplace. She took up the position Detective

Jackson had occupied only a few minutes ago and surveyed Gary's collection.

Eventually she shook her head. "None of this makes any sense. Why would somebody...why would anyone hurt Gary?"

And in what Allister guessed was a rare moment of compassion for Devane, the detective joined her at the mantel.

"We'll know more once we can talk to Ms. Falcioni," he repeated quietly. "If my hunch is right, she'll be able to finger your husband's killer for us. Trust me, Mrs. Palmer, we'll get this guy. With Ms. Falcioni as our eye witness, we'll put him behind bars for a long, long time."

STEVIE COULDN'T STOP shaking. Her hand trembled when she lifted it to her eyes. She expected to find gauze, bandages, *some*thing covering them, anything that would explain this horror.

There was nothing.

"Paige, I can't see." The words had become a desperate chant now. "I can't see." She tried to sit up again, still believing that this had to be some sort of nightmare, that it wasn't real, that if only she could sit up—

"Stevie, please." Paige held her down. "Dr. Sterling's here. Let him explain."

"Stevie?" The male voice again. Stevie tried to locate him in the dizzying blackness and imagined him to her left. "Stevie, I know this is a shock," he said, "but just try to relax and I'll explain."

"Paige?" Stevie reached out to where her friend had been before. She found only a crisp edge of the hospital sheet. "Paige, are you still here?"

"I'm right beside you, honey. I'm not going anywhere." A hand took hers, and Stevie clung to it as though it was her only lifeline in this terrifying sea of darkness.

"Stevie," the doctor continued, "you've been unconscious for over twenty hours now. That's why we've had you on an IV. Do you remember anything about last night?"

Stevie nodded—the jammed film, the storm, the warehouse. Gary. "I think so." She swallowed dry. "But what happened? I mean, why can't I see?"

"You've suffered a severe concussion, either from a fall or being struck with a blunt object. We've already run a CAT scan, and there's no evidence of skull fractures or intercerebral bleeding. Nor are there signs of any subdural hematomas, which indicates to me that any damage isn't likely to be permanent. You're extremely lucky, Stevie."

"How is this lucky? I'm blind!"

"Stevie, your loss of vision won't be permanent. You have a certain degree of swelling, bruising of the occipital lobe. That's the area that controls your vision. With the severity of the injury you've suffered, there is generally the possibility of a certain degree of visual impairment, of damage that the scans can't pick up. I still want to run an EEG, possibly today, to establish that there isn't any damage to the cerebral cortex."

"So my blindness . . . is temporary, then, right? That's what you're saying?"

Of course that was what he was saying. She'd heard of this kind of thing before, hadn't she? It was just a temporary condition. That was all. Not permanent. It couldn't be. She had the Armatrading shoot to finish, and there were other contracts waiting back at the studio. There was her career—her whole *life*—waiting for her.

Paige shifted her hand in hers. Stevie slackened her hold, wondering if she'd gripped her friend's hand so hard she'd hurt her.

"I can't say anything for certain, Stevie," the doctor answered. "But yes, more than likely this is just a temporary condition caused by the swelling."

"So, what are we talking about? A couple of days?"

"I really can't say, Stevie. With injuries like this, no two cases are alike. But I'm optimistic with yours. I'd say that after a week or so the bruising should resolve, and all, or part, of your vision should return. In fact, I don't see why you can't go home as soon as tomorrow afternoon, providing you have someone to take care of you."

"I'll be with her, Doctor," Paige offered.

"Good. I'll want to see you a couple of times over the next little while for reassessment. After two weeks, if there's still no resolution of your vision, we'll repeat the CAT scan and run another EEG. Even then, you have to understand that the bruising *may* take even longer than two weeks to clear up. But things should start to improve by that time...."

"And if they don't?" she asked, struggling against the quiver in her voice. "If I don't regain my vision, and a new CAT scan and EEG show nothing, what then?"

Her question was met with silence. Stevie felt her panic rise and a wave of nausea crash over her.

"Doctor, please. I need the truth."

"We'll have to cross that bridge when we come to it, Stevie. In situations like this, each case is unique. As much as I'd like to be able to give you a simple answer, I just can't. Your sight could start to return by tomorrow morning or next week or the week after."

"Or not at all?"

"Stevie—"

"No, Paige. Please. I have to know. Dr. Sterling? What *is* the likelihood that this is permanent?"

Beyond the hospital room, Stevie heard warbling phones and chimes, and the crackle of a PA system. There were other voices and laughter. And then the doctor's long intake of breath before he spoke again.

"Stevie, in all honesty, I just don't know. There's no way to tell at this point. Everything depends on the degree of the swelling and the rate at which it diminishes. So I can't answer your questions. I'm sorry. I can recommend another specialist for a second opinion if you like...."

"So my blindness *could* be permanent then." It wasn't a question, but a cold statement.

There was a dreadful silence again, and then Stevie felt the doctor's hand on her arm.

"Stevie, I know this is a shock for you, but please, try not to worry. We're doing everything we can. You just need time to heal. That's the best prescription I can give you right now."

Stevie tried to find a thin shred of comfort in his words. Only in her worst nightmares, in her darkest thoughts, had she ever imagined something like this. Just last year, a high-school friend from Chicago had nearly died in a car accident. Now her friend saw life from a wheelchair, was completely dependent on a live-in nurse. It had haunted Stevie for months afterward, the thought of being suddenly and completely dependent on others, of having the life you knew snatched away in one senseless flash, altering everything you'd known and worked for, and to never again see or perceive the world in the same way you once had.

"I'm going to arrange for that EEG," Dr. Sterling told her finally, removing his hand. "I'll be back shortly."

The door swung quietly in its frame a few times and then was still. She wasn't certain how long she lay there listening to the buzzing in her head, to the wild pounding of her heart, but it was Paige who eventually drew her out of the dark silence.

"Honey?" She rubbed Stevie's shoulder as if this could possibly ease the fears that raged through her mind. "You're going to be all right."

Stevie felt herself about to cry. She shook her head, fighting back the tears.

"Tell me I'm dreaming, Paige." Her voice trembled. "Tell me this is just a really bad dream."

"Stevie, listen to me, you have to think positively. Like Dr. Sterling said, it has to do with the swelling or whatever. It'll go down. You'll be fine."

That was Paige—the eternal optimist. Three years ago, not long before Stevie's father had died, when the contracts had been stacking up and she had been working twenty-hour days, Stevie had recognized the need for help around the studio. She'd placed the ad, and the instant Paige Carpenter had arrived at Images, fifteen minutes late and more than a little windblown, her hair a vibrant orange cascade of curls and her face glowing with an apologetic smile, Stevie knew there was no need to look any farther. From the start, Paige exuded the confidence and fresh talent Stevie had been looking for in an assistant, not to mention an enthusiasm and commitment that sometimes exceeded even her own. Within weeks of working together, Paige had proved herself the greatest assistant and friend Stevie could have hoped for.

"Do you want to sit up, Stevie?"

She barely nodded, and immediately Paige was at her side, rearranging pillows and drawing up the blanket.

"Listen, Stevie, I should tell you, the police have been lurking around. They even have an officer posted at the door. A Detective Devane said he'd be by to ask questions about last night."

"Gary's dead, isn't he?"

"I'm sorry, Stevie."

Stevie bit her lower lip. In spite of the darkness around her, she could still see the office, how everything had been thrown about, papers scattered, furniture tossed aside like toys, and Gary...lying unmoving on the floor. Then the man at the doorway, the man who had attacked her, and her race along the catwalk. And finally, nothing.

"How did I get here, Paige?"

"Someone brought you in last night."

"Who?"

"They don't know, Stevie. The police are still trying to find out, I guess."

She wished she could remember more, wished that last night wasn't such a blur. Then again, did she really want to conjure up those images? Perhaps the details of the ordeal were best forgotten.

"Barb's called a couple of times," Paige said. "She wanted to come by, but...she has a lot of arrangements to make."

Stevie nodded.

"She said she'd try to stop in later."

"I want to go home, Paige."

"I know."

She wanted to be in her own bed, away from the phones and the bells, from IVs and EEGs. She wanted to turn on the stereo and block out the rest of the world. Pull the duvet over her head and not come out for two weeks.

"Uh, Stevie?"

Paige was pacing. Stevie heard the soft squeak of her leather soles on the linoleum and the jangle of her bracelets.

"Paige, what's wrong?"

The squeaking stopped, and Stevie imagined her friend standing in the middle of the room. Knowing Paige, she probably wore an oversize shirt and vest, a pair of black tights and socks bunched up at the tops of her ankle boots. Her hands would be buried deep in the pockets of a man's tweed jacket she'd picked up at the thrift shop downtown. Her carrot-colored hair was most likely disheveled and pulled up in a wild ponytail after her long vigil at the hospital, and her pale complexion no doubt appeared paler still with lack of sleep.

"Paige?" she prompted.

"Stevie, listen, I'm sorry, but I . . . I called your mom."

"Oh, Paige."

"I know, I know. You always say you don't want to worry her. But Stevie, you . . . well . . . dammit, Stevie, you scared the hell out of me." Her voice wavered now, and Stevie wondered if Paige was crying. "I mean, the doctors . . . they were going on about you, talking about comas and brain damage and hematomas. I—"

"Paige, it's all right. *I'm* all right." But she heard the tremor in her voice and doubted her words were any more convincing for Paige than they were for her right now. She reached out for her friend, needing comfort as much as Paige seemed to.

Stevie felt the bed shift as Paige sat next to her and slid her hand into hers.

"Thanks for staying with me, Paige. For being here."

"I wouldn't have been anywhere else."

And then Paige's arms were around her before she could reply, giving her a reassuring embrace.

"God, you really had me scared," Paige murmured, pulling away but keeping her hand in Stevie's, and Stevie could tell that, for her sake, Paige was only telling the half of it.

"I'll be okay, Paige. You're right, I'll be fine. But I think I'd better call Ma before she jumps on the next plane from Tampa."

"Wait, Stevie."

"What?"

"There's something else." Paige stood and started to pace again.

"My mother's already here?"

"No, Stevie. No, it's not about your mother. It's...it's the studio."

"The Armatrading film?"

"Well, sort of. We had a break-in. It must have been late last night or early this morning when I was here. I went to the studio this morning to make a couple of calls and—"

Stevie was already shaking her head. "No, Paige. No."

"It's not that bad, Stevie, really. I called the police and filed a report. The insurance will cover the stolen equipment. It wasn't as bad as it could have been. They got away with a few of the cameras and one of the bags, but...we've lost the film from the Armatrading shoot."

"All of it?" This couldn't be happening, Stevie thought. It was like an endless nightmare, one horror following the next.

"I'm afraid so," Paige answered.

"Dammit, Paige. I don't believe this. What the hell is going on?"

"Stevie, listen to me. I don't want you to worry. I took care of everything. I called Brian this morning and he understands. He wants us to take whatever time we need to reshoot, and he promises that a couple of weeks won't make any difference to him."

Stevie rubbed her forehead. Well, maybe a couple of weeks didn't make any difference to Brian Armatrading. But according to Dr. Sterling's prognosis, two weeks meant the world to her. If, after that time, her sight hadn't returned, her blindness could very well be permanent. And then worrying about the reshoot for Brian Armatrading—or any other contract—would be immaterial.

VINCE FENTON felt more than a little proud of himself as he swilled back the rest of his beer and motioned to the night bartender of Mario's for a refill. It had been so easy.

First, getting the name of the photographer—that had been a simple matter of seeing the company name on the personalized plates of the Volvo when he'd sneaked out of the warehouse yesterday afternoon. Second, finding the studio and getting in—again, a piece of cake. He'd waited until the redhead left for the night, and without any kind of security system to contend with, he jimmied the back door of the converted warehouse. Then he'd grabbed all the cameras he could find, loaded them into his car in the alley behind the building and drove them to his buddy Stan Swanson.

In exchange for developing the film for him, Stan could keep the stolen goods. But Vince wanted to see the film himself, be sure that he'd stolen the right one, the one used for the shoot at Palmer's warehouse. After that, he'd have covered all his tracks.

Maybe then Vince could finally get out of Danby. Bainbridge and his precious coins were starting to piss him off. It wasn't worth the money anymore, not with Palmer's murder on top of everything else. All he needed was the film—the right film—and he was gone.

IT HAD BEEN a long day, followed by an equally long night. After the EEG, Stevie had been returned to her room and told to rest, as if she'd been able to do anything else. She had called Tampa and assured her mother that there was no need to fly all the way up to Danby. She'd listened patiently to her mother ramble on about the new condo, her neighbors and the weather. And when she'd asked once again about flying up to Danby, Stevie had promised her she was fine and would call again soon.

Before he left for the day, Dr. Sterling had spoken to the floor nurses. Paige had been allowed to stay past visiting hours, and for this Stevie was grateful. Paige had helped her with dinner and had guided her to the washroom a couple of times.

But eventually even Paige had been forced to leave. Reluctantly she'd said good-night with promises of sneaking in a large coffee for Stevie in the morning. After that, Stevie had lain awake listening to the sounds of the hospital.

At one point during the night, when the corridor outside her door had fallen almost completely silent, Stevie had decided to brave the short trip across her room to the washroom unaided. But within moments of leaving the bed, a wave of dizziness swept through her, and when she flailed out to stop her fall, Stevie thought she'd woken the entire wing. Stainless-steel pans crashed across the linoleum.

Seconds later one of the night nurses had rushed in to find Stevie on the floor clutching her hands to one throbbing knee and letting out such a string of expletives she was certain the nurse must have had second thoughts about coming to her aid.

After that, Stevie had slipped in and out of sleep, never really knowing whether it was day or night, trying to judge time by the sounds of the hospital around her. She'd even taken to counting seconds out loud after another nurse had told her it was 2:00 a.m.

In the morning, Barb had called, saying she was tied up with various arrangements. She voiced her relief that Stevie was all right, and at the same time stated how sorry she was that something so terrible as her blindness had happened. She'd mentioned briefly the plans for the funeral, that

Gary's friend Allister was helping her out with the business, and once again how sorry she was.

There had been more tests, followed by enough of Dr. Sterling's optimism to see Stevie through another week, or at least until her next scheduled appointment.

Only when Paige had arrived for her second visit in the afternoon, with a change of clothes and another smuggled coffee, did Stevie begin to feel a little more on track. Paige had helped her dress, and by the time Dr. Sterling arrived to sign her out, Stevie was more than ready to go home.

"So, we need to book a follow-up appointment, Stevie," Dr. Sterling told her. "There's a conference I have to be at in Seattle early next week, so I'm taking appointments on Saturday. How would late morning be for you?"

"Should be fine." Stevie shrugged, then added a quick smile. "But only if you promise to give me some good news then."

"I'll see what I can do." Stevie wondered what his smile looked like; she imagined it was as gentle as his voice. "So, next Saturday, eleven-thirty, in my office upstairs. I've given Paige a prescription for you. Just a mild sedative to help you sleep, if you feel you need it, and a painkiller. Other than that, you're formally discharged."

"Thanks, Doc." Stevie managed another smile for his benefit. She shifted in the chair next to the bed, the chrome armrests cold against her wrists.

"And, Stevie, I've also given Paige my card. I want you to feel free to call me day or night if there's any change, or if you have even the smallest concern."

"I will. Thanks."

"Now the only other matter of business is the police," he said as she heard him click his pen a few times. "A couple of detectives have been anxious to talk to you. And now that you're discharged, I don't have the authority to keep them out anymore."

"Are they here now?"

"I'm afraid so."

She had to talk to them. For Gary's sake. She appreciated Dr. Sterling's efforts to protect her from the countless questions they undoubtedly had, but she was going to have to face them sooner or later, no matter how tired and disoriented she felt.

"Well, I may as well get it over with," she said.

Dr. Sterling had been gone less than a minute before the door swung open. Stevie heard them come in, hard soles against the floor, and one of them cleared his throat.

"Ms. Falcioni?" His voice was rough, and when he cleared his throat a second time Stevie suspected he was a smoker. "Ms. Falcioni, I'm Detective Devane, and this is Detective Jackson."

Stevie nodded, her hands firmly gripping the chrome armrests.

"This is my friend, Paige Carpenter," she said.

"Yes, we've . . . met."

Stevie couldn't resist an inward smile. Paige had mentioned to Stevie this morning that she'd had "words" with Detective Devane. Now, by the momentary awkwardness in the silence between them, Stevie didn't doubt the content of those words.

"Ms. Falcioni, we have a few questions we need to ask you about Friday night . . ."

SHE TOLD the detectives everything she remembered—the drive to the warehouse because she'd forgotten her bag, going upstairs to Gary's office, seeing his body on the floor, and then the man who attacked her.

"So this guy with the fire extinguisher," Devane asked a second time, "before he took a swing at you, did you get a good look at him?"

Stevie shook her head. "Not really. I had just stepped into the office when he came at me. It was only a split second."

"So how would you describe him, then?"

"I really can't be sure. He was tall, over six feet, I'd guess. Average build. Dark hair, dark eyes."

"And you say there was blood on his hands?"

"Yes. On his gloves."

"But nothing else? Do you remember any distinguishing features?"

Again Stevie shook her head. She'd racked her brains, sifting through the hazy and disjointed memories of that night, but the only image she'd been able to conjure up of the man was based on that one instant when she'd stepped into the office and seen him about to swing the fire extinguisher at her.

Dr. Sterling had tried to assure Stevie that, given time, further memory of that night could return. She was likely experiencing a type of selective amnesia—blocking out certain details of the attack that were too frightening for her to deal with—and she might never recall every second of that night.

"No, Detective, I can't remember any distinguishing features."

"Ms. Falcioni, do you think you got a good enough look at this guy that you might be able to, say, pick him out of a lineup?"

Stevie let out a short laugh, a combination of wry amusement and resentment curling the corners of her lips as she shook her head. "Under the circumstances, Detective, I think I'd have to say no to the lineup."

"What I mean is—" he stumbled with his words "—perhaps, when your sight returns, do you think you might be able to?"

"*If* my sight returns, yes, maybe I'd be able to ID him for you. But I can't make any promises."

"Fine. That's all I'm asking. And in the meantime, you might remember something else about this man."

Stevie heard the detective moving around the room. She tried to follow his path by the sound of his tread and the soft rustle of paper as he leafed through his notebook. But when he finally spoke again, his voice came from the far left, instead of in front of her where she'd expected him to be. Stevie shifted uneasily in the chair and massaged her temple. The painkiller was wearing off.

"The man who brought you in the other night," Devane was saying, "he told the attending physician that you fell. Do you remember falling?"

"Like I said before, Detective, all I remember is running along the catwalk away from Gary's office."

"So this man, he was chasing you?"

"Yes." Impatience and exhaustion sharpened her tone. How many times would she have to answer the same questions? "Yes, I'd assume he was chasing me. And then... I think he grabbed me. That's it. I can't tell you if he hit me, or I fell, or what happened. I'm sorry. I just can't remember."

"And what about Mr. Palmer? You were at the warehouse for a few hours earlier in the day, doing a photo shoot, right?"

"Yes. Both Paige and I and our hired crew."

"Did you speak with Mr. Palmer then?"

"Yes, a couple of times."

"And did he seem out of sorts at all?"

Throughout the night as Stevie had lain awake, wishing for sleep, she'd thought a lot about Gary and the last time she'd spoken to him. She remembered how, shortly after the Nikon jammed, Gary had come out of his office. He'd crossed the loading area to where she worked and told her that he was going out for a bit, that if anyone needed him he'd be back in twenty minutes. He *had* seemed "out of sorts." Preoccupied, almost nervous. And when he headed to the side door, Stevie noticed how he'd glanced over his shoulder a couple of times.

"Was there anything unusual about his behavior, Ms. Falcioni?"

Stevie nodded, recalling how later she'd gone up to see Gary. "When I stopped in his office after the shoot was done, he practically jumped out of his skin. I asked if there was anything wrong, but he said he was just tired."

She could still picture how his exhausted smile had done little to mask his obvious anxiety. "But looking back now, I don't know, it almost seemed as though Gary had known something was going to happen."

"And did you talk about anything that last time you saw Mr. Palmer?"

"No, not really," she replied. "I think I suggested he take a holiday or something."

"And what was his response?"

"He said he couldn't leave the business, that there was too much going on. And then I suggested he get Allister to handle things for a while."

"So you know Allister Quaid?"

Stevie shook her head. "No, not personally. I know of him through Gary, that's all. I know they were friends since childhood and that he's been helping out with the company for the past few months. But I haven't met him."

There was a long lull. Paige, apparently recognizing Stevie's fatigue, placed one hand on her shoulder and gave it a gentle rub. Stevie wondered if Paige made some sort of gesture to the detectives, because Devane suddenly cleared his throat and said, "Well, Ms. Falcioni, thank you for your time. Here's my card. I guess your friend here can..." He didn't bother to finish. "If you remember anything else, any other details, you'll be sure to call me?"

Stevie reached out and accepted the card that Devane slipped into her hand. She fingered the embossed surface.

"I will, Detective."

"Very good."

She heard them walk to the door, heard it swing open to the clamor of the corridor, and then there was Devane's voice again.

"One more thing, Ms. Falcioni. About Mr. Palmer...did he by chance give you anything? A package perhaps?"

"A package?"

"Yeah. Or maybe an envelope? For safekeeping?"

"No, Detective." Stevie shook her head, puzzled by this shift in Devane's questioning. "Gary didn't give me anything. Does this have something to do with his death?"

"No, probably not. It's just that with Mr. Palmer's office being ransacked and then the break-in of your studio later that night...well, it's probably just coincidence, you know? I was only wondering. Thanks again for your time, Ms. Falcioni. We'll be in touch."

As the door swung lazily in its frame, Stevie wondered if her expression reflected her confusion at Detective Devane's parting question. A package? Safekeeping? *Was* there some connection between Gary's murder and the studio break-in, after all?

And for the first time, Stevie realized how distant she and Gary had become. What had he been into? What was Devane looking for? And was it the reason Gary had been killed?

CHAPTER FOUR

ALLISTER HAD GIVEN Mrs. Dorsey the day off. Out of all the Palmer Shipping employees, Gary's secretary had taken the news the hardest. Even five days after Gary's murder, the staff still seemed to be functioning in a state of shock and disbelief. And with many of them planning to attend Gary's funeral this afternoon, Allister had let most of them go for the day, leaving only a skeleton staff.

From behind the secretary's cluttered desk, Allister glanced up at the wall clock and watched the steady sweep of the second hand. He needn't have looked to know that it was almost one. After four years of measuring time, four years of counting each minute, each second until the day he'd walked away from that prison cell, Allister had developed an inner clock that rarely failed him.

Absently he drummed a chewed ballpoint against the edge of the desk. In one hour he'd be standing at the podium next to Gary's closed casket delivering the eulogy, gazing out at the faces of friends and family, faces torn by disbelief and shock, begging for an explanation for the violence that had touched all their lives.

Faces like Stevie Falcioni's.

Allister could still feel twinges of the remorse that had flooded him three nights ago when Barb had called to give him the news. She'd just received word from the hospital, from Stevie's friend Paige Carpenter. Stevie had regained consciousness. But even before the implication of this news hit home, Allister had been shocked to learn of her condition.

Blind.

Temporarily blind was what Barb said the doctors were hoping. But Stevie's friend had implied that there might not be a change for days or even weeks.

And then this morning, when he'd gone to the house for Barb's signature on several forms, finalizing the transfer of signing authority on the company's accounts to him, Barb had been visibly distressed by more than the impending funeral.

"They don't know anything yet, Allister," she'd told him, her hand shaking while she systematically signed each form. "I phoned Stevie yesterday afternoon. She's home from the hospital at least, and her friend Paige is staying with her, but she's... My God, Allister, I just don't know what to say to her. I mean, she's blind. What do you... what do you say to someone who..."

"I don't know, Barb."

"It's just not fair, Al. She's always been so full of life, so happy, so energetic. And her photography. God, it's her life. I just can't imagine what she's going through. What she's going to do now that—"

"But you said they thought it was temporary."

Barb shook her head. "They can't tell yet. Stevie said it could still be a couple of weeks before they know if she will ever regain her vision."

A couple of weeks. Allister wondered if that would be enough time to find Bainbridge's coins, enough time to find even a shred of evidence against the antiquities collector that would clear Allister of any suspicion. In a couple of weeks, when—*if*—Stevie's sight returned, it could be only a matter of time before she identified him as the man who'd attacked her. The man she undoubtedly believed to be Gary's killer. After that, there'd be no hope of proving his innocence—either to her or to the authorities.

Yet Allister knew that somehow, in some way, Stevie held the key. Gary wouldn't have mentioned her otherwise. She was inextricably bound up in Bainbridge's deal, whether she knew it or not.

Or maybe she'd been in on Gary's scheme from the start. Maybe she even had the coins.

Allister had already inspected the shipping bin he'd come to check the night of Gary's murder. Of course it was empty. He'd spent several hours over the past couple of days searching all the likely places Gary might have stashed the shipment. Still nothing. Apart from going through Gary's office, which had been secured and taped off by the police, there was nowhere else to look. Surely Gary wouldn't have taken Bainbridge's package to his home. Even Bainbridge must have known Gary wasn't that foolish, otherwise the house would already have been ransacked, just like the office.

Then there was the box that Mrs. Dorsey had mentioned the other day—a large box, she'd told him, with some of Gary's office things that the police had taken with them the morning after the murder. But if the coins had been among those belongings, there would have been word of their recovery by now in the local paper.

No, the coins were still out there. Somewhere. And it was only a matter of time before Bainbridge started to get really antsy—and, with any luck, even careless.

In the silence of the office, Allister withdrew a sheet of paper from the breast pocket of his suit jacket and unfolded it. Gary's eulogy. His last words for a friend he thought he'd known. A friend who'd quite literally taken his life in his hands when he'd agreed to do business with Edward Bainbridge.

When he got up from the desk, Allister heard someone call his name. He left the office and headed to the catwalk overlooking the loading bay.

One of the workers below gave Allister a quick wave. Beside him was Detective Devane. "Mr. Quaid, someone here to see you," the worker said before nodding in the direction of the stairs for the detective.

Allister watched Devane take the steps two at a time and follow the catwalk to where he stood at the railing. Already Allister could feel cords of tension tighten along the back of his neck.

"Good afternoon, Detective."

"Mr. Quaid." Devane nodded.

"I hope this won't take long," Allister said flatly as he headed back into the office, the burly detective on his heels. "I was on my way out. I have a funeral to attend."

"Shouldn't take more than a minute, Mr. Quaid. I just need you to listen to something for me."

Allister turned as Devane drew a microcassette recorder from his coat pocket. With one fleshy thumb the detective jabbed the play button and set the compact recorder on the desk. The hiss of the tape sliced through the room's silence. Devane crossed his arms over his broad chest and watched Allister.

Allister focused on the small black recorder. The tape crackled a few times and then he heard Gary's muffled voice.

"It's me," Gary said through the hiss. "We've got to talk."

"About what?" another voice asked, more distant, rather fuzzy, as though it came through some cheap portable phone. "You told me everything was taken care of."

Bainbridge. If Gary hadn't told him about Bainbridge and the coins, Allister would never have recognized the voice.

"Not quite," Gary answered. "We've got a couple loose ends."

"How the hell can there be loose ends? What are you talking about, Palmer? I thought you said the shipment was going out today. What is it? Customs?"

"No. Not customs."

"What then?"

"It's a matter of the shipment's contents. I...I don't make a habit of shipping stolen goods."

There was scuffling noise then, as though one of them had covered the mouthpiece of the phone, and then more hissing.

"But I think we can come to some sort of arrangement. Perhaps we should talk."

"Damn right we need to talk, Palmer. I thought we had a deal. If you think you can—"

"I just want to talk, that's it."

"I'll send Vince."

"No, I want—" But Gary's last words were swallowed by a dial tone.

Devane reached for the recorder and turned it off. When Allister looked up, the detective's expression was something between expectation and challenge.

"So, Mr. Quaid, what do you know about stolen goods being shipped out of this warehouse?"

Allister shook his head. "Absolutely nothing."

Devane's skepticism lifted his thick brows. "Nothing, hmm?"

"No."

"We found this tape in Gary Palmer's office, along with a telephone recording device. You know anything about that?"

"No." Allister didn't have to lie.

"Do you know anyone named Vince?"

"No."

"Seems to me your friend was in over his head. Looks like maybe he was dabbling in a bit of blackmail, wouldn't you say?"

"Why don't you tell me? You're the detective."

Devane returned the recorder to his pocket and started to pace the small office. "Even more interesting, we found these in Mr. Palmer's desk." He withdrew several photocopied newspaper clippings and tossed them onto Mrs. Dorsey's desktop.

"Mean anything to you, Mr. Quaid?"

Allister glanced at the articles, but he didn't need to. He knew what they were—stories from seven months ago announcing the theft of a collection of rare Spanish coins from a traveling exhibit, which had stopped at the Danby Museum.

Dammit, Gary, Allister thought, clenching his jaw, *what the hell were you thinking? What did you get yourself into?*

"Mr. Quaid?"

Allister nodded. "Yes, I heard about the robbery."

"Pretty big heist," Devane continued, retrieving the photocopies from the desk. "Happened last May. That'd be what? Five, six weeks after your release?"

"If you've got something to say, Detective . . ."

Devane waved his hand dismissively. "Just thinking out loud," he said. "And what was that you were serving time for again, Mr. Quaid? Grand theft, wasn't it? Something to do with stolen gems, if I remember correctly."

Devane stopped pacing and turned to look squarely at Allister, sizing him up. If the detective was hoping he would lash out, trip up somehow, he was going to be disappointed, Allister thought, clenching his fists in the pockets of his jacket.

"But they never did recover the rest of those gems, did they? Just the ones from your car, am I right? You still claiming you didn't do it?"

Allister refused to respond. But Devane seemed undaunted.

"And what was that? Four, five years ago? Gosh, seems like only yesterday, and here you are, out on the streets again. Gotta love our justice system, huh?"

"Listen, Detective, if I'm a suspect, why don't you come right out and say it. In fact, why don't you go and get a warrant, and then you and your men can go over to my apartment and search it like you did the last time."

"Actually, Mr. Quaid, it would be a lot easier if you just told me where the coins are."

Allister shook his head. "And I suppose next you'll be accusing me of killing Gary, right?"

Devane gave a shrug, but it was the accompanying sneer that grated on Allister's patience.

"Are you finished, Detective?" he asked, swallowing his anger. "Like I said before, I have to bury a friend today."

STEVIE SHIFTED on the hard wooden chair. Sliding one hand along her thigh, she felt for the hem of her dress, making sure it was in place as she crossed her legs. Next to her, Paige must have sensed her restlessness. She laid her hand over Stevie's.

"How are you doing?" she whispered.

Stevie nodded and offered a quick smile to reassure her. But the truth was, she couldn't remember if she'd ever felt as uncomfortable as she did right now.

Arriving a few minutes late had given Stevie the perfect excuse for taking a back-row seat, closer to the door in case she started to feel sick again from the painkillers, and out of sight of the rest of the mourners. When they'd sat down initially, Stevie had caught snippets of the whispered conversations—words of grief, murmurs of comfort. But without a visual context of who was speaking, that was all they were to Stevie—disjointed voices reeling dizzyingly around her.

She wanted to be home in the security of her apartment over the studio. She felt exposed here, completely vulnerable, naked in the eyes of people she could not see.

No, she would just as soon have stayed in bed, with Puccini blaring on the stereo, until Saturday, until her appointment with Dr. Sterling.

But Paige hadn't let her.

Within minutes of returning home from the hospital three days ago, Paige had tossed Stevie's bag in the corner and guided her through both the studio and the apartment. She'd cleaned the night before, she warned Stevie. She'd straightened the frightful mess that Stevie's apartment tended to fall prey to whenever contracts piled up and had proudly shown her how she'd organized the place, so Stevie would be less apt to trip over things.

After that, Stevie had spent a good two hours on the phone to Chicago assuring her brothers and sister that she was fine. If it hadn't been for Paige staying with her, Stevie was certain the entire Falcioni family, aunt and uncle and cousins included, would have been on her doorstep within hours wanting to cater to her every need. Instead, she'd been able to find comfort in her own surroundings with just her good friend around.

Paige knew Stevie well enough to recognize when she needed to be alone and when she was on the verge of wallowing in self-pity. And it was at those moments that Paige had been her savior. She'd put Stevie to work in the studio, rolling film and helping out with other tasks that required darkness. Even yesterday Paige sat her down with the jammed Nikon so that Stevie could salvage the film from the broken camera.

Yes, Paige had been more than a friend through this. She'd been a saint.

Stevie gave her friend's hand a gentle squeeze now, appreciative of her presence. She couldn't have come here without Paige. She couldn't have attended Gary's funeral. And, as uncomfortable as she was, if Paige hadn't dragged her here today, Stevie would later have regretted not coming.

Stevie heard a man clear his throat near a mike at the front of the room.

"Seems like I've known Gary all my life," she heard him begin, his deep fluid voice catching only slightly. He paused, took a breath and then went on. "In fact, I don't remember much before the day his family moved into the house across the street on Birch, and this cocky freckle-faced kid walked right up to me and introduced himself. 'We're gonna be best friends, you and me, Al,' he'd told me. And I believed him. I mean, I didn't even know this kid, but I believed him. Gary always was so sure of himself even back then..."

So this was Allister Quaid, Gary's best friend. After years of hearing about him, this was the closest Stevie had come to actually meeting the man.

His voice reached out across the congregation, its sooth-ing and heartfelt tone touching Stevie in a way she hadn't thought possible, stirring her own memories of Gary and bringing a painful lump to her throat.

He spoke of their childhood together, shared exploits and conquests, followed by humorous and fond anecdotes. He spoke of Gary the friend, Gary the loving husband to Barb, and Gary the person they'd all known. And throughout, Stevie tried to envision the man behind the voice.

In spite of his closeness to Gary, Stevie couldn't remem-ber if she'd even seen a picture of Allister Quaid in all those years. She imagined him tall. And she imagined him dark. But most of all, she imagined warm sincere eyes as she lis-tened to him speak so lovingly of their mutual friend.

"...and I think I speak for everyone here today, for ev-eryone who had the good fortune of knowing Gary, when I say that he will be greatly missed among us. His loss is truly tragic, and we are all lesser people in his absence."

WHEN ALLISTER STEPPED back from the podium and re-turned the folded sheet of paper to his pocket, a somber hush hung over the congregation. At last, though, the ser-vice was finished, and people rose from their seats, many of them stopping to murmur words of condolence to Barb.

Allister stayed with her, his hand resting on the small of her back, lending her support as she thanked Gary's friends for their attendance. But Allister's attention was elsewhere.

From the podium minutes ago, he thought he'd seen Stevie Falcioni seated near the back, but now as he scanned the room, the only face that caught his attention was De-tective Devane's. He saw the man scowl and slip out the door. He'd been right behind Allister on his way to the fu-neral home, and judging by the scowl, Allister could only assume that Devane hadn't seen anything during the service that resembled a possible lead.

It was then, as Allister resigned himself to the fact that Stevie must have already left, that he saw her at the side of the room. In one heart-stopping moment, an unexpected flood of memories from that night came hammering back—how he'd lifted her unconscious body from the catwalk and carried her to his car, how he'd held her in his arms, her head resting against his chest, and how he'd smelled her perfume on his own skin even after he'd fled the hospital.

Today she wore a short form-fitting black dress that emphasized her gentle curves. She was striking, with her olive complexion and sleek chin-length black hair. Standing next to her, with one hand on Stevie's arm, was a taller fair-complexioned woman with a long mop of tight orange curls.

He watched them for a moment, but it wasn't until the woman at Stevie's side whispered something to her and proceeded to guide her toward the front that Allister felt the sickening swell of remorse twist up from his gut.

He had to get out of here somehow, before Stevie reached Barb to offer her condolences.

"Allister?"

It was Barb. She looked up at him, her pale blue eyes glistening slightly, her expression drawn with exhaustion.

"Thank you for the eulogy, Al. It was beautiful. And thanks for not . . . for not mentioning the divorce."

He nodded.

"And thank you for everything else. Taking care of the business and the funeral arrangements. I . . . I couldn't have done it without you."

"Barb, you don't need to thank me, you know that."

They were drawing nearer, Stevie and the other woman, skirting the perimeter of the room. Allister doubted that

Barb had seen them yet, but they were only seconds away now.

He tried to reason with himself. Stevie Falcioni was blind. There was no way she could recognize him. He had to relax.

Still...

"Listen, Barb, I have to go out for a minute," he said, taking a step back. "I won't be long."

"Oh, wait, Allister."

He was too late.

"There's Stevie. Just let me introduce you."

There was nothing he could do but stand and watch as Barb threw her arms around Stevie and hugged her. Heartfelt whispers passed between the two women, and when Barb drew away, Allister saw her dab at her eyes.

"I'm so sorry, Stevie," Barb said. "I just... Do the doctors know anything else? Do they know when...?"

Stevie shook her head, and Allister noted how forced her fleeting smile was. But it was her eyes that sent another nauseating wave of guilt crashing through him. Wide, almost black, beneath dark brows. Eyes that no doubt were normally bright and alert, but now were eerily unfocused. In them he saw fear and uncertainty—an uncertainty, he was sure, that reached far beyond her immediate surroundings and situation.

"Is there anything you need, Stevie?" Allister marveled at Barb's ability to turn her own sorrow and loss into compassion. "Anything I can do?"

"No, Barb, really. But thank you."

Her voice. Allister swallowed hard. He'd been so close to her the other night, memorized almost every line and every angle of her face, and yet he hadn't heard her voice. Now its soft tone cut like a knife through his chest.

"Paige is taking good care of me," she said. "So you're returning to Baltimore with your family, then?"

Barb nodded. "The day after tomorrow. I'll be back in Danby at some point to pack up the house and finalize things before I move there. In the meantime, Allister is going to take care of the business for me. I don't think you two have ever actually met, have you?" she asked, turning to Allister.

"NO. NO, I DON'T BELIEVE we *have* met," the man replied. For Stevie there was no mistaking the smooth male voice that had delivered Gary's eulogy.

As Barb made the requisite introductions, Stevie turned in the direction of the voice. She hoped her guess was good. When she extended her hand in greeting, she was relieved when it was enclosed in warm flesh.

His hand was large, his grasp firm and instantly reassuring. And for a moment, Stevie wondered if it was just her imagination that the handshake was lasting longer than a customary greeting warranted.

"It's great to finally meet you, Allister," she said, her hand still lost in his. "After hearing Gary sing your praises all these years and never meeting you, well, I was starting to believe you were some imaginary friend left over from his childhood."

She heard a quick exhalation of breath and guessed that she'd managed to elicit a smile from the man. He finally released her hand.

"It was a beautiful eulogy," she added in the brief silence that fell between them.

"I was just commenting on that myself," Barb added. "Gary would have liked it."

"I'm glad you think so," he said. There was something in his voice, a hesitancy, a slight awkwardness, that made Stevie suspect her blindness made him nervous.

"Oh, Stevie," Barb said, "you mentioned something about needing to use the warehouse again. With me out of town, maybe you should make arrangements with Allister."

"Gary told me about your photo shoot," Allister put in. "It must have gone well if you're wanting to use the warehouse for another."

"Actually, it's the same shoot," she explained. "Seems we're going to have to redo it." But even as Stevie said the words, she couldn't help thinking it could very well be Paige who'd be doing the reshooting, not her.

"Why?" he asked. "The pictures didn't turn out?"

"Oh, I'm sure they were fine." She sighed. "It's just that we don't exactly have them anymore."

"Our studio was broken into a couple nights ago," Paige explained.

Allister didn't respond to that, and in the awkward silence that fell, Stevie felt obliged to clarify.

"It wasn't too bad, really. We're insured. It's just that the cameras that were stolen were the ones we'd used for the shoot at the warehouse, so we've lost all the film."

"When did this happen?"

"The day after... I mean, Saturday sometime," Stevie said.

Allister watched Stevie bite her bottom lip, and another flood of guilt forced him to look away from her, as images from that night shuddered through his mind again.

"I'm sorry to hear that," he offered, his words sounding weak. "Of course you're welcome to use the warehouse whenever you need."

"Thank you." She combed her fingers back through her luxuriant jet black hair and seemed to search for Paige's arm. Her friend was quick to respond, but not quick enough.

Whether it was a lack of balance caused by her blindness or perhaps fatigue from the past few days, Stevie faltered as she turned. In a flash, Allister was at her side. With one arm around her small waist and the other catching her hand, he felt her familiar weight sag momentarily against his chest. A combination of surprise and relief washed across her face, and her grip tightened on his arm as she steadied herself.

"I'm sorry," she murmured, her lips trembling into a smile.

"It's all right," he told her. "I've got you."

"I . . . I get a little dizzy sometimes. Not sure if it's the painkillers or just . . ."

Or just that she was blind, Allister thought when it was obvious Stevie couldn't bring herself to finish the statement. Her hand lingered on his arm a moment longer before he guided her to Paige, and as he did he caught the faint yet familiar scent of her perfume.

"We should probably get going," Paige suggested.

Stevie seemed to withdraw suddenly, as though embarrassed by her momentary weakness and her dependency on her friend, and Paige handled the goodbyes. Stevie murmured some parting words to Barb, followed by something about being glad to have finally met Allister, and then they moved away. He watched the pair weave their way carefully through the remaining mourners who waited to extend their condolences to Barb.

Allister felt sick seeing Stevie's utter helplessness and knowing he was the cause. That proud tilt of her head, that air of fierce independence, made him realize that Stevie Falcioni was not the type of person who took well to relying on others.

Still, he couldn't ignore one crucial fact—her blindness, the condition that brought such an acrid taste of remorse to his mouth, was the one guarantee that Stevie Falcioni could not place him at Gary's warehouse the night of the murder. Her blindness, which was a dreadful curse to her, was now almost a blessing to him.

"And on top of everything else, to have her studio broken into," Barb was saying as she followed his gaze.

Allister nodded.

The break-in. Could he really believe that it was just coincidence? Could he believe that Bainbridge had nothing to do with it? That the man didn't suspect a connection between Gary and Stevie?

If it wasn't coincidence, it could mean only one thing. Someone, whether Bainbridge or not, somehow recognized the possibility that Stevie was linked to Gary and the coins. And if indeed Stevie was the key to the missing shipment, then she was the one person who could help Allister recover the coins and prove Bainbridge's corruption once and for all. Unless, of course, Stevie Falcioni knew far more than she was letting on. There was a possibility that Stevie knew all about the coins and Gary's involvement with Bainbridge. And maybe she even had the coins herself; maybe she had her own agenda.

If that was the case, Allister could only wonder whether Stevie realized the dangerous game she was playing.

"WHAT DO YOU MEAN, you don't have them yet?" Edward Bainbridge stood with his cordless phone at the patio doors and looked out at the slate gray sky. His last words had sent a shower of spittle against the glass. He didn't wipe it off. "Dammit, Fenton, what the hell's taking so long? I've got a buyer waiting in—"

"Hey, I'll get them," Vince Fenton said. "Just let me do my job, all right? I know what I'm doing. Man, you really gotta relax."

"Relax? I'm not paying you to be my therapist, Fenton, you hear me? This has gone on too long now."

"Look, I don't need this aggro, okay? I got shit of my own to take care of, too, you know."

"Not while you're on my payroll, you don't."

Fenton didn't respond. In the silence over the line, Edward Bainbridge realized that no matter whose payroll Fenton was on, the man was not about to make a move on the coins until it suited him.

"So what the hell's happening with Quaid?" he asked Fenton now. "Does he have them or not?"

"Yeah, he's got them. I'm sure of it. I'm just not sure yet *where* he's got them. You don't want me moving in on Quaid before I know where the coins are, do you?"

Right. Another Gary Palmer. That was all he needed. If it hadn't been for Fenton's overzealous nature to begin with, he'd never be in this mess now. The coins would be in his buyer's hands overseas, and he'd already have collected the prearranged sum.

"Look, Fenton, I just want my stuff, okay? I don't care what you have to do to Quaid to get it. Remember our deal. Until I see that shipment, you don't see the final instalment of your fee."

Even across the bad connection he could hear Fenton's sharp intake of breath. He should have never hired him. The ex-con had too quick a temper, too great a liking for violence.

God help anyone who got in the man's way.

God help Allister Quaid, Bainbridge thought, as he hung up the phone.

CHAPTER FIVE

WHIRLWINDS OF SNOW danced along the empty street, shimmering momentarily in the headlights of the Explorer before being whisked off into the darkness. It had snowed most of the day, light crystalline flakes that accumulated along the banks formed by the plows after that first storm six days ago.

Allister pulled the vehicle to a stop, killed the headlights and turned off the ignition. Across the street, the squat two-story converted warehouse appeared vacant. Its facade, illuminated by three covered bulbs mounted over the Images Studio sign, had been stuccoed and painted an unusual shade of apricot that reminded him of a New Mexico desert. In the heat of a Danby summer, Allister didn't doubt that the color had its appeal, but tonight, with the mercury dipping to a frigid nine degrees, it seemed decidedly at odds with its surroundings.

A second Images sign was mounted in one of the two wide windows that flanked the double doors. This one was in soft pink neon letters that swirled in a graceful arc over a pale blue slash. But the neon sign was the only discernible light from within the studio where Barb said Stevie had her apartment.

Allister angled his wrist to catch the light of a street lamp. Just after nine. Perhaps he should have called first. But then, he hadn't wanted to make his visit seem like anything other than a casual coincidence.

"I was just in the area," he planned to tell Stevie when he handed her the light meter he'd found at the warehouse this morning. Obviously the piece of equipment was not irreplaceable, otherwise she would have made arrangements to retrieve it by now. And had he called first, Allister was certain she wouldn't have wanted him to come all the way across the city to return it.

But he needed to see her.

Gazing at the dark building, Allister wondered if the drive had been for nothing. Still, he'd come all this way, he thought, tugging at the car's door handle and shoving it open to the numbingly cold night. The least he could do was try. And if she was home, he just might get the answers he needed.

In seconds he was across the street and knocking at the door. He cupped his bare hands over his breath to warm them as he stamped the snow from his boots. It was a good minute before he knocked again, and this time he was rewarded by the sound of movement on the other side of the door.

There was a heavy thump, followed by a muffled curse, and in another second he recognized Stevie's voice asking, "Who is it?"

"Stevie? It's Allister Quaid."

He heard the scrape of metal against metal, followed by the slap of a door chain and finally the thud of the dead bolt.

"Allister?" With one hand on the door handle, Stevie used her free arm to hug herself against the cold. She wore a large faded NYU sweatshirt over a pair of gray tights, and in a sudden burst of snow-laden air, she shivered.

"Hi, Stevie. Look, I'm sorry it's late—"

"No, not at all, Allister." She smiled. "It's not late. Come in. I've just made a fresh pot of coffee. At least, I think I did. Smells like it, anyway, if you'd like some."

"Sounds great," he said, and stepped into the darkness of the front hall. He unzipped his leather bomber as he watched her fumble with the door chain and turn the dead bolt.

"I was just in the area," he lied, wondering if he sounded at all convincing, "making a delivery. So I thought I'd drop off your light meter. You left it at the warehouse."

"Oh, thanks." In the liquid neon glow of the sign in the window, Allister saw her stretch out one hand. When he put the small instrument into her palm, delicate fingers closed around it.

"Actually I didn't think you were home. The lights are all off."

"They are? Sorry about that." She reached for a bank of switches next to the door, and the studio's entrance flooded with light from strategically placed halogens. "Afraid I hadn't noticed. And Paige has been locked away in the darkroom since dinner, developing negatives. Oh, and watch your step," she warned. "I think I killed the coat tree when I went to the door."

"Dead in its tracks," he joked, lifting the heavy wooden rack from the floor, coats and all. "You've got a good aim."

She returned his smile. "I'm getting better. I only managed to maim the umbrella stand the other day."

Allister couldn't remember if he'd ever seen a smile like Stevie's before, or if one had ever had the same effect hers had on him now. It curled her exquisite lips into a sensuous curve and drew up the corners of her eyes, where it set off sparks of amusement her entire face.

She broke the magical silence. "Come on. Let me show you upstairs."

Allister followed her through the studio's plush reception area.

"You'll have to excuse the cold in this place," she told him as they crossed the wide expanse of the main studio, her wool-stockinged feet shuffling over the hardwood flooring. "Our furnace has a mind of its own, I'm afraid. It's one of those early all-or-nothing models. We're either turning blue from hypothermia, or Paige and I are prancing around here in our bikinis in the middle of January." She turned briefly to flash him another quick smile.

She slowed as they neared a metal staircase that spiraled up to the second floor. Casually, as though not wanting him to notice, Stevie reached out for the handrail but groped only air.

"One more step," Allister offered, taking her hand in his. She didn't seem startled by his touch but allowed him to guide her forward and settle her hand on the cool railing.

"Thanks," she said, her voice little more than a whisper, and immediately he regretted having interfered. She could have done it on her own, he realized. She would have taken another step and found the railing herself. And no doubt she would have preferred it that way.

When they reached the top of the steel staircase and Stevie hit another bank of light switches, Allister was immediately impressed by the decor of the second-floor apartment. The high-ceilinged kitchen, dining and living rooms worked together as a single open area. Its focal point was a virtual oasis of large potted plants that thrived beneath a huge skylight bordered by an elaborate pattern in stained glass.

He followed Stevie to the kitchen, admiring the skill with which she navigated around the furniture by touch: running her hand along the back of the couch, tracing her fingers over the kitchen bar and finally turning to rest her hip against the counter.

"I probably should have called first," Allister said, feeling the need to let her know where he was by the sound of his voice. "I hope I didn't interrupt anything."

"Not at all." She took two mugs from their hooks under the cupboard and handed him one. "In fact, you rescued me, in a sense. Out of sheer boredom, I was going to pop *Casablanca* in the VCR one more time. I've seen it so often I figured I could do without the picture, you know?"

Allister watched her take the coffeepot from its hot plate and set it on the kitchen bar.

"You'd probably do better pouring your own coffee," she recommended. "Less chance of my spilling it all over you. What do you take?"

"Just black, thanks."

"You might want to check for grounds, as well. I'm still working out the kinks in this coffee-making process. Paige doesn't exactly condone my caffeine addiction, so I'm pretty much left to my own devices in that department."

"Coffee's fine," he assured her, filling her cup, too.

She motioned to the living-room area. "Would you like to sit down?"

"Sure. I'll take the cups," he offered. "It looks like your place has recovered from the break-in. I take it there wasn't much damage?"

"Not upstairs," she explained as she felt her way across the wide room. "They got in through the back door on the first floor. The police figure that whoever it was must have scoped the place first. They knew what they were looking for. They went through the studio and the darkroom. Took most of the cameras, but that was it. Could have been worse, I guess."

"What about your security system?"

"Up until now, we've relied on dead bolts and chains. But Paige has made arrangements with a company the police recommended to us. We're supposed to have some new state-of-the-art system in here by the end of the week. Knowing my luck, though, I'll be tripping the thing every ten minutes."

She had found her way to the large armchair next to the couch, and it was when she started to sit that Allister spotted the furry mass curled up on the cushion.

"Hang on, Stevie." In a second he was beside her, grasping her shoulders in his hands. Through the heavy sweatshirt, he could feel her body tense as he pulled her back from the chair, and her hand shot out to grasp his forearm. She must have sensed how close they were, how a few more inches would have constituted an embrace, yet she did not pull away.

In that suspended moment, as Allister looked down into her perfect face, he remembered the feel of her body cradled in his arms, the tickle of her soft hair against his cheek and her warm breath on his neck. At the time, six nights ago, he hadn't considered their contact enticing, but now, with Stevie less than a breath away, he felt a sudden and unexpected arousal.

It would take nothing to lean over and lift that proud chin of hers, to taste those lips and feather his fingers through that glossy black hair.

Embarrassed by his rampant thoughts, Allister took a step back, steadying Stevie as he released her shoulders.

"It's your cat," he explained. "On the chair."

"Oh. Tiny," she said, turning to scoop the massive Persian from the cushion and ease him to the floor. "It's all right. I've been stepping and sitting on him ever since I got home from the hospital. He's resilient."

Tiny moved indignantly to the middle of the room where he stretched across the area rug.

"Actually he acts like he owns the place," Stevie added as she lowered herself into the chair and pulled her legs up beneath her, "ever since he showed up on the doorstep last year. All in all, this has been a very humbling experience for him, having me step all over him. So, how's the coffee?"

He'd been staring again, Allister realized. Being so close to her, able to openly admire her beauty, had to be as unsettling for her as it was for him. Ashamed, he turned his attention to the mugs on the table.

"Let me hand you your cup," he offered. But as he tried to ease it into her outstretched hand, the cup jerked and the coffee nearly splashed over the rim. Allister noticed for the first time how her hands trembled.

"This blind business," she admitted, as she took firm hold of the warm cup, "makes life a bitch."

But her flippant remark and quick smile couldn't hide the frustration she undoubtedly felt now, especially in his presence, Allister realized, a person she'd never met and therefore couldn't envision, a person she knew only through Gary.

"I have to hand it to you, Stevie," he said, taking a seat on the couch, "and I hope I don't sound too intrusive, but I think you're doing amazingly well. Adjusting and all. The courage it must take to go on . . . it's very admirable."

She took a sip of coffee and then smiled. Once again Allister could tell it was forced. "Well, I haven't broken any of the equipment in the darkroom yet, and I still haven't burned the place down. So if that's any indication, I guess I can't be doing too badly. Then again, Paige follows me almost every second of the day and picks up after me."

"What do the doctors say? Have they given you anything more concrete about when you might regain your vision?"

Stevie shrugged. "The closest they've been able to pinpoint is somewhere between a couple of days and never."

But as soon as the words slipped from her lips, Allister sensed that she regretted the moment of bitterness she'd allowed herself.

"I'm sorry, Allister," she said quickly. "I didn't mean to sound—"

"It's all right, Stevie. You don't have to apologize. Really." *Not to me,* he added in his thoughts, *especially not to me, the person who did this to you.* "I . . . I can't imagine what it must be like for you."

He fought the impulse to reach out and touch her now, to put his hand on her arm, comfort her.

"You're very courageous, Stevie. I mean, if it were me, I think I'd be lying in bed with the covers over my head."

"Oh, well, don't think for one second that I'd rather be anywhere else if I actually had a choice in the matter. It's Paige who's been keeping me on my feet."

"So what do the doctors say is wrong then?"

She balanced the mug on her knee and nervously wound a short strand of hair around one finger.

"They don't really know. But from what I understand, it has to do with swelling around the occipital lobe or something, and they won't know the extent of the damage until the swelling goes down. I have to go for more tests the day after tomorrow. . . ." Her voice trailed off.

He looked away, regretting his question because of the obvious discomfort it caused her. On the opposite wall was a series of framed black-and-white photographs. Allister didn't need to move closer to admire the unique camera work or to recognize the family resemblance of most of the people in the portraits. All dark-haired and dark-eyed, and all possessing Stevie's arresting beauty.

"I see you have a big family," he commented. "Those photographs are beautiful." When he glanced at her again, she appeared grateful for the change of topic.

"Three older brothers and one sister. Not to mention my aunt and uncle who came over from Sicily, along with my parents. There's all my cousins, as well. My father and my uncle ran a deli together back in Chicago, so we were one big family. In fact, that was the main reason I accepted the scholarship from NYU. With a family that big, as much as I love them, I needed to get away on my own, at least for a while. I always figured I'd go back someday, but I don't know now. I'm comfortable here."

"So why Danby?"

Stevie shrugged. "A guy. Nick Ditaranto." The name rolled off her tongue so easily it was obvious she looked back on the relationship as little more than a mistake. There was no trace of bitterness, no twinge of sentimentality. She'd gone on with her life, it appeared, a stronger person for her experiences and mistakes.

"We dated during our last couple of years of college, and when he accepted a position with an engineering firm here in town, we decided to move together, share an apartment. But after a year he accepted a transfer. Things weren't working out between us, anyway, and I'd already started to establish myself, so I stayed. It was just luck that this was Gary's hometown and he'd moved back here. During my first couple of years in Danby, I saw a lot of Gary and Barb. But gradually work got in the way, and we hardly saw each other socially at all. In fact, until I set up the shoot at the warehouse, I hadn't seen either of them in several months."

"You knew Gary from college, right?" Allister ventured.

"He dated my roommate for a bit. Then we ended up in a couple of English lit classes together, shared notes, studied together, that sort of thing. We were close back then." Her smile faded. "I wish...I wish I hadn't let my work come in the way of our friendship like it did the past couple of years."

She fell silent for a moment, lifting her mug to her lips, and when she looked up again, she seemed to push her regret away.

"So what about you? You grew up in Danby. Is your family still here?"

Allister gazed at the cup in his own hands for a moment. His family. A far cry from the smiling faces of Stevie's.

"Gary and Barb are...were pretty much it. My dad left when I was four and my mother raised me herself. She moved down to California a few years ago, remarried and started over. No brothers or sisters. Just Gary."

"I'm sorry," Stevie whispered across the sudden quiet. "His death must be really hard on you."

"No more than anyone else, I suppose. It's hardest on Barb."

He watched Stevie nod. He wondered if she'd known about the impending divorce, if she'd been aware of the discord in Barb and Gary's marriage, or if she had any idea of the risks Gary had taken with his life because of it.

"And Barb's leaving for Baltimore?"

Allister nodded. "She's catching the noon flight with her mother tomorrow."

"And she's really going to stay there?"

"I'm pretty sure. With Gary gone, I don't think she feels there's too much left for her here in Danby. She's already talked about closing her counseling practice and starting up fresh down there. I think she needs her family right now."

"I wish I could have been of more comfort to her," Stevie admitted. "Barb and I weren't . . . well, I wasn't as close to her as I was to Gary really. But . . . I'm going to miss her." She took another sip of coffee and seemed to lose herself momentarily in her memories.

"You're going to manage the business for Barb then?" she asked eventually.

"Until she decides what to do with it. I've been helping out for the past few months, anyway, so I'm familiar with the employees and some of the larger clients."

"I'm still surprised that we never actually met before. After all this time, after everything Gary's told me about you . . ."

Allister wondered exactly what Gary *had* told her. "I've been out of town for the past few years," he offered, realizing that Stevie had been fishing for an explanation and hoping she wasn't seeking a more detailed one.

"Gary said you'd been traveling."

Allister shifted uneasily on the couch. What could he say now? How far should the lies go? And why was it he felt this sudden guilt in deceiving Stevie? After all, wasn't *everything* he said to her a lie in a way, given that his only reason for being here tonight was to find out her connection to Bainbridge's coins? Given that he was the man, if anyone, responsible for the loss of her sight?

And then, just as Allister thought he'd have to add yet another lie to the pack, he heard Paige on the stairs.

"Hey, Stevie," she called out. "Did I hear someone at the—" She stopped when she reached the landing. "Oh, Allister. Hi."

"Hello, Paige."

"Sorry I didn't come up sooner. The slave driver here had me working up these proofs."

Allister watched the affectionate smiles the two women exchanged.

"And hey," she said to Stevie as she crossed the room and fell into a wing chair, "that had better be decaf you're drinking. I am *not* spending another night with you stumbling around this apartment because you can't sleep. Or worse, listening to one of those old movies of yours for the hundredth time."

Stevie's only answer was a grin and another sip of coffee.

"So how did the proofs turn out?" she asked.

Paige tossed the contact prints on the coffee table, and Allister caught a glimpse of them, recognizing the backdrops as Gary's warehouse.

"Well, in spite of your mangling the film out of that useless camera, they're actually pretty great. You really should see them."

Stevie grimaced while Paige gave Allister a wink. Obviously this kind of ribbing was a feature of their friendship. He smiled.

"Still," Stevie said, "we're going to have to reshoot the entire thing. Is your offer of the warehouse still open, Allister?"

"Whenever you need it." He nodded and got to his feet. "But we can talk about that some other time. I really should get going. It's late, and I'm sure you two have things to do."

Stevie set her mug on the table and stood up, too, steadying herself on the arm of the chair for a second as though finding her bearings. "I'll walk you to the door, Allister."

As STEVIE FOLLOWED him through the apartment and down the stairs, she found herself disappointed that Allister was leaving so soon. She tried to convince herself that her disappointment had to do with Gary; that somehow, because of Allister's link to her friend, Gary didn't seem quite so gone from her life with Allister around. But she suspected there was more to it than that.

"It was nice of you to stop by, Allister," she told him once they'd reached the front hall. "I hope this isn't just a one-time occurrence, your 'being in the area.'"

"No, I don't think it is," he said after a moment's pause, during which Stevie tried to conjure up the smile she heard in his voice.

"I appreciate your concern, Allister. Really I do. Coming down here and all. But I have to ask you something—and I hope you don't take this the wrong way, but why do I get the feeling there's more behind your visit than returning my light meter?"

His silence was unsettling, and Stevie regretted her bluntness. It was a trait of hers that often took people by surprise, and now it made her sound ungrateful, which was far from the truth.

"What I mean is," she tried to explain, "well, this isn't just about my using the warehouse again or about checking up on Gary's blind friend, is it?"

She was relieved when he finally did speak.

"No, Stevie," he admitted. "No, you're right. I wanted to ask you something. About Gary."

"So ask."

Another pause. Obviously it was not something that Allister found easy to discuss.

"It's about his death. I don't . . . I don't believe it was the result of some random burglary like the police are saying."

"I kind of figured it wasn't, either."

"Why's that?"

"The police. A detective—Devane—has been asking me questions. A lot about Gary."

"I think Gary was in trouble." There was a reluctance in Allister's voice. "I think he was into something, and he was in too deep."

"You mean drugs? Money? What?"

"I don't know exactly. But...listen, Gary didn't...he didn't give you anything, did he? A package, maybe, to hang on to for him?"

It was the same question Devane had asked at the hospital. He, too, had wanted to know whether Gary had given her anything before his murder.

"No." Stevie shook her head and hoped her surprise at the question wasn't apparent. "No, Gary didn't give me anything. Do you think—"

"Forget it, Stevie. It's probably nothing. Listen, I should go. Thanks for the coffee. I'm glad you're feeling a bit better."

She felt his hand on her shoulder then, and in spite of his evident awkwardness, his touch felt sincere.

"Take care of yourself, Stevie. I'll...I'll stop by again?"

"Sure, Allister. That would be great. And thanks for dropping off the light meter."

"Good night, Stevie."

The door swung open to a blast of frigid air, and she heard the high-pitched squeak of his boots on the packed snow covering the walk.

But even as she closed the door, Stevie could still hear Allister's voice in her mind. When he'd said good-night, oddly, she'd thought about radio announcers, how you always created a mental image of what they looked like and then were shocked to discover how different they were from those expectations.

Paige had been extremely brief and not very helpful in her description of Allister after the funeral. "Tall, dark and handsome," was all she'd said. But it was Allister's voice—

deep and soothing and seductively familiar—that had a way of making Stevie's imagination run rampant, she thought now as her hand lingered on the door handle.

IT TOOK TWENTY MINUTES to drive from Stevie's apartment to his own building, during which time Allister had not been able to let go of thoughts of Stevie—or the guilt he felt about lying to her. But it wasn't just guilt that had made him leave her so abruptly. Nor was it that Stevie was the one person who could put him at the warehouse the night of Gary's murder, the person who could essentially send him back to the very place he'd lost four years of his life to.

More than those, it was his unexpected attraction to her that had driven him from Stevie's tonight.

Yes, somehow she held the answer, and he should have questioned her further when she'd walked him to her door. But he hadn't been able to go through with it—partly because of the close quarters of the front hall and his overwhelming desire to hold her in his arms again, to confess his role in her blindness and beg her forgiveness.

Fortunately, reason had won out.

Reason—and experience.

People were unpredictable. He'd learned that the hard way. And Stevie could not be considered an exception to that rule. He'd trusted people before. He'd told the truth before. Both had gotten him a four-year prison term. Not even Michelle had believed him—the one person whose trust he'd thought he could count on.

That moment when Michelle had been unable to look him in the eye, when she'd handed him back the engagement ring, she had not only shattered his ideas of trust, but she'd also taught him the hard lesson of conditional love. And Allister had sworn never again to count on or trust anyone. Now that had to include Stevie. He couldn't tell her the truth about what happened at the warehouse last week. There was no way of knowing how she would react if he did.

As he steered the Explorer onto Cardinal Drive, Allister checked his rearview mirror. He'd noticed a car a couple of blocks from Stevie's that had seemed to be following him. It was still there, its headlights shimmering through the glittering veil of snow a block back.

When Allister drew up to his building, he saw the other driver flip off the headlights and pull the car to the curb. From this distance, there was no hope of discerning the type of vehicle it was, other than a dark sedan. And there was certainly no hope in making out the driver. Still, Allister had a pretty good idea it could be only one of two people—Detective Devane or Bainbridge's hired man, for surely the collector would have employed someone to do his dirty work.

Either way, Allister was grateful for the security entrance of his apartment building. Then again, he thought as he pulled into the parking garage, how secure was any building from someone as ruthless as Gary's killer?

STEVIE YANKED the cushions from the couch and ran her fingers behind the seat. The stereo's remote control wasn't to be found. Maybe Paige had hidden it because of the hours of opera Stevie had listened to.

Stevie replaced the cushions and straightened. She shook her head and smiled. She couldn't really blame Paige. Paige hated Puccini.

Initially Stevie had hoped that playing her father's favorite opera would take her mind off her blindness and the murder of her friend. But it hadn't.

Then there was Allister Quaid and his surprising visit last night. She'd tried to convince herself that it had to do with their mutual connection to, and loss of, Gary. But there was more to it than that, and more to it than the way Allister's presence consoled her or his voice enticed her.

It was Allister's parting question that kept running through her head. Like Detective Devane, he'd asked if Gary had given her anything for safekeeping. There was something neither Devane nor Allister was telling her about Gary, something that obviously had to do with his death.

It had bothered Stevie so much throughout the day in fact, that several times she'd wanted to call the warehouse and ask Allister exactly what it was he expected Gary had given her.

But she hadn't. Instead, she'd surrendered to Paige's insistence that she help out around the studio: developing negatives after Paige set out all the premeasured chemicals, rolling film and whatever else would normally have been done in the darkroom with no more than the red light.

The paces Paige put her through today were nothing more than a diversion tactic, Stevie thought now as she redirected her search to the coffee table. Tomorrow was Saturday—her follow-up appointment with Dr. Sterling—and clearly Paige had hoped to keep Stevie's mind off it.

The tactic had worked, until of course this evening when Paige had pronounced the cupboards bare and had headed out on a quick grocery run. That had to have been less than fifteen minutes ago, and already Stevie's thoughts were darkening with worries of tomorrow's appointment. What if the news wasn't good? What if Dr. Sterling had gotten another opinion on the scans and told her that, contrary to the sliver of hope he'd given her before, there was no possibility of her sight ever returning?

For almost a week now, Stevie had put up a front for Paige, and yes, a front even for herself. She'd pretended to believe that her condition was only temporary, pretended to have faith that, when the swelling finally went down, she'd be able to see perfectly. And sometimes, just sometimes, the pretending almost convinced her.

Each morning, when Stevie opened her eyes after yet another night filled with bad dreams and horrifying images of Gary and the man who had attacked her, she prayed she would open her eyes and see again. But each morning she was greeted only by darkness.

Too often lately, Stevie had allowed herself to lapse into speculation of the future, of the possibility of being blind for the rest of her life. Usually those times were in the middle of the night, when Paige was asleep out on the sofa bed, when her friend wouldn't see her tears.

Times like now, Stevie thought as she swiped at the moisture that had gathered beneath her eyes.

She couldn't think like this. Paige would be home soon. She needed a distraction.

Finding the remote at last on one of the side tables, Stevie was feeling for the on button when she heard a crash downstairs. Her heart skipped and she let out a gasp.

It was far too soon for Paige to be back.

Tiny had been sleeping at the end of the couch. He'd been contentedly minding his own business when she'd begun her search for the remote, tossing pillows and shoving cushions. But when she reached for the cat now, he was gone. Her fingers found only the warm spot where he'd been.

That had to be it, she convinced herself. Tiny, the obese but brilliant feline, had finally come to realize that he could take advantage of Stevie's situation in Paige's absence. He'd probably trundled off downstairs to wreak havoc on the studio as retribution for being disturbed. She was about to yell out a warning to the cat when she heard a second crash.

There was no telling exactly what had caused the resounding thud this time, but Stevie was certain it had come from the office. It sounded like the supply cabinets.

That was not Tiny.

The next crash convinced her—someone was in the studio.

Stevie should have felt fear, but instead she felt anger—anger at the violation. Not one, but *two* break-ins?

She had to do something. Whoever it was down in the studio could decide to come upstairs. And standing here in the middle of her apartment completely defenseless was not where she wanted to be when that happened.

The phone.

She had to get to the phone. Call the police. Hadn't Paige programmed Detective Devane's number into the memory keys on the bedroom phone the day she came home from the hospital?

The only trick was getting to the bedroom without alerting the intruder.

It was when Stevie turned, almost tripping over a stray pillow on the floor, that the first wave of panic hit her. She was defenseless, a concept she hadn't fully comprehended until now.

Her hands shook as she groped her way from the couch toward the hall. And with each shuffling step Stevie prayed that Tiny was not in her way, that she wouldn't topple one of the floor lamps or bump into anything that would draw the intruder's attention.

She wouldn't stand a chance in hell if he came upstairs. She understood that now. How could she fight off an assailant she couldn't even see?

When she reached the hall, she fumbled for the light switches and pushed them off. Darkness was her only defense.

Steadily she worked her way down the hall. For a heart-stopping moment, she thought she heard footsteps in the main studio area.

She had to keep moving.

And then, when she stepped on the one and only squeaky board in the entire corridor, Stevie thought the world had split open beneath her foot.

Finally she stubbed a finger sharply against the wooden jamb of the bedroom door. She bit her lip to keep from crying out at the jolt of pain. She was almost there. Half-walking, half-crawling, her hands sweeping the black abyss in front of her, she inched her way across the bedroom until at last she reached the nightstand. In her anxiousness to find the phone, her hand knocked over the bedside lamp.

Incredibly she caught the lamp before it clattered to the floor and righted it. For a long moment she did not remove her trembling hands from its smooth base. She listened, straining through the heavy stillness, her ears ringing.

Perhaps he was listening for her, as well. Downstairs at the bottom of the steps, or maybe even in the apartment with her.

No, she tried to calm her panicked mind, he couldn't be upstairs. Surely she would have heard him come up.

She groped for the phone now. As soon as her fingers curled around the receiver, Stevie felt her knees weaken. She lowered herself to the floor, wedging herself between the nightstand and the wall.

The dial tone blared like a homing beacon. Stevie covered the earpiece as her fingers fluttered over the keypad. What number had Paige told her she'd programmed Devane as? Three? It had to be three. One had always been reserved for her mother. And two was Paige. It had to be three.

With a silent prayer, Stevie pressed the third key. As she listened to each hollow ring, she wondered if Devane was even in. And if he wasn't, would someone else pick up his line?

"Please, please, please . . ." she mouthed, too terrified to utter a sound until absolutely necessary.

And then, "Homicide. Jackson here."

Devane's partner.

But her words froze in her throat, choking her, cutting off her breath.

"Hello? Is anyone there?" he asked.

"Detective Jackson. It's Stevie Falcioni." Her voice was barely a whisper, and still she imagined that the whole world could hear her.

"Ms. Falcioni? Are you all right?"

"I'm . . . There's someone in my studio."

"Are you there now, Ms. Falcioni?"

"Yes."

She heard him yell across the mouthpiece of his own phone. "I need all available patrols in the Brandon area to respond to a B and E in progress at eighteen Whitby. Intruder is on the premises right now. Move it!"

Then his voice lowered. "Ms. Falcioni? We'll be right there. Just hang on, okay? We'll—"

Footsteps sounded on the steel staircase. Stevie was certain of it.

Not waiting to find out if Detective Jackson wanted her to stay on the line, Stevie hung up. She couldn't afford to have anything give away her location.

With a sudden jolt of panic, she wondered about the lamp on the night table. Was it on? Was she huddled here on the floor completely exposed by the glow of its bulb?

She bit her lower lip and reached for the shade. Her heart slammed against her ribs, and lines of sweat trickled down her skin beneath her sweatshirt. Her hands shook so much now she was certain she'd send the lamp flying this time, but when her fingers touched the cool bulb, she breathed a momentary sigh of relief.

A small voice in her head urged her to move, to crawl under the bed, anywhere. Even to grab the lamp in an effort to arm herself. Anything, instead of just sitting here and waiting.

But the fear was too great.

A blind paralyzing fear.

And then she detected the faint smell of a man's cologne.

CHAPTER SIX

SIRENS SHATTERED the night. Their distant wail grew steadily louder, piercing through her darkness and drowning out all other sounds.

Stevie concentrated on that approaching wail.

But there was another sound above the sirens, above the pounding of her heart. A banging sound she couldn't ignore. And then a crash.

In moments she heard heavy footfalls on the stairs. Voices. Doors opening and closing. And still more sirens.

There was someone moving down the hallway now coming into the bedroom. When she felt a hand touch her shoulder, she jerked back.

"Miss? Miss, it's all right. I'm Officer Barratt. Are you all right, miss?"

She was nodding, trying to stand, but her legs were wobbly. Her whole body felt as if it wasn't even hers, her shaking was so violent.

"Miss, are you hurt?"

"No," she managed to say. She felt tears on her cheeks and swiped angrily at them.

"Let me help you, miss." Hands grasped her shoulders, guiding her to her feet and over to the bed. Through the rest of the apartment, she heard other officers' voices now, the squawk of police radios and boots thudding against the hardwood flooring.

"Are you sure you're all right, miss?"

When Stevie nodded this time, she clenched her jaw, biting down on the residual fear that had paralyzed her only moments before. "I'm fine."

The officer crossed the room. She heard him speak in a harsh whisper with another officer—something about her being in shock and the need to call the paramedics.

"I told you, I'm all right," she said, loudly. "I don't need an ambulance. I'm not in shock. I'm *blind*." The anger in her voice seemed to silence the two officers, and in the sudden hush, Stevie heard Devane's rasping voice downstairs in the studio.

Moments later he was standing over her where she still sat on the edge of the bed. "Ms. Falcioni, are you okay?"

She sighed. "Yes, Detective, I'm okay."

"Can you tell me what happened?"

Stevie nodded. She told him everything, from the moment she'd heard the first crash downstairs in the studio to when the officers had come through the front door. And when she was finished, she heard Paige's voice.

"I'm her *friend*, dammit! Now either you let me through or I'll—"

"It's all right, Roberts. Let her in."

"Stevie?" Paige was beside her then. "Honey? What happened? Are you okay?"

A nod was all Stevie had the energy for as she fell into Paige's embrace.

"Seems like someone decided they'd try your place again," Devane explained. "It was the back door like before. But this time they came prepared. Looks like they brought some tools. Picked the lock, then cut the chain."

"So you think it was the same person?" Paige asked, her arm still around Stevie's shoulder.

"Most likely," he offered gruffly. "Hits like the one you had a few nights ago are often the work of repeat offenders. They'll break into a place, grab whatever they can and scope the place for a second hit. Granted, they usually wait a little longer between jobs, but still..."

Devane was minimizing what had happened, Stevie was sure. He had to suspect that the break-ins were connected to Gary's murder, otherwise he would have left it to the uniformed officers to respond to the call.

"We'll send some men over in the morning to dust the place for prints again and—"

"Detective? There's nothing out back," an officer told him. "All we got was the cutters and a couple of partial foot prints that could belong to the perpetrator. The place is secure."

"Thanks, Novak. You guys can clear out. I think we're done for now."

Stevie stood up from the bed, and Paige, recognizing her restlessness, guided her to the living room. Devane followed.

"Look, Ms. Falcioni," he said, "I don't think you have to worry about this guy coming back. All the same, I can have a patrol car park out front if you like. But for your own peace of mind, perhaps you'd be better off staying the night someplace else. Is there somewhere you can go?"

Paige's hand tightened around her arm. "She'll be staying at my place tonight, Detective."

"Good. Leave a couple of lights on here. I'll have a car pass by once in a while through the night to keep an eye on the place."

"Thank you, Detective."

"What about that alarm system? I thought you were going to contact Ace Security," Devane asked, referring to the company he'd recommended after the first break-in.

"We did. They're supposed to be installing the system tomorrow sometime."

"Good." She heard Devane start for the stairs. Then his rough voice grated through the quiet that had descended on the studio when the officers cleared out. "I'll speak to my friend at Ace Security and see what he can do about making sure your system is in and operating tomorrow morning. Do you want a patrol to escort the two of you to Ms. Carpenter's?"

"Thank you, Detective, but I think we'll manage. Besides, I need to pack a few things."

Stevie hoped her smile at least appeared grateful. When she thanked the detective before he left, she couldn't help thinking that the only reason Devane displayed the concern he did was because she was his key witness. Only she could ID Gary's killer, and Devane was not about to let anything jeopardize that.

WHEN ALLISTER TURNED onto Stevie's street and passed the second patrol car within a three-block distance, he was willing to write it off as coincidence. But then, as the Images studio came into view and he saw a final cruiser back away from the building followed by a dark sedan, he thought his heart had stopped.

This time when he parked next to the studio-apartment, it was lit up like the Fourth of July. Yanking the keys from the ignition, he raced across the street and down the snow-packed walk. He was short of breath when he started pounding on the front door, but it wasn't because of the run. Icy fingers of dread wrapped around his throat, choking each gulp of cold air. And by the time Paige opened the door, Allister was already expecting the worst.

"What happened?" he blurted before Paige had even managed to utter a greeting.

"I saw the cruisers leave. Are you guys— Where's Stevie?"

"Upstairs—she's fine, Allister," Paige assured him, stepping aside to let him in. "We had another break-in. I...I was out getting groceries. Stevie...was alone when it happened."

Paige blamed herself, Allister realized. Blamed herself because she'd left Stevie on her own.

He saw her need for comfort and took her shoulders in his hands. "Paige, it's not your fault."

Her eyes filled with tears. "I still shouldn't have left her. She...she was here all alone when the guy broke in. She could have..."

Allister released her shoulders and gave her arm a final reassuring squeeze before rushing across the studio and up the stairs, only vaguely aware that Paige followed him. Stevie stood at the kitchen bar. Her back was to him, and her arms were wrapped around herself.

"Stevie?"

She didn't move.

"Stevie? It's Allister," he said, crossing the room as she turned toward him at last. "Are you all right?"

Allister couldn't recall ever seeing an expression alter as rapidly as hers did just then. Fear and trepidation were replaced by a defiant strength; he could see she had mustered her courage and was forcing back tears.

"Stevie?" He reached out to take her hand, desperate to make physical contact with her, to get past that stubborn facade of independence.

Her hand trembled in his.

"I'm okay, Allister," she said at last, her chin lifting a fraction of an inch. "The police were here almost immediately. And we don't think anything was stolen this time."

She withdrew her hand from his and worked her way across the room as though needing to put space between them, to stand on her own.

Paige broke the silence. "Stevie and I were just going to pack a few things. Detective Devane offered to have a patrol car stationed out front, but Stevie agrees she'd feel safer staying at my place tonight. Just in case the burglars come back."

He nodded. "I think that's a good idea."

"They weren't burglars," Stevie said.

"What do you mean?" Allister crossed to her side once again. This time she did not move away from him.

"This is about Gary's murder," she stated so matter-of-factly Allister was taken aback.

"Stevie—"

"Whoever killed Gary thinks I have something. That's why they broke in when I was in the hospital. That's why they broke in again tonight."

She paused for a breath, then went on, "The lights were off, like they were last night. You remember, Allister, you thought no one was home. Whoever broke in here tonight thought the same thing. They figured the place was empty. They figured they could get whatever it was they didn't find the first time."

Allister stared at her. He should have guessed that Stevie would make the connection sooner or later. He just hadn't counted on it being sooner.

"What is it, Allister? Tell me. What are they after?"

"I...I don't know what you're talking about, Stevie."

She took an abrupt step backward, barely missing an end table, and when she crossed her arms over her chest, Allister was struck by her sudden flare of anger.

"Don't play me for stupid, Allister. You know *exactly* what it is. You and Devane. Both of you know. You were asking me about a package or something just last night. Asking if Gary had left anything with me. Given me something for safekeeping."

"Stevie, listen to me—"

"Only if you're going to give me some answers. I want to know what the hell is happening. And I want to know exactly what it is you and the police seem to think I have."

Even Paige looked surprised by Stevie's ignited wrath, Allister noted as he glanced from Stevie to Paige and then back again. This was it, he thought. There was no way out now.

He had to tell Stevie about the coins. It was clear she knew nothing about them. And since, according to Gary, she was involved, Allister had to come clean with the one person who could, just maybe, help him find Bainbridge's shipment.

"Okay," he said, his hands curling into fists at his sides. "Okay, Stevie. I'll tell you what I know. But not here. My place."

Paige looked at him in astonishment. "But—"

"My apartment has a security entrance. Does yours?"

"Well, no, but..."

For almost ten minutes Allister and Paige debated over where Stevie would spend the night. And the longer they argued, the more Stevie felt like a child caught between two bickering parents, until finally she'd shouted at both of them to stop. She told them she would accept Allister's offer. Her lingering fear gave his place with it's tight security a certain appeal. Besides at Allister's, she would finally get the answers she'd been seeking.

Minutes later Paige tossed Stevie's overnight bag into the Explorer, then gave her a quick hug and drove off in her own car.

The trip to Allister's was silent. Stevie wasn't sure if it was because he wasn't ready to discuss what he had promised, or if he actually recognized how shaken she was. Either way, she was grateful for the silence.

He still wasn't forthcoming when he took her up to his small one-bedroom apartment and led her through it. She was aware of him picking things up as they went, pausing several times to shove boxes out of the way. When she asked how long he'd lived there, he'd ashamedly admitted eight months.

He guided her to the couch and offered to make tea, but Stevie convinced him that it wasn't too late for coffee. Soon she could hear the last gurgles of the coffeemaker from the kitchen, followed by the clatter of ceramic mugs and finally Allister's footfalls as he came back into the living room.

"Black, right?" he asked as he took her hand and put it around the warm mug.

"Black's great." Stevie sipped the brew, welcoming the caffeine that would see her through the explanations Allister had promised her.

"So," she said, "why were you on your way to my place tonight?"

"Tonight?" His voice came from her right and she turned toward it. "Tonight . . . I was just coming over. Barb had asked after you, and I'd promised I would stop by. That's all."

But Stevie had to wonder if Barb even remotely figured in Allister's reasons.

"About Gary . . ."

She heard his quick exhale and took it as amusement at her directness.

"What is it you seem to think Gary gave me, anyway?"

There was a pause, then finally, "Coins."

"Coins? I don't understand."

"Do you remember that burglary at the museum last May?"

"Vaguely."

"A collection of rare Spanish coins was stolen from a traveling exhibit. Their worth was estimated at anywhere from four to five million dollars."

"You're not going to tell me Gary was mixed up with that, are you?"

"Not directly," Allister said. "But from what I can figure, Gary was hired to ship the coins overseas. I think he had his suspicions about the shipment and checked the contents. When he discovered the stolen coins, it seems he decided to blackmail the shipper."

"Gary?" Stevie shook her head. That did not sound like the Gary she'd known. Allister had to be wrong. "I don't believe it. How do you know this, Allister? Do you have proof?"

"Actually, Stevie, it's the police who have the proof. They searched Gary's office at the warehouse and found a tape of a phone call between him and the man behind the shipment. They were talking about stolen goods, although there was no mention of what those goods actually were. But the police also found a bunch of newspaper clippings about the museum robbery."

"Well, have they identified the other man on the tape?"

"Not as far as I know. And I don't think they will. It was too fuzzy. Even I hardly recognized the voice."

"Wait a second, Allister. *You* know who hired Gary to ship the coins?"

He hesitated, and then, "Yes, I know the man behind the entire operation, Stevie. It's a wealthy collector by the name of Edward Bainbridge."

Stevie's fingers tightened around her mug. None of this made sense. It all sounded too crazy. Allister was talking about her friend Gary and this Edward Bainbridge as though they were active members of some shady Danby underworld she'd never even realized existed.

"Once Gary discovered the contents of the shipment," Allister continued, "he tried to make a deal with Bainbridge. That's what their phone call was about. But Gary got in too deep. I tried to warn him about Bainbridge, but I was obviously too late. Stevie, it was Bainbridge who was behind Gary's death. I'm sure of it."

Stevie shuddered. This was the stuff of nightmares, men plotting to kill other men . . . to kill Gary. This wasn't reality—at least no reality she'd ever known.

She shook her head again.

"Stevie." Allister moved closer to her on the couch and laid a hand on her shoulder. "Stevie, I'm sorry. I know this isn't easy to hear, but it's the truth."

She was afraid to ask, but knew she had to. "So how does this relate to me, Allister?"

"I think the problem now is that Bainbridge doesn't have his coins. I don't think Gary was supposed to have been killed—at least, not until Bainbridge had the coins again. But whoever he'd sent to Gary's office that night must have gotten carried away. And, he didn't get the package."

"And that's what you think Gary gave me? Why, Allister? I mean, Gary had an entire warehouse to hide the coins in, so why would he give them to me?"

"I don't know. Maybe because he knew he was in over his head, because he knew Bainbridge was going to come after him and he needed to get them out of the warehouse."

"Bainbridge and Devane—you think they believe this, too, that I've somehow got these coins?"

"Yes."

"But why? I don't see the connection."

"Because you were there that night, Stevie. You and Paige. The photo shoot. You were there after the staff had already all gone home. As far as anyone can tell, you were probably the last person to see Gary alive."

"Except for his killer," Stevie added, remembering how she'd barely stepped into Gary's office that night, how she'd seen his body by the desk seconds before she'd been attacked. No, she wasn't the last person to see Gary alive.

"Except for his killer," Allister repeated. "If anyone was watching Gary, they would have known you were at the warehouse, Stevie, and if they were desperate to find the coins, they might think he gave them to you."

"But he didn't, Allister. Gary didn't give me anything."

"Did he say anything to you that last day? Anything that seemed odd or out of the ordinary?"

"No. Gary was...I don't know, he seemed really nervous the last time I saw him. He didn't say much at all. I saw him for maybe five or ten minutes after the shoot. That was it."

Allister was silent for a long time. His hand was still on Stevie's shoulder, and he was close enough that she could hear his breathing. Beyond that, there were only muffled street noises: cars passing outside the building, a distant horn, a late-night sander.

"Look, Allister, I have to be honest," she said finally. "All of this sounds a bit farfetched. I mean, don't you think that Bainbridge, or whoever is after these coins, would search Gary's warehouse first before breaking into my place? It just doesn't make sense."

But it did make sense. To Allister, who'd held Gary through his final breaths, it made perfect sense. Gary had given him Stevie's name for one reason and one reason alone —the coins.

But this was not something Allister could tell Stevie.

As though seeking solace from him, Stevie brought her hand to his where it rested on her shoulder. He was surprised by its soft warmth.

"You do believe me, don't you, Allister? About the coins? You don't think I—"

"Stevie, no. Of course I believe you. But that's not the point here. It's Bainbridge who obviously assumes you have the coins. You said yourself you don't believe those two break-ins were random. And if he thinks you have the coins, or even something that might lead to them, trust me, he's not going to stop at a couple of break-ins."

He took her hand in his then and lowered it to her lap. Her fingers slid easily between his, and he stared at their hands—hers so delicate, his so strong—entwined, as though they belonged together.

"I don't mean to frighten you, Stevie. It's just that with a man like Edward Bainbridge, you can't be too careful."

"Sounds like you know this guy pretty well," she murmured, her voice as soft as her touch.

"Yeah, you could say that."

Perhaps the bitterness in his voice was warning enough that she not press him on the subject.

"So why don't you take all this to the police, Allister? If you know about Bainbridge and the coins, and if you think this man is dangerous, why not tell Devane and let him handle it?"

He sighed. "There's a lot you don't know, Stevie."

"Well, perhaps you should enlighten me."

He withdrew his hand and stood up, abruptly. When he glanced at her again, she seemed a bit startled by his action. But he couldn't be physically close to her right now, not while he told her what he had to.

And he *had* to tell her—about Bainbridge and about his prison-term—because if he didn't, Devane would. The detective would warn Stevie about Allister the second he found out where she'd spent the night; Devane would say anything necessary to keep his key witness away from his prime suspect. And if that happened, if Allister wasn't the one to tell Stevie about his past, then Stevie's trust would be lost forever. He'd never get the coins or the evidence he needed.

"Allister?"

"Stevie...I'm not sure what Barb and Gary told you about me. About where I've been the past few years and why you never met me before now."

"They said you'd been traveling."

"I wasn't, Stevie. Up until eight months ago, I..." He let out his breath in a rush and shoved his fingers through his hair. To tell her the truth, where he'd been, what he'd gone through, now seemed almost harder than actually serving the time. At least then, surrounded by convicted burglars, drug pushers, rapists and even murderers, he wasn't worried about how others would perceive him. But Stevie...he wasn't sure why her opinion of him should matter so much, but it did—almost more than anything else at this moment.

Still, it had to be said.

"Stevie, I wasn't traveling. I was in a state penitentiary for four years. I was released eight months ago."

She didn't say anything. But, she didn't need to. Her face said it all. Shock, disbelief, even a flicker of fear.

"Six years ago, I owned my own shipping company, one like Gary's," he explained. "It had been a family business, handed down to my mother. The man who was managing it for her was bleeding her dry, so I took over right after high school. I put years into that business, and Bainbridge was just one of my regular clients.

"I handled a lot of packages for him over the years. Some for his antiques company, and others that I never questioned. That was my big mistake—trusting a man like Bainbridge. He had this shipment to go to Buenos Aires. Some antique jewelry and rare gems. I should have guessed that something was up when he told me there was no rush on the shipment. He usually wanted his stuff handled as quickly as possible. But this one he brought in past the deadline, and we couldn't get it out until the Monday morning."

Allister told her about the burglary, how the company had been ransacked sometime during the Sunday night before the package was to go out, and how Bainbridge's shipment of precious gems had been stolen. And then Allister told her how the investigation had gone sour.

"I was living with my fiancée at the time," Allister said, swallowing his animosity. "And four days after the burglary, we were packing for a long weekend out of town when the police came banging on our door. They'd received accusations from Bainbridge and handed me a search warrant. They tore the place apart. Went through everything right there in front of Michelle and me. But they didn't find anything."

Allister would never forget how they'd practically dragged him from the apartment then, how he'd told Michelle to call Gary, to have him get a hold of his lawyer. And he'd never forget the shock on Michelle's face as she stood there in the middle of all their stuff—clothes and books, the contents of their medicine chest, broken dishes, everything—strewn about the apartment. It was almost as if the police had done it on purpose, as though they knew that it was a frame-up and that they'd never have to answer for their overzealous search.

"And then they searched my car," he said. "When they pulled three of the missing gems from the trunk, I knew that both the heist and the search had been an elaborate setup. The entire process had been too slick to suspect that anyone but the police themselves had planted those gems."

Stevie remained silent and motionless on the couch.

"Bainbridge had a hefty insurance policy on the contents of that shipment. He collected all of it, minus the three lesser gems he'd arranged to have planted in my car. And God knows he probably turned around only a few weeks later and sold the other gems to the originally intended buyer."

Allister went on to tell Stevie about the trial, how the physical evidence had been too damning, how he'd been convicted, and finally how he'd lost the business and everything else in his life. He could still feel his numbing horror when the judge handed down the sentence that morning. But even that hadn't been half as sickening as the moment Michelle told him it was over between them.

And the biggest shock hadn't been the broken engagement; much worse was Michelle's reason: she simply did not believe Allister was innocent.

"Gary was the only person who stuck by me through it all," he told Stevie as he stopped pacing and looked through the frosted window. He watched the glimmer of snowflakes in the yellow sodium glow of a street lamp. "Gary was the only one who really believed in my innocence. Even Barb, I think, has always harbored some doubts, although she's never come right out and said so. But Gary... I don't think there was ever any question in his mind. That was the one and only thing I could count on in all those years."

Stevie was pretty sure Allister was turned away from her, and she was glad. She didn't want him to see her wipe at the stray tear that slid down her cheek. She swallowed hard, but the painful lump remained. No, she couldn't allow Allister to see how deeply his story had affected her. Compassion and sympathy were not what he'd been seeking when telling her what he had.

It was understanding he was after.

Now, in the swell of silence that grew between them, Stevie hoped Allister recognized that she *did* understand.

After all he'd been through, after everything he'd worked for had been taken away from him because of something he didn't do, after those around him hadn't even kept faith, Allister still possessed the courage and the stamina to go on.

The hatred he must harbor for Edward Bainbridge! The man had snatched away everything Allister had known and loved. He'd altered Allister's life forever, stolen four years that could never be replaced.

It was the kind of hatred Stevie could understand.

The same hatred darkened her own heart now—hatred for the man who had taken her sight. The man who had ended the world she'd known and taken from her everything she'd lived for.

Setting her mug on the coffee table, she stood and stepped in the direction she'd last heard Allister's voice. With one hand she reached out and connected with Allister's arm, then lowered her hand to his. Strong broad fingers wove between hers once again, but there was a familiarity about it this time—the same kind of familiarity that prompted her to step into the inverted V of his long legs and made it feel so absolutely right.

She felt the whisper of his breath against her hair, and the heat of his body beckoning her even closer.

"Allister..." she whispered, but could think of nothing to say that might possibly express the connection she felt with him now, this common understanding.

Instead, she brought her other hand up to his chest. Through the soft flannel of his shirt, she felt a quick quiver of muscle and then the rhythm of his heart, beating as urgently as her own. Her hip pressing into his thigh now, Stevie moved her hand farther up his chest.

It was when she started to reach for his face that he caught her hand in his, and for one heart-sinking moment Stevie wondered if he was going to stop her. She needed Allister, needed his embrace, his closeness, to share their losses and their suffering.

And then she felt his lips brush her palm.

A hot rush of desire swept through her, and her fingertips trembled against his lips. She slid her fingers through his thick silky hair, drawing him nearer still. For a brief moment Stevie questioned her impulse to allow such closeness to a man she barely knew, had never seen.

But when she felt his mouth move above hers and she heard him murmur her name, all hesitations were cast from Stevie's mind.

With one hand cupping her chin, Allister drew her into his kiss. His lips, at first gentle and testing, became more demanding, and Stevie matched his eagerness. And when his mouth left hers, Stevie bit back her disappointment. But within seconds she felt his lips press fervent kisses along the sensitive skin at the base of her throat.

She was unable to suppress the moan that escaped her lips, and Allister seemed moved by the honest expression. He drew her closer still, pressing his strong body into her curves, igniting even more sparks of desire. His mouth found hers again, and this time their hunger was so acute, so desperate, that Stevie thought she couldn't bear it.

It was Allister who pulled back finally, his groan heavy with frustration.

"I . . . I'm sorry, Allister," Stevie whispered, still held loosely in his arms. "I honestly don't know where that came from, I guess—"

"You don't have to apologize, Stevie."

"Oh, I think I do. I mean, just because my place was broken into tonight... I'm on edge, but that doesn't give me the right to throw myself at you." She started to back away, but Allister caught her.

"I don't think that was your only reason for kissing me, Stevie."

She shook her head and immediately wished she could see Allister's eyes. She wished she could see the way he must be looking at her now.

"If it makes you feel any better," he confided softly, every word whispering warmly across her cheek, "I've been wanting to kiss you all night."

He continued to hold her, his embrace tender, warm. Stevie felt so very right here in his arms. Nothing had felt that right in years. And not seeing him was something she should get used to, Stevie thought as she drank in his tenderness now, because she might *never* see this man.

CHAPTER SEVEN

"No. STILL NOTHING, Doc."

"How about now?"

"Nothing."

"And now?"

Stevie let out a sigh of frustration. "No."

She had no idea how long she'd been at the hospital, only that it seemed like hours. Initially she'd been subjected to more scans, after which Dr. Sterling informed her that the swelling had indeed gone down. He'd then launched into his medical babble, talking about tissue damage and the occipital lobe and visual cortex.

None of which sounded remotely optimistic. At least, not from where Stevie sat.

She lifted her hand off the vinyl armrest of the examining chair intending to brush her bangs from her forehead, but her wrist struck the corner of a stainless-steel tray. She jumped at the resounding clatter of metal instruments.

"Sorry about that, Stevie. Let me move this out of your way." Dr. Sterling's voice was low and calm, as it had been throughout his examination. "We're through with this, anyway."

There was another reverberating clatter of the tray, followed by the harsh grating of Dr. Sterling's stool against the linoleum flooring, and then the click of his hard-soled shoes.

"It doesn't look good, does it, Doc?"

"I didn't say that, Stevie."

"But there hasn't been any improvement, has there?"

"Of course there has. You said yourself you no longer need the painkillers, the headaches have eased up and so has the dizziness."

"But I still can't see."

His footsteps came closer, and she sensed him beside her. The hydraulic chair she'd been half reclining in was gradually righted. Sitting in the almost tomblike silence of the room, Stevie imagined that Dr. Sterling was studying her.

She prompted him again. "My sight's still not returning."

"It's only been a week, Stevie."

"You said—"

"I *said* it could take a week. I also said it could take a couple of weeks. Or more. Stevie, you have to be patient."

"Oh, sure." Resentful sarcasm sharpened her voice. How could she be patient when her career, her entire life, hinged on her vision?

She sighed. "I'm sorry, Doc. I didn't mean to—"

"That's all right, Stevie." She heard him pull up the stool once more. "I realize this is very difficult for you. But you have to keep faith. Just because there hasn't been any visual recovery yet doesn't mean that there still won't be."

She nodded. It was all she could do.

Perhaps it was the quiet understanding in his voice, or maybe the fact that, unlike Paige and even Allister now, Dr. Sterling was a stranger, but here in his examining room on the twelfth floor of Danby General, Stevie no longer felt the need to be strong. From the moment she'd left Allister in the waiting room and stepped into the doctor's office, her facade had steadily crumbled.

Yes, she was terrified. And here, she no longer had the energy to mask her terror.

For a week, Stevie had tried to turn off the fear of never regaining her vision, of never again gazing through a camera lens, the overwhelming dread of her future—but the nightmares had persisted. The worst was the darkness she always awoke to. It was constant. Not so much as a glimmer of light. Nor a glimmer of hope.

Now, hearing the concern in Dr. Sterling's voice, it took everything Stevie had to hold back her tears. He must have seen them well up in her eyes, because the next thing she knew, he was pressing a tissue into her hand.

"Stevie, listen to me. I realize it probably feels as if your life is over, as if you have nothing to live for, but trust me, that isn't the case."

"It is if my sight doesn't return. Doc, I'm a photographer," she reminded him. Her voice wavered. She hated the sound of it. "Somehow I don't think I'll have quite the same edge as others in my field with a handicap like this, if you know what I mean."

But there was no responding chuckle. Obviously Dr. Sterling saw through her attempts at humor. His silence was unnerving, and Stevie squirmed in the big chair. When she lifted the tissue to her eyes, she knew he would notice her hand shaking.

"Well, if nothing else," she said, "my photography will certainly take on a unique angle. Who knows, it might just work."

Still no response.

No, there was no fooling the good doctor with her offhand quips. Unlike Paige, who accepted her humor because she recognized it as Stevie's way of coping, Dr. Sterling seemed determined to get to the heart of the matter.

"Okay, Stevie," he said at last, "what's the worst that can happen? In all honesty. Between you and me and these four walls, let's say your vision doesn't return and your photography career ends prematurely. The main thing is, you're alive, right? That's got to count for something, doesn't it?''

Stevie bit her lower lip. "I'll have to get back to you on that one, Doc." And she meant it, she realized. Without her photography, what *would* her life mean to her? There was no way she could answer that. No way she'd dare. Not yet.

"Fine then. So let's talk about when you *do* regain your vision." His stool scraped back and she heard him move through the room, putting away instruments and closing drawers. "In most cases like this, although each is unique, there are some common experiences you should be aware of. Usually, at first, you'll distinguish only light, most likely starting with your peripheral. Shortly after that, you should be able to discern movement. But this will be very blurred, and I'll warn you, it can be very disorienting and you're probably better off staying in bed during this period."

"How long should all this take? If...when my sight does start to come back?"

"Generally ten to twelve hours. Sometimes longer."

"And then what? I'll just be able to see again?"

"Best-case scenario, yes. Of course, as I warned you earlier, if there is damage to the cerebellum, there's the threat of double vision or other complications. But I'm not anticipating that," he added, his tone lifting encouragingly. "You'll get better, Stevie. Trust me. You just need time. And faith."

"You think you could bottle me some of that optimism of yours, Doc? I mean, for the ride home and all?" she asked as he guided her to his adjoining office.

Now he chuckled and showed her to a chair. "I'll work on it." He patted her shoulder "Just sit tight. I'll find your friend so you can go home."

Her friend. Poor Allister. No doubt, he hadn't banked on spending hours in the twelfth-floor waiting room when he'd offered to bring Stevie to the hospital this morning.

Then again, he hadn't had much choice. After another sleepless night, this one in Allister's bed while he slept on the living-room sofa, Stevie had just managed to doze off when Paige's phone call had woken her. She'd heard the ring, and through the closed door of the bedroom, she listened to Allister's muffled voice coming from the kitchen. Then there had been the welcome aroma of fresh coffee, and that was all the encouragement Stevie had needed. She'd slipped into Allister's robe, which he'd left at the foot of the bed, and headed to the kitchen.

She'd been foolish enough to believe she could make it all the way through his apartment unaided. It was when she groped her way past the couch that she reacquainted herself with the coffee table.

Her shin had collided with one sharp corner, and her curses carried easily to the kitchen. By the time Allister rushed in, Stevie was already on the couch, sitting amongst his rumpled sheets and blankets.

Just another bruise to add to all the others, she'd told him, and cursed some more as he led her to the kitchen for a badly needed coffee. When he told her about Paige's call, reminding her of today's appointment, there was no arguing with him about how she was to get to the hospital, in spite of Paige's offer to come and pick her up. They were already running late.

During their rushed breakfast, neither of them mentioned what had happened between them the night before. Even when Allister had pointed out the misaligned buttons on her shirt, and had discreetly adjusted them for her, even then he hadn't made any move to kiss her again.

In fact, had it not been for the way he'd held her hand in the waiting room or the gentle squeeze he'd given it when the doctor had called her in, Stevie would have begun to suspect that last night's kiss had been a figment of her rampant imagination.

But it hadn't been. The second she heard Allister's voice as Dr. Sterling led him in now, Stevie felt a hot pulse of excitement quiver through her. Surely no imagination, even a rampant one, could generate such an acute response.

"HOW ARE YOU DOING?" Allister placed a hand on Stevie's shoulder.

"I'm okay," she said, the waver in her voice barely perceptible.

"I think Stevie's ready to go home," Dr. Sterling said for her. "I'm sure you've had enough prodding and poking to last you for another week, am I right?"

Stevie nodded, and Allister took her hand in his, again squeezing it gently.

"Just take it easy, Stevie." Dr. Sterling looked directly at her, as though he expected her to return his smile. "I'll see you next week."

"Thanks, Doc."

Allister watched her fleeting smile. But he knew it was an act. He'd seen the worry that drew delicate lines across Stevie's brow and tightened the corners of her mouth. The expression was so dark and so drawn that for a moment he expected to be told that the tests had all been negative, and that there was no hope for any improvement.

But then, hadn't that been what he'd been hoping for in a way? For two hours he'd sat out there in the waiting room; he'd leafed through an entire stack of torn and dog-eared magazines but it might as well have been the same issue over and over again; he'd paced the corridors, bought a candy bar from the vending machine down the hall and drunk bitter coffee from a paper cup. And throughout the wait, there had been only one thought filling his mind—Stevie's blindness.

He hated himself for wishing what he did. But until he managed to find the coins or any evidence against Edward Bainbridge, he secretly prayed that Stevie's condition did not improve. And it was that thought that made him feel physically ill. It wasn't bad enough that he was the man responsible for her blindness, but here he was dreading even the slightest sign of improvement.

Still, no matter what feelings he was beginning to have for Stevie, especially after last night, Allister could not allow himself to forget that she was the one person who could send him back to prison. If her sight returned and she saw who he really was . . . well, they might as well throw away the key to the cell this time.

He helped Stevie on with her coat and guided her from the elevator to the main doors. "So how did it go?" he asked once they were in the Explorer and he'd turned on the ignition.

"Still no change," she said matter-of-factly.

"They couldn't tell anything from the tests?"

"Nothing yet. Dr. Sterling says it could still take time."

"I'm sorry, Stevie," he said, hoping his voice sounded sincere. He reached across to place his hand over hers.

She said nothing. The smile slipped away, leaving the haunting blankness of her unfixed gaze.

"Did you want me to drive you home, Stevie? Or would you prefer coming back to my place?"

"I think home, Allister." Her hands didn't move beneath his.

"Would you like to call Paige first at the studio? Just in case the police are still there or the security-system people?

The place could be a bit of a madhouse if they haven't finished.''

She nodded, and Allister reached for his cellular phone. He punched out the number she dictated to him, and when he slipped the phone into her hand, the line was already ringing.

"Paige? It's Stevie... Yes, we're just leaving now. I know... No, they ran all kinds of tests again. But I can tell you about it later. Uh-huh. Yes... I know.''

Allister looked past Stevie through the passenger window. Beyond the parking lot, the emergency entrance sat vacant, unlike last week. He'd worried about going into the hospital with Stevie this morning, worried he might be recognized from that crazy night. But he'd been lucky.

"So they're just about finished?" Stevie was asking Paige. "Uh-huh...okay. No, I'll come home... Yeah, okay, I'll tell him. I'll see you soon.''

Stevie handed him the phone, and Allister returned it to the dash mount. "What did she want you to tell me?''

"Oh, the roads. She says they haven't been sanded out there yet.''

"And the security system?''

"They're just finishing up. Detective Devane pulled some strings and had them put us at the top of their list this morning.''

The muscle along the back of Allister's neck tensed at the mention of the detective's name.

"Well, I guess I'd better get you home then,'' he said, and reached for Stevie's seat belt.

In the close quarters of the vehicle's interior, with only inches between them, memories of last night flared again. He'd tried to push them aside, tried to convince himself that their kiss hadn't affected him as much as it had. But even now he was so drawn to Stevie, his desire to take her into his arms so undeniable, that it took every ounce of restraint he had to do nothing more than clip her seat belt.

Last night, long after he'd shown Stevie to his bedroom, Allister had lain awake on the couch. Over and over in his mind he had tried to rationalize what had happened, what their kiss meant. God knew they'd both wanted it. He'd felt her longing, as strong as his own. There had been more behind Stevie's kiss than her fright at the studio and more than compassion at hearing his story. There had been an honesty in her kiss, a raw and heartfelt affection that had reawakened his own bleak remorse.

In the end he'd eventually found sleep, but it was the morning light that had brought a reality check to his emotions. As sunshine flooded the apartment and the smell of brewing coffee offered a new lucidity to his thoughts, Allister realized that, no matter how much he might have wanted to, kissing Stevie had been wrong. How could he lead her on like that? How could he give in to his own selfish longings after everything he wasn't telling her? After what he'd done to her?

Still, when Stevie had come to him last night, when she'd stepped into his arms and whispered his name, Allister couldn't remember if his own name had ever sounded the way it did coming from her lips.

Banishing those memories as best he could, Allister put the vehicle into Drive. As he steered out of the hospital parking lot and merged with the northbound traffic, he snatched quick glances at Stevie. Her hands were still clasped in her lap, and her lips were pursed as though she was deep in thought.

"Stevie?"

She turned her face, her eyes directed past him.

"Stevie, listen, about Devane. I know he's helped you and Paige out with this security company and all, but I have to

warn you about him. Or at least tell you that...that he
suspects I'm mixed up with these stolen coins."

"Because you'd been working with Gary?"

"Partly. But also because of my criminal record."

She faced forward again and nodded once, as though she
understood and no further explanation was required.

"I just thought you ought to know," he said. "Especially since Devane's likely to say some things...when he
finds out that you've been with me."

She gave him another nod, but remained silent.

"Stevie? Are you okay?"

"I'm fine, Allister." Again, the quick unconvincing smile.

"So what are you thinking about?"

She was silent as they waited at an intersection for a green
light. Only once they were moving again, did she turn in her
seat toward him.

"I was thinking about the break-in last night," she said.

"What about it?"

"Paige says she's gone through everything and nothing's
been taken this time."

"That's good."

"But then with the first break-in, while I was at the hospital, only the cameras were stolen."

"Right. So?"

"So, if you think about it, it doesn't really make sense,
does it?" she asked. "I mean, all coincidences aside, Allister, if it was a genuine robbery and nothing to do with
Bainbridge, then why didn't they take more the first time?
There was no one home. They had time. No one interrupted them. And yet, they bypassed a lot of other very
valuable equipment and went only for the cameras. They
didn't so much as go through the drawers to look for a cash
box or anything. Didn't go into the filing cabinets or even
the front desk for that matter. It just doesn't add up."

"And if it was Bainbridge or his hired thug?"

"Well, that's just it. If it *was* Bainbridge, then you'd think the whole place would have been torn apart. If he believes that I somehow have the coins, wouldn't they have searched the apartment, as well?"

"You'd think so, yes."

"It was as though they were after something in particular. Not the coins at all."

"You mean, the cameras?"

She nodded. "Or maybe what was *in* those cameras."

Allister braked sharply for a red light. He'd been so caught up in Stevie's analysis that he hadn't noticed it until the last second. His arm shot out to stop her from lurching forward, and at the same time, out of instinct, he checked his rearview mirror. That was when he noticed the dark sedan several cars back.

"Sorry, Stevie," he apologized, removing his arm, his gaze still fixed on the roof of the sedan.

He was being paranoid, he tried to convince himself, and glanced at Stevie again.

What she'd said made sense—perfect sense. He hadn't thought about the break-ins like that. He'd just figured that if Bainbridge's thug had broken into Stevie's to search for the coins, he'd taken the cameras simply to make it look as though it was a random burglary. But Stevie was right. It didn't add up. The apartment should have been literally torn apart, too.

"So you think that whoever broke in might actually have been after the film?"

"I don't know, Allister. But it's the only thing that makes sense."

"And why would somebody want your film?"

Stevie shook her head, and Allister eased the Explorer through the intersection. The sedan followed.

"I'm not sure. But you said yourself that if someone had been following Gary, if they had been watching the warehouse, then they would have known I was there. And they might have known *why* I was there. What if...what if somehow this person thinks there's something incriminating on the film? The film I shot at the warehouse?"

She had a point.

"Then what about the break-in last night?"

"I'm not sure about that...." Her voice trailed off.

Still heading north, Allister left the downtown core of Danby behind, along with most of the traffic. He glanced again in the rearview mirror. There was only one car between them and the dark brown sedan now. Even so, the driver of the sedan maintained a respectable distance. And when Allister steered onto Fisher Street, heading toward Stevie's studio, the sedan also made the turn.

"Allister." Stevie reached across to put a hand on his arm. "What if it *is* the film? What if I really did manage to shoot something I wasn't supposed to at the warehouse? And what if they stole the cameras hoping to get it? Whoever it was would want to know if they'd gotten the correct film, right? So maybe they had it developed. Well, what if they found out that they *hadn't* gotten the right film? They'd have to come back. They'd have to look for the rest of it."

"But you said they took all the cameras."

"Not all of them."

Allister steered the Explorer into another turn. The sedan followed. It lagged half a block back, but it was there.

"I still have the camera that jammed during the shoot at the warehouse. I'd put it in my black duffel, Allister, the bag I went back to Gary's to get that night, the bag that was with me at the hospital. Remember when you were over the other night and Paige was in the darkroom? That's what she was working on—the film from that camera."

"And she has the proofs from that film?"

Stevie nodded. "They're in my apartment."

He glanced at her again and now, more than ever, wanted to kiss her. He wanted to kiss her because she was brilliant, and he wanted to kiss her because there was a real possibility she might be right.

"Well, I'd say we're going to have to take a look at those proofs. As soon as we get you home."

Stevie settled back in her seat, no doubt as anxious as he was to discover the content of the film.

When Allister checked the rearview mirror again, the sedan was still there. He slowed, hoping to close the gap, hoping to catch even a glimpse of the vehicle's plate, or better yet, its driver. But the sedan slowed, as well, maintaining its distance.

And when he accelerated, the other car followed suit.

"Allister, what's wrong?" Obviously Stevie had noticed his erratic driving.

"We're being followed. Since the hospital, I think."

"Can you see who it is?"

"No, but I'm sure it's the same car that's been tailing me for the past couple of days. And I think right now," he said, as he took the wheel firmly with both hands, "I want to get a better look at this guy. Hang on, Stevie," he warned, and waited for her to grip the door's armrest.

He glanced once more in the mirror, gauged the distance and braked sharply as he forced the wheel all the way to the left. The heavy vehicle responded well, the tires grabbing what residual sand there was on the otherwise slippery road, and Allister managed the 180-degree turn with little more than a sideways shimmy.

The wheels spun briefly against the slick surface, and then the big vehicle lurched forward. Allister accelerated toward the sedan. The other driver had already begun to brake, and by the time Allister was within range, was already trying to turn around.

But the surface here was slicker, Allister noticed as he struggled with his own vehicle. He saw the sedan's back end swerve uselessly as snow and ice flew out from behind its churning tires.

Then he was within range. He could make out the license plate and he memorized the number. Still he barreled toward the sedan, and still the other driver tried to bring the car around. And then Allister saw the man at the wheel.

It wasn't anyone he recognized.

At that moment, as Allister started to brake, as he snatched a glance at Stevie and saw her ashen expression, he felt the Explorer begin to slide.

"Stevie, hang on." But Allister realized his warning was pointless.

In sickeningly slow motion, the big vehicle started to swerve. Allister eased his foot on the brake, not daring to jam it to the floor for fear the Explorer would go into a deadly spin. But in spite of his efforts, the vehicle's tail end glided over the greasy surface.

The steering wheel became useless in his hands as the car careened into its first nauseating 360-degree turn. There was a blur of white, and through it Allister saw the sedan's taillights as it pulled away. He saw a flash of guardrail, and then more white.

He fought with the wheel, but it dragged uselessly in his hands, skinning his palms.

And then there was the embankment. The second shuddering rotation brought them even closer to it. He saw the railing again.

This time it was too close.

The right front end caught it first, whipping the Explorer around sharply. There was a piercing shriek of metal, and for one second Allister imagined that the guardrail would stop their momentum.

He was wrong.

The corroded railing was no match for the combined speed and weight of the Explorer. And in that instant, as it tore loose from its posts and the vehicle pitched through the jagged opening, Allister's only thought was for Stevie.

As they plunged down the ice-encrusted slope, he reached for her. The vehicle bounced violently once to the left, and Allister was thrown forward.

There was a flash of pain.

And then only darkness.

CHAPTER EIGHT

LEFT AND RIGHT lost all relevance. As far as Stevie could tell, the world still reeled around her. The scream of tortured metal still rang in her ears. And her breath still came in shallow frantic gulps.

She couldn't be sure if the car had swerved, spun or even rolled. But at last, it had come to a rest. Exactly where, though, she had no idea.

It was pitched forward—she knew that much—nose first. An embankment. They must have gone off the road and down into a ravine. Although she hadn't been paying attention during the drive, she was sure they couldn't be farther than five or ten minutes from the studio. Frantically Stevie tried to lay out a map in her mind.

She pushed back against the bucket seat, fighting the steep cant of the vehicle. Immediately she winced. Her hip and thigh burned with pain, and the right side of her jaw throbbed. She remembered she'd been slammed against the passenger door and window.

"Allister?" she said into the silence. She took a ragged breath. "Allister?"

No reply.

Her heart hammered against her ribs.

"Allister!"

Still no response.

Stevie reached across the center console. He was slumped forward. Her hand skimmed over the slick leather of his jacket, traveling upward to his shoulders. His face was turned to her.

"Allister?"

His skin felt hot under her cold hands. Her fingers trembled so fiercely now she could barely control them.

Then she felt something hot and sticky along his forehead. Blood.

"Oh, God. Allister. Allister."

She was chanting his name now. Over and over. And she was rocking him, as though she was trying to wake him from a nap, instead of this nightmare they were in.

"Allister, please..."

Her fingertips fluttered to his throat, and she gave a small whimper of relief when she found his pulse.

She tried to pull him away from the steering wheel. The seat belt gouged painfully into her neck. Fumbling with the clip, her fingers slippery with Allister's blood, Stevie cried out with frustration. When the snap released, she untangled herself and twisted around in the bucket seat.

Whether or not it was her sudden movement within the cab, the Explorer shifted, and instantly there was a low gut-wrenching groan from beneath the big vehicle. Stevie froze and felt it again—a slight jostle.

Panic clawed at her throat. She imagined teetering on the brink of one of the deep ravines she knew flanked the route to the studio.

The ominous grinding sound that ripped through the momentary hush then was only a fleeting warning for what happened next.

With barely enough time to brace herself, Stevie felt the vehicle shudder, release and plunge forward. Her scream was lost in the earsplitting roar. Snow and rocks and everything else in the vehicle's path scraped its wide underbelly as it plowed its way downward until finally, with a thunderous crack and a spine-jolting lurch, it came to a halt.

Whether or not they were firmly wedged this time, Stevie had no way of knowing, but the tilt of the vehicle was less severe. Cautiously she moved in her seat. The car stayed. She reached for Allister again.

His body was still slumped forward against the steering wheel. She grabbed the collar of his jacket and pulled him back.

"Allister, please. You've got to help me out," she said, knowing he couldn't hear her, but needing to speak in order to subdue her panic.

She traced her fingers across his forehead again and found the gash just below his hairline. It didn't seem serious. "Come on, Allister. If you think I can do this by myself, you've got to be—"

She stopped abruptly. There was another sound now. A sound far more sinister than the crushing groan of metal against rock. A sound that clarified for Stevie exactly where they were.

It was the low gurgle of water—lapping against the sides of the vehicle, sucking hungrily at the wheel wells.

The river. Its banks usually froze by midwinter, but here at the north end of Danby, the center always ran open— open and deep.

How far had the vehicle ground its way down the bank? She knew these embankments well enough. They were steep, the drop to the river practically sheer, as was the riverbed itself.

Still, they couldn't be in too far, Stevie thought. Already she could feel hot tears of fear on her cheeks. She wiped at them with the back of her hand. No, she had to stay calm. She had to think.

The Explorer seemed stable enough. If they were actually immersed in the river, surely she should feel the vehicle sway in the current. Still, she had to get Allister out. There was no way of knowing when the bank might give way again. If she couldn't rouse him, she'd have to climb over him, drag him, somehow, to the shore.

Stevie reached across him and groped for the driver's-side door handle. Immediately the door swung open, allowing in a blast of cold air.

"Okay, Allister," she said, clamping down on her terror, "this is it. Are you with me or not?"

She turned all the way in her seat now, feeling for the center console. She slipped her right leg over it. Bracing herself, one hand on the back of her seat, the other on Allister's, she eased herself across the console until she was straddling his lap, her back against the steering wheel.

Again, Stevie tried to bring him to consciousness. She touched his face and spoke loudly, close to his ear. "Please, Allister. I can't do this on my own. You've got to wake up!" She was practically screaming at him, she realized. Screaming above the rush of the river and the wail of the wind howling through the car's interior. But more than that, she was screaming above her own fear.

And then the car shifted again.

Stevie heard her own terrified cry over the now-familiar groan of metal, and she threw her arms around Allister and the seat to brace both of them. But the vehicle lurched only a couple of feet this time.

Stevie let out a shaky breath of relief.

Then she felt the water. Freezing water.

It slapped angrily against the sides of the vehicle, and rushed in through the open door. In seconds it flooded the floor, soaking her boots, her jeans. The shock of its cold threatened to paralyze her.

And still it rushed in. She could feel it lapping at the edge of the seat.

"Allister!" His name burst from her throat in a gasp, the cold knocking the wind out of her lungs. "Allister, dammit! Wake up!" She was crying.

She had to get him out. It could be only a matter of seconds before the swift current filled the car and dragged it loose. Then there'd be no chance of rescuing him. Or saving herself.

In that instant, Stevie remembered the cellular phone. With hands flailing across the dash behind her, she found the unit and yanked it from its mount. Her teeth chattered as she shoved the phone inside her jacket with numbed fingers.

But first Allister. She had to get him out. The water rose past the seat.

Struggling with the clip to his seat belt, Stevie released him. He sagged forward, against her, and for the first time she wondered if she could handle his dead weight.

"Okay, Allister, this is it," she said. Her voice was ragged with cold.

She slid out from under him then and grabbed the sides of the doorway. Before her was the familiar chasm of blackness, but this time it was accompanied by the roar of churning water.

Stevie had no idea what to expect when she dropped over the side of the vehicle and into the crippling cold of the river. She let out a thin whimper of relief when her boots found bottom. Almost waist-deep in the frigid current, she had to literally force herself to breathe.

By the tilt of the car and the sharp angle of the riverbed, Stevie guessed that the bank lay to her right. She'd have to get Allister out and to that bank. She prayed it wasn't too far.

She reached into the vehicle. His jeans were soaked, making him even heavier as she pulled him toward her. She grabbed a fistful of jacket and eventually slid his right arm over her shoulder.

When she finally managed to pull him out the door, she thought she'd been prepared to take his weight. And for a brief moment she was. But then she lost her balance, and in that instant Allister slipped from her grasp.

Stevie tried to scream, but the cold locked it in her throat. She spun around, thrashing at the frigid water for him, terrified that the current had dragged him under.

And then she heard a sputtering cough.

Her hand found his jacket, soaked and heavy now, like the rest of his clothes, dragging him down. Her fingers glided uselessly across the slick surface, until she managed to hook her arms under his.

"Allister," she gasped. "Allister!"

He coughed again. Choking on icy water.

He grabbed her shoulders, using her to pull himself up. And as she half-dragged, half-guided him to where she imagined the bank, she heard him mumble her name.

He was barely conscious, she realized, and how long it would last, she didn't know. But he managed to stay with her long enough for them to reach the shore. Once there, as she started to lower him to the snow, Stevie felt him collapse.

Hypothermia was the fear that drove through her numbed mind now. The cold was almost painful and her muscles ached. But she wasn't as wet as Allister who had been completely immersed in that deadly cold.

Stevie shivered and eased herself to the ground next to him. She had to keep him warm. Unzipping her own coat, shaking uncontrollably, she slid it off her shoulders and covered him with it. When she touched his lips they felt cool.

The cellular. With trembling fingers she found it where it had fallen next to her and searched for the right numbers.

She waited.

And when she heard the recording, Stevie could no longer suppress her tears.

"You've reached the 911 emergency line. All operators are busy. Please stand by..."

"STEVIE?" PAIGE'S VOICE cut through the haze. "Stevie? Honey, listen, he's going to be all right."

Paige touched her cheek. Her hand was warm. Even now, in dry clothes and wrapped in the wool hospital blanket, Stevie felt chilled to the bone.

She had huddled against Allister's still body long after the sirens had stopped at the top of the embankment. And when the rescue crew had clambered down, they'd had to pry her off him so they could lift him into the basket and hoist him up the slope. He hadn't regained consciousness, even in the ambulance, but the paramedics had tried to assure her he'd be fine.

At the hospital, they'd taken him away. An intern had examined Stevie, and then—at her insistence—had led her to a phone. After calling Paige, she'd been promptly returned to her bed in the ER, sounds of the ward reeling around her. And when Paige tracked her down at last, Stevie had collapsed in her friend's arms.

"I'm sure if it was serious, they would have told us by now. Can I get you anything, honey?" she asked.

"No, I'm fine, Paige, really. You haven't seen Dr. Sterling again, have you?"

"No. I haven't."

Dr. Sterling had come down to the ER shortly after Paige had arrived. He'd heard about Stevie's daring rescue, he said, through the hospital grapevine and had slipped out of his office as soon as he'd been able. Assured that she was uninjured, he'd promised to find out what he could about Allister's condition.

That had been hours ago—at least, to Stevie, it felt that long.

"Here he is." Paige left the side of the hospital bed and stood. Stevie followed suit, letting the blanket fall away from her shoulders.

"How are you doing, Stevie?" Dr. Sterling asked, taking both her hands in his.

"Fine, Doc. I'm just...worried about Allister. Did you find out—"

"Allister's fine, Stevie. I'm sorry, I got tied up with another situation. I would have thought you'd've been informed by now."

"No, we haven't been told anything."

"Well, let me assure you, Stevie, he's all right. He's got a mild concussion. That's it. And they want to keep him overnight."

"Can I see him?"

"Of course. He's probably resting, but you can go in."

Paige draped the blanket over her shoulders again as Dr. Sterling started to lead her out. "I'll wait for you, Stevie," she heard her say.

"Paige, no. I...I want to stay. That's all right, isn't it, Doc? They'll let me stay with Allister?"

No one spoke, and for a moment there was only the chiming of elevator bells, warbling phones and the shuffle of people around her. Stevie tried to imagine the glances exchanged by Dr. Sterling and Paige, and hoped that neither of them was willing to argue with her.

Dr. Sterling spoke first. "I'm sure I can arrange something. In the meantime I'll show you to Allister's room."

"I'll call you, Paige, later," Stevie told her friend before she was led from the ward.

They'd given him a semiprivate room, Dr. Sterling informed her, but the other bed was empty. After guiding her to Allister's bedside and pulling up a chair for her, Dr. Sterling promised to speak with the floor nurses on duty to see what could be arranged for Stevie to stay the night.

"Feel free to use the extra bed," he told her. "It's just a few steps to your left, but I'm sure the night nurse will be in sometime later."

"Thanks, Doc. Thank you for everything."

He gave her hand a squeeze, then left the room. The sound of the door swinging in its frame brought back memories of a week ago.

Only a week. And yet it seemed a lifetime since she'd first heard Dr. Sterling's voice and been given the horrifying diagnosis. Did it seem like such a long time because of the blindness? Stevie wondered. Or was it because of Allister, because she seemed to know him so much better than one week should allow?

She dragged the cushioned chair close to his bed. She could hear him breathing, low and deep. She felt the cool sheets, crisp against her palm, and finally she found the warmth of Allister's hand.

Stevie took it in hers—caressing it and turning it over. Tenderly she pressed a kiss into his palm. And when she whispered his name, she wondered if he heard.

DETECTIVE DEVANE had had a long day. All he could think of now, as he went through this morning's results from Falcioni's studio, was getting home to a hot meal. He checked his digital watch—five-eleven. Mary would be wondering where he was if he didn't head out soon.

But he'd wanted to go through the report once more, before he wrote it off as a complete waste of time. Whoever had broken into Falcioni's studio last night hadn't been an amateur. The lock had been picked with great skill before the chain was cut. And not one print anywhere, other than a couple of smudged glove prints, which, on their own, didn't stand a chance in hell of leading to anything.

The investigation was going nowhere. Just this morning, after the chief had come down on him again for results, Devane had gone over all the case notes one more time, hoping to find something he'd missed before—some link between the stolen coins, Palmer and Stephanie Falcioni. The morning after the murder, after they'd found the microcassette with Palmer's and the unidentified client's conversation, after they'd found the newspaper clippings and knew that somehow the stolen coins figured into the shipper's murder, he had asked Falcioni if Palmer had given her anything for safekeeping. It had been a long shot, of course, but not entirely unreasonable. If Palmer had wanted to get the coins out of his warehouse, he *might* have given them to Falcioni. After all, she was likely the last person to see him alive. Apart from the murderer.

And obviously, considering the two break-ins into the studio, he was not the only person who believed that the Falcioni woman might somehow be connected to Palmer's murder and the coins.

"Hey, Devane." Tony Martinez sauntered into the squad room, a smug grin on his thin face. "Did you hear about that accident out on Shelton this afternoon?"

Devane shook his head and turned back to the report.

"Car spun off the road and went down the ravine."

Devane shrugged, but wouldn't look up. No wonder no one on the squad wanted Martinez as a partner, he thought, as the newest member on the Danby force sidled up to his desk. It wasn't just the nagging whine in the younger detective's voice; it was the way everything he said sounded so taunting.

"Yeah, they had to drag it out of the river. Real mess."

"Look, Martinez, is there a point to this little discussion, or are you just jabbering 'cause you like the sound of your own voice?" Devane afforded him one sideways glower and hoped that it was enough to get rid of the annoyance once and for all.

"No, just thought you'd be interested. Seems your blind eyewitness was in the car."

"What the hell are you talking about, Martinez? You sure it was her?" Devane stood now, towering over the junior detective. The effect seemed to work. Martinez backed off.

"Yeah, it was her. Stephanie Falcioni, right?"

"When did this happen?"

"Few hours ago. Report came in after two sometime, I guess. You were out."

"She all right?"

"Yeah, far as I know."

"Who was the driver?"

"Owner of the vehicle. Some guy—Quaid or something."

"Allister Quaid?"

"Yeah, that's it."

"For crying out loud!" Devane closed the report on his desk and slammed out of the office.

ALLISTER REMEMBERED the accident.

He remembered speeding toward the dark sedan, remembered the man's face and the license number. The rest was only blurred images of the crash—the whole world spinning in slow motion, metal screeching against metal, and finally a great thundering explosion as the Explorer ground its way down the slope. Until there had been only darkness.

He lifted a hand to his forehead and felt the neat bandage there. He'd hit his head on the steering wheel, he was pretty certain, and then he'd lost consciousness.

But somehow he remembered water. Black icy water, tugging at his clothes, dragging him down. And he'd been choking on it. Then Stevie had been calling his name, lifting him from the water.

Yes, he remembered Stevie—her arms around him, dragging him to the bank, screaming his name even when the darkness took him one more time. She'd saved his life.

He opened his eyes now, already recognizing where he was by the muffled sounds from the corridor and the odor of antiseptic. Except for a low light on the side table, the room lay in shadows. The blinds on the wide window were open to a night sky.

Beside him, half on the chair and half on the bed, Stevie held his hand in hers. She was asleep. Her cheek was warm in his palm, and he could feel her breath whisper across his wrist.

As the soft glow of the lamp touched her face, Allister wondered if he'd ever seen a more welcome sight. She was all right, he kept saying over and over in his mind. She was all right. Stevie had saved his life. And she was all right.

He shifted on the bed and felt every muscle in his body ache. Stevie didn't wake up. Only when he reached over and caressed her hair did she stir.

In that gray portal between dream and reality, Allister saw her momentary confusion as her head come up. Her face twisted with the dark memory of fear, and she gasped his name.

"Stevie." He clutched her hands and felt them shake briefly. "Stevie, I'm here. It's all right. I'm right here."

"Allister." She let out a breath, collecting herself, and pulled her hand from his to run it back through her hair. "You're awake."

"Yeah."

It was relief, he guessed, that suddenly moistened her eyes. He lifted a finger to her cheek to wipe away the first tear, and when he did, her back straightened and she pulled away. With her own hand, she swiped at the second tear.

"Are you all right, Stevie?"

He could see her tremble when she nodded.

But as she tilted her head slightly, Allister saw the purplish tinge of a bruise along the right side of her jaw. He took her chin in his hand and turned her to the light.

"It's nothing, Allister," she said when he touched it. She took his hand. "Just a bruise."

Still, she was on the verge of tears. And it was because of him.

"Stevie, I'm okay," he said, giving her hand a squeeze. "I'm sorry I put your life at risk. I'm sorry I scared you. I don't . . . I don't think I can ever forgive myself for that."

She nodded weakly and bit her lip.

"Stevie?"

"I thought you were dead, Allister."

"Oh, Stevie." She was shaking when he drew her into his arms and onto the bed alongside him. "I'm not. I'm very much alive, Stevie, thanks to you." Their closeness seemed so natural. Her small frame was pressed against him, and with one arm around her, holding her tight, Allister stroked her hair.

When she eventually spoke again, her voice was stronger. "Promise me you'll never do that again."

"What? Drive you into a river?"

He was sure she smiled.

"You know what I mean."

"I promise," he said, feeling her heat against his chest.

"You know," she said, "I'm really getting tired of this place."

"Yeah?"

She nodded. "Uh-huh."

"Well, you're lucky."

"And how's that?"

"At least you don't have to look at the godawful color scheme they've got going here."

Her gentle laughter rocked her delicate body, and Allister found a deep contentment in its sound and in the feel of her in his arms.

They lay together in silence for a long time, both taking comfort in the closeness of the other, both realizing how lucky they'd been this afternoon. Eventually Stevie reached up to find his hand. She wove her fingers through his, holding tight.

"So who was the man in the car, Allister?"

He peered over her shoulder, watching her thumb caress the back of his hand. "I don't know, Stevie."

"Who had you thought he might have been?"

"I figured Devane had been tailing me. But it wasn't."

"Could it have been another cop?"

"I don't know," he said again. "I doubt it. I don't think a cop would have hightailed it out of there, unless it was a cop on Bainbridge's payroll. I think whoever was driving that car today is working for Bainbridge."

"But you said this guy's been following you for a couple of days. Why? I mean, you thought it was me Bainbridge wanted. That he thought *I* somehow had his coins."

"I know."

"So what would Bainbridge want with you?"

Only to frame me for my best friend's murder, Allister thought for one bitter moment.

"I don't know, Stevie," he told her, instead. "Maybe he thinks I've got the coins. Who knows?"

There was another long spell of silence, and Allister wondered if Stevie had fallen asleep. She hadn't.

"So what are you going to do, Allister?"

"Well, I'm going to find out who was driving that brown sedan—I've got his license-plate number memorized. There's this guy at the Department of Motor Vehicles who takes care of our shipping trucks. I can get him to run a check on the plate for me tomorrow."

"Then what?"

"Then I have to see if my tail is linked to Bainbridge."

"And *then* you'll go to the police?"

"No!" His response was almost explosive in the hush of the room, and he wondered if he'd frightened her. He softened his voice. "No, I can't do that, Stevie. It's too risky. There's no way of knowing at this point who's on Bainbridge's payroll. And that includes Devane."

She didn't reply.

"Stevie?"

Finally she nodded, but Allister could feel the tension along her back, almost rigid against his chest.

"You're right, Allister." Her voice lowered to a whisper as though she were giving a confessional. "It's just . . . I'm afraid."

"I know, Stevie. I know." He drew closer to her then, pressing his cheek against hers. "But I promise I won't let anything happen to you."

He caressed her hair, wishing there was something he could do to ease her worry.

Certainly, she had a right to worry. There were risks involved. But for Allister, there was much more at stake than proving his innocence or seeing Bainbridge brought to justice after all these years.

There was Stevie now.

And for Stevie, he realized, he'd risk just about everything, even his life, if necessary. He'd done enough to her already.

CHAPTER NINE

IT TOOK SEVERAL MINUTES for Stevie to realize it was morning. She listened to the muffled sounds of the hospital around her, and then she heard the breakfast trolleys trundle by in the corridor beyond the closed door.

Only once had she and Allister been woken by the night nurse. Stevie had no idea what time it had been, but shortly after, groggy with sleep, she was certain she'd heard Dr. Sterling whisper something to the nurse about their "needing their sleep" and that they should be left alone. And it was in the undisturbed silence of their hospital room, in Allister's embrace, that Stevie had found solace and a sense of security that had finally enabled her to sleep for the first time without nightmares since her blindness had begun.

She had no idea when they'd eventually fallen asleep or who had drifted off first. They'd talked for a long time. Locked in each other's arms, Allister had asked about Stevie's family, her childhood, her career. He hadn't pressed her about her future, about the blindness and her very real fears of its possible permanence or the end of her career. And for that, Stevie had been grateful.

Likewise, she hadn't asked Allister for details about his prison term and what his life had been like for those four years of unjust hell. What little he did divulge was enough for her to realize that the experience had been something he'd found difficult to deal with and now was almost impossible to forget.

Allister's fervent bitterness toward Bainbridge and the police, who he believed had planted the stolen gems in his car years ago, had been painfully obvious. And he'd held Stevie even tighter then, as though having her there with him somehow offered him the peace he'd needed but been denied all those years.

A week ago, had someone asked her if it was possible to fall in love with someone she'd never seen, perhaps might never see, Stevie would have scoffed and given a resolute no. But listening to the low rhythm of Allister's breathing behind her, feeling it fan the back of her neck, Stevie realized her answer would be different now.

After the crash, when she'd lost Allister in the icy current of the river for that one frantic moment, Stevie honestly couldn't remember ever being so afraid. And then last night, lying in each other's arms in the hospital bed, their embrace had changed from one of comfort to one that stirred deeper feelings and roused long-dormant desires that Stevie had kept in check these past few years while her career took priority.

Allister had become strangely silent after a while, as though he, too, sensed this deeper intimacy and shared Stevie's longings. But if he did, he never acted upon them.

Still, Stevie wondered, if it hadn't been a hospital bed they'd shared last night, would things have gone farther? Even now, with Allister asleep and a barrier of sheets and blankets between them, Stevie longed to feel his body, feel that strong chest press against hers, and feel the heat of his skin tingle across her own.

She turned slightly in his arms, easing her weight from her stiff shoulder, and as she did, Allister stirred. She pushed back the blanket that covered her, realizing he must have taken the one at the foot of the bed and drawn it over her sometime in the night.

"Allister." She'd only whispered his name, but instantly he was awake.

"Allister, I think it's morning."

"What time is it?" His voice, thick with sleep, murmured softly across her ear, sending another shiver of yearning through her.

Stevie pulled away from his embrace far enough to reach the side table. Next to the lamp, she found the strap of his watch and managed to grab it before he pulled her back into his arms.

She handed it to him.

"Quarter to eight," he told her, and then nuzzled the nape of her neck. "When is Paige coming for us?"

"She said quarter past. We'd better get ready. Paige's New Year's resolution was to be on time. Now she's almost always early for everything."

Still Allister held her securely against his chest, molding his body into hers, and there was no way Stevie was going to argue with that.

"How are you doing?" he asked.

"I'm fine." Beneath her fingertips she felt the iron-hard muscles along his forearm, wondering why it should feel so right to be here in his embrace this way. "More to the point, how are you?"

"A bit bruised and battered. But I'll live." He propped himself up on one elbow and fondled a strand of her hair for a moment before she felt the gentle brush of his lips on her forehead. He was staring at her, she could tell. She could almost feel his admiring gaze sweep over her, and she turned her face toward him, as though she could gaze back.

"Stevie," he said quietly, "thanks for staying with me last night." He traced her lips with the soft pad of his thumb.

"Where else would I have been?" she answered seconds before she felt his lips on hers.

There seemed a quiet desperation about him suddenly, an intensity in his kiss that left Stevie breathless.

His big hands caressed her face at the same time, and a small moan slipped from Stevie's throat. She pulled herself to him, responding to his hunger, feeling deeper cravings of her own calling out. She was aware of him moving above her and the sheets falling to one side. When she reached out, her hand skimmed across the hard ripple of muscle beneath the soft curling hair on his chest.

Last night's restraint was forgotten. Allister's heart beat urgently under her palm as he shifted above her once again, and his thigh, still bound by the hospital blanket, pressed agonizingly against hers. His entire body, strong and solid, covered hers, so that it seemed as if every part of him touched her in some way, as though no amount of contact could possibly be enough. His power consumed her; his yearning enveloped her.

And just when Stevie found herself gasping under the force of his advances, Allister eased off. He must have sensed her apprehension, her surprise at this unexpected and almost violent passion. His low groan broke the hush of the hospital room, and he drew back far enough that she could breathe again but could still feel the heat emanating from his body.

Stevie slid her hand over his muscular shoulder and wove her fingers through his thick hair. She wrapped her other arm around his waist. They said nothing for a long time, and as she felt him gradually calm in her embrace, she wondered about the time he'd spent in prison and afterward. How long was it since he'd been with a woman? Again, Stevie found herself blinking back tears—tears for Allister and what he had lost.

"I'm sorry, Stevie." His whisper was ragged, and he pressed a tender kiss to her temple before drawing away.

"No, Allister." She shook her head, reaching a hand to his face and touching her fingers lightly to the same lips that had only moments ago expressed such passion. "Don't be."

He was looking at her, she was certain. She gave him a quick smile and it was answered with another kiss—gentle, almost careful this time.

"Now, what was that you were saying before about hating this place?" he asked.

Stevie was grateful for the lighthearted change of subject. Grateful that neither an apology nor an explanation was due.

"Yes, well, it doesn't matter how good the, ah, service is here," she said, "you still can't get a decent cup of coffee in this place."

"Okay, okay. I get the hint. We'll get you some bona fide caffeine."

She felt him leave the bed and immediately missed the contact.

She could hear him dress, and as he did, Stevie brushed at the shirt Paige had brought her yesterday. No doubt it was hopelessly rumpled—as she herself felt right now. She ran her fingers through her hair and wished she could see herself in a mirror.

Then Allister was beside her again. He brushed aside a stray wisp from her forehead and touched her cheek with one finger. "Don't worry, Stevie," he said as though he'd read her mind, "you look fine. In fact, you look beautiful." And another hot shiver of desire went through her when he dropped a sweet kiss on her lips.

As PREDICTED, Paige was early—by ten minutes. What Stevie hadn't predicted was the two cups of steaming coffee that were waiting for them in the car. Paige obviously had been feeling sorry enough for Stevie to give in to her addiction.

Paige had brought the Volvo, claiming she'd pulled an all-nighter at the studio, working on prints from another contract, and then hadn't been able to start her Tercel in the cold this morning. They dropped Paige at her apartment on the west side after she carefully described the new security system at the studio and gave them the pass code, and finally Allister headed to the Palmer Storage and Shipping warehouse. He had some calls to make, he told Stevie as he steered the Volvo into the parking lot and turned off the engine.

By Allister's hesitation, Stevie knew that he recognized her reluctance. She hadn't been in Gary's warehouse since that night more than a week ago, and now even the thought of walking into the building made her feel queasy. She had to struggle to keep down her coffee.

"Did you want to wait in the car, Stevie? I can leave it running if—"

"No, Allister. It's all right." She opened the passenger door quickly before she could change her mind. Allister guided her through the side door of the warehouse, and when Stevie heard their footsteps echo through the cavernous building, memories of that night came thundering back. She shivered.

"Come upstairs, Stevie." Allister took her by the arm. "It's warmer there."

But even on the second floor, Stevie couldn't shake the chill that gripped her. As she sat in the secretary's office, she listened to Allister rummage through one of the adjoining rooms. Then she heard him on the phone in the office across the walkway.

Gary's office. Where she'd seen his bleeding body, where she'd seen his killer seconds before she'd been attacked herself.

Even now, nine days later, Stevie could still remember the deadly intent she'd seen in the man's dark eyes. Or had it been fear? No, she distinctly remembered the rage that had twisted the man's face. And it was that look of rage she wasn't soon to forget, a face she would be able to identify for police once her sight returned. Then, and only then, with Gary's killer behind bars, would she begin to feel safe again.

The sound of Allister's footfalls against the steel walkway wrenched another haunting memory up from her gut. Unconsciously Stevie's fingers tightened on the chair's armrests, and her spine went rigid against the hard back.

It wasn't until they were back in the car heading to her studio that Stevie was able to shake the ghosts from that night.

"Looks like you've got company," Allister told her as he slowed the car and pulled it into the driveway.

"Who is it?"

"Gray Buick. My bet's on Devane."

He was right.

Stevie had barely stepped from the Volvo when she heard the slam of a car door. The sound was followed by the detective's unmistakable growl.

"Morning, Ms. Falcioni." The soles of his boots squeaked against the packed snow as he came toward them.

"Good morning, Detective."

"Heard you had an accident yesterday afternoon. I hope you're all right?"

"We're both fine, thank you, Detective." She felt Allister's hand on her arm then and welcomed his guidance to the door.

Devane was behind them.

"I saw where they hauled your truck out of the river, Mr. Quaid. Looks like the two of you were pretty damned lucky to walk out of that one. How'd it happen?"

"Road conditions," Allister told him as he worked the key in the lock. "Must have been a patch of ice."

Stevie didn't need to see the two men to recognize the tension that crackled between them, the distrust and the suspicion.

"Allister, the alarm," Stevie reminded him quietly when they stepped through the door. She heard him punch several keys as Paige had instructed, and then there was a short beep.

"Was there something on your mind, Detective?" Allister asked him. They moved from the front hall into the main studio area, and as they did, Allister released Stevie's arm. She wondered if it had anything to do with Devane.

"Actually," the detective said, clearing his throat, "I just wanted to check on you, Ms. Falcioni, see how you were doing. And I thought you should know that our boys came up negative yesterday when they dusted for prints. I'm sorry. But your partner assures me that nothing was stolen this time."

Stevie nodded.

"Well, at least you've got the new security system. You shouldn't be having any more problems with break-ins, and if you do, we'll know about it right away."

"Thank you, Detective, for making all the arrangements. I'll feel much safer now."

"Good."

There was a heavy silence then, a silence that had nothing to do with her, she realized, and everything to do with Allister. Just when she was about to break it, Devane cleared his throat and said, "Could I speak to you alone, Ms. Falcioni?"

She hesitated, wishing that Allister hadn't let go of her arm. She felt almost lost without him beside her now. "I don't see how anything you need to ask me can't be asked in Allister's presence."

"That's all right, Stevie," Allister said. "I'll be upstairs if you need me." He touched her shoulder briefly before heading to the stairs.

"Detective?" Stevie turned to where she thought he stood, but then she heard him pace for a moment. When he finally stopped, she'd lost track of him. "There's something you wanted to say?"

"Yeah, Ms. Falcioni, there is."

She heard the soft brush of nylon and imagined his black-blue police parka. Then he started to pace again, but this time, he came toward her. When he stopped, Stevie could have sworn he stood within inches of her, but she held her ground.

"Ms. Falcioni, I don't know what kind of relationship you've got going with Allister Quaid, but there's something I think you should know about him before—"

"Are you going to tell me about his time in prison, Detective?"

He seemed surprised, but didn't back off. "Ah, so he's told you," he said. There was the smell of cigarettes on Devane's breath as he moved even closer. "Well, wise move on his part, I'll give him that much."

"Yes, Detective, Allister's told me about the four years he spent in prison for a crime he didn't commit." Stevie didn't know why she felt the fierce compulsion to defend Allister now, especially to a man who suspected him of being involved with the stolen coins simply because of his record. But between her own exhaustion and Devane's heavy-handed scare tactics, Stevie had had about all she could take.

"So that's what he told you, did he?" Devane went on. "Well, let me just say one thing, Ms. Falcioni. Don't let Allister Quaid's good looks fool you."

"I hardly think you need worry about *me* being taken in by anyone's good looks, Detective."

"What I meant to say, Ms. Falcioni, is that given Mr. Quaid's criminal record, I feel it's my responsibility to warn you—"

"Detective," she interrupted, "as far as I'm concerned, I'm a lot safer with Allister than with anyone else right now. He's done far more to protect me than the police have. So if there's nothing else..." Stevie brushed past him and headed to the front door planning to open it for him to leave. She prayed she wouldn't trip over anything on the way and shatter her image of complete control.

Devane was right behind her as she grappled for the door.

"Just remember one thing, Ms. Falcioni. It wasn't the police who almost got you killed in that river yesterday."

"And just what the hell is that supposed to mean? You don't honestly expect me to believe that Allister did that deliberately, do you?"

"No. What I'm saying is Allister Quaid is a dangerous man. I don't think you're aware of what he's capable of."

"And you are, right?"

Devane had helped her and Paige out, Stevie remembered as she took a steadying breath. He'd made all the arrangements with the security company. He'd responded to her call the other night. She had no justification to feel such animosity, but she did. Was it simply because of his suspicions of Allister?

"Listen, Detective—" she held up a hand as a gesture of apology "—I'm sorry, but I've had a really bad week. So maybe you should just concentrate on finding the man who killed Gary, and let me worry about the company I keep, all right? Good day, Detective.''

ALLISTER HEARD the front door close, and moments later Stevie was up the stairs and entering the apartment.

"I'm over here," he called and then watched her feel her way through the living-room area to where he sat at the kitchen bar. She looked tired.

"You all right?" he asked, touching her cheek with the back of his hand.

She nodded, but it did little to reassure him. Only once had he seen her complexion so pale.

"I think you should rest, Stevie. You've been through a lot."

"I'm all right." She took his hand from her cheek and gave it a reassuring squeeze before she turned to a small writing desk in the corner of the room.

As he watched her riffle through the papers there, Allister wondered exactly what Devane had told her downstairs. Had he said something to upset her, or worse, turn her against him?

"These must be the ones," she said at last, pulling a contact sheet from the pile and handing it to Allister. "The proofs from the jammed camera. Pictures taken in the warehouse."

"Looks like it," he told her.

There were only half-a-dozen shots on the page. In each frame, several long-legged models posed in various dramatic stances, and at the top of each shot was the steel walkway.

Allister brought the sheet closer, studying each frame. And then he saw it. There was a man on the catwalk in the last frame. He appeared to be a big man, wearing a heavy fatigue-style coat that hung off broad shoulders.

"Stevie, there's a man in this last shot, up on the cat-walk."

She drew in a sharp breath. "Do you recognize him? Is he one of Gary's staff?"

"I don't think so."

"Is he the man you saw in the car yesterday?"

"It's hard to tell."

Stevie turned to the desk again, tugged open the top drawer and after a moment of fumbling handed him a magnifying glass.

"How about now?" she asked.

Tilting the sheet to the light, Allister zeroed in on the figure on the catwalk. Even with the play of shadows, he didn't need a blowup of the shot to recognize the man's hardened features. That square jaw, the thin lips and those sunken eyes. He'd seen them before.

"Yes, that's our man, all right. That's the guy who's been following us."

PAIGE HAD TAKEN a cab to the studio later in the day, and after several hours in the darkroom, she'd come upstairs where the three of them had shared a pizza for dinner. Now, almost an hour later, Allister was becoming anxious.

Stevie and Paige were lounging on the couch, sipping the remains of a bottle of chablis, while an opera Allister had forgotten the name of played on the stereo. With only half an ear, he listened to Stevie describe for them what was happening in each scene. Any other time, he would have been enthralled by Stevie's animated description of these Italian lovers' demise, but tonight, there were other things on his mind.

Pulling back one of the blinds that covered the living-room window, Allister peered out into the still night. On the quiet snow-covered street, almost out of visual range from the studio, he saw the dark sedan. He'd noticed it parked there, behind a couple of other cars down the street, when he'd gone downstairs to pay the pizza-delivery boy. It hadn't moved.

Allister let the blind snap back into place. Stevie must have heard it, because she stopped her narration. "What is it, Allister?"

"It's nothing, Stevie. Go on."

He should have received the call hours ago. Now it was almost eight.

From the warehouse earlier today, he'd called Danny James, his contact at the DMV downtown, and had given him the sedan's plate number. Danny hadn't been too keen about searching for the information, but his reluctance had come mostly from the fact that Allister had dragged him off his break.

He would try his best, Danny had promised. Then he'd warned Allister that he'd probably not be able to do it until the end of the day, so Allister had given him Stevie's number.

At last the phone rang, and sure enough it was for Allister.

"Danny?"

"Oh, hey, Allister, listen man, I'm really sorry I didn't get to you sooner. My kid got sick at school and my wife's out of town, so I been running around all afternoon. You wouldn't believe the day I had."

"Sorry to hear that."

"Yeah, well, kids, you know?"

"Did you get that name for me?"

"Oh, yeah. No problem. The car's registered to a guy by the name of Vince Fenton."

Allister found a pen amongst the bills and other papers on the corner desk and jotted the name on an old envelope.

"You didn't happen to get an address, too, did you?"

"Yup. Fifty-six Adelle Avenue. Apartment 2C. Hope that helps you out, man."

"More than you know. I owe you for this."

"Yeah, well, I like Jack Daniel's. Talk to you later, man."

"Thanks, Danny."

Fenton. Vince Fenton. Allister ran the name through his mind a few times. It meant nothing to him. But if he was the man Stevie had photographed on the catwalk and the driver of the sedan parked outside right now, he quite likely was the man who had beaten the life out of Gary. The man who'd killed his best friend. Allister folded the envelope and shoved it into his back pocket.

What was to stop him from going out there right now? Just walking straight across the street, dragging this Fenton son of a bitch from his damned car and beating the life out of *him*. After what he'd done to Gary—

"Allister?"

"Yeah?" He spun around, his turbulent thoughts fragmented by Stevie's voice.

"I asked if you were up to the final act of *La Bohème*."

"Uh, no, Stevie. I'll have to pass tonight."

"Are you all right?"

"Sure." But judging by the look that Paige gave him then, Allister wasn't doing a very good job at convincing either of them. "Listen, guys, I've got to go out for a bit. Couple of errands I have to run."

"What? This late?" Stevie aimed the remote and turned off the stereo. The silence was startling.

"I won't be long, Stevie."

"What's this about, Allister?"

It took all of one second for Paige to recognize the challenging tone in her friend's voice, and she was off the couch in a shot. "I'll be in the darkroom if anyone needs me,"

Paige said before giving Allister a you're-on-your-own look and heading downstairs.

"Stevie—"

"This is about the coins, isn't it?"

"I don't know. Probably not. I just want to check on a few things, that's all."

"Who was on the phone?"

"Stevie, it's nothing. Really."

"Allister." She stood up abruptly, and when she did her knee struck the empty wine bottle. It toppled to the area rug and rolled away, rattling loudly across the hardwood flooring. She waited until it came to rest against one of the ceramic plant pots. "Please, don't keep secrets from me, Allister. It's about this guy, isn't it? The man in the proofs."

He crossed the room toward her, wishing to hell that she wasn't so damned intuitive. Why couldn't she have just believed him when he'd said he had to run some errands?

"Who was on the phone?" she demanded again.

He didn't answer, just took her shoulders in his hands and gazed down at her. Now he knew what was stopping him from going out there and dealing with Vince Fenton with his own bare hands. For the first time in what felt like forever, Allister had a reason to look forward to the future, a reason to tame the vengeance that seethed in him whenever he thought of the police or Bainbridge, and now Fenton. And that reason was Stevie.

He lifted her chin with a finger, and tilted her face so he could brush a kiss across her lips. She tasted sweet.

"Stevie, it's nothing," he said softly. "I just want to—"

"For crying out loud, Allister. Don't you *dare* patronize me." She pulled away from him then with such force that for a moment he thought she might take a step back and crash into the coffee table. He was about to reach for her again when he realized the extent of her anger and decided he'd best stay clear.

"If there's something you know about Gary or the coins, I think I should be informed, Allister. This involves me, too."

"No, Stevie. It *doesn't* involve you. You have nothing to do with Bainbridge, do you hear me?" Even the thought of it made Allister sick to his stomach.

"So I'm right. That phone call—it was about Bainbridge, about the coins, wasn't it?"

"Stevie, I don't want to argue about this."

"Then don't. Just tell me and we won't have to argue about anything. Who was on the phone?"

He was close enough to reach out, take a hold of her and shake some sense into her. Couldn't she see that he didn't want to put her life in any more danger than he already had? That he was only doing this for her own good? His hands balled into fists at his sides and he turned from her.

"Allister?"

He let out a long breath. "That was Danny James, the person I'd mentioned before at the DMV."

"He got the name of the man who owns the car?"

Allister nodded. "Yeah. Vince Fenton."

When he looked at Stevie again, her expression didn't reveal any recognition of the name.

"So what are you going to do?"

"I don't know exactly. But this doesn't involve you, Stevie, okay?" When he tried to brush past her to head for the stairs, she must have felt his closeness, because in a flash she'd grabbed his arm.

"Allister, I'm already involved. *I'm* the one whose place has been broken into twice. *I'm* the one who found Gary dead. And *I'm* the one who saw his killer. Now whether you like it not, Allister, I am involved in this thing, and no matter how hard you try, there's nothing you can do to *un*involve me at this point.''

"I won't put your life at risk, Stevie."

"Well, it's a bit late for that, isn't it?"

Her words hit their intended mark and Allister flinched. Yes, he could have killed her with that stunt of his yesterday. He should never have taken the risk he had, not with Stevie in the Explorer. But this was different. This involved Vince Fenton, the man who might very well have murdered Gary.

"Stevie, what I have to do—"

"And what would that be? What is you have to do?"

But he didn't even know that himself yet. "That's not what's important right now. What's important is that you stay here where it's safe." He pulled away from her and again headed to the stairs. He had to get out. If he stayed another moment, he knew there would be no winning this argument.

"Allister!"

He could hear her come through the apartment and down the stairs after him. He didn't look back.

"Paige." He crossed the studio to the darkroom at the back. The door was open. "Paige."

Paige looked up from the light table. "Yeah?"

"I have a favor to ask."

"Sure. Anything."

"Your car's out back in the alley, right?"

She nodded. "Why?"

"I need to borrow it, if you don't mind."

"Sure," she said, getting her purse from one of the stainless-steel tables and rummaging through it. "One condition, though."

"What's that?"

"I don't want you driving it into some river, okay? I mean, I just finished paying off that damned junker."

Allister caught her wink and gave her a quick smile. In that same second, Stevie came around the corner.

"Paige, don't do it," she said.

"What?"

"Don't lend him your car."

Allister glared at her. "Stevie, listen to me—"

"Paige, don't lend him your car unless he agrees to take me along."

"Stevie—"

"No, Allister. If you think you're going to just leave me here like some invalid while you're out—"

"That's not what—"

"I can take care of myself, Allister. Just remember who it was that pulled you out of that river yesterday."

"Look, guys." Paige stepped between them, her hands in the air. "Guys! I have no idea what this is about, but, Allister, I'm sorry, my loyalties lie with Stevie first." She placed the keys in Stevie's hand. "There're the keys. The car's out back. You two do what you have to. Now clear out. I've got work to finish here."

She bustled them out of the darkroom and started to close the door before she added with a smirk, "Oh, and, Allister? One more thing. Whatever you do, don't let her drive, okay?"

With no other choice, Allister guided Stevie out to Paige's car, put her in the passenger seat and cleaned off the windshield as the engine warmed up. When they pulled out of the back alley, Allister drove slowly, but Stevie guessed it had nothing to do with his unfamiliarity with the Tercel.

Allister was also silent, and he stayed that way for the next fifteen minutes. Stevie tried to imagine what he was planning. He'd wanted Paige's car, instead of the Volvo, because it had been parked at the back, out of sight from the street. He'd driven slowly from the alley, and she guessed that he'd left the headlights off so as not to draw attention as they pulled onto the side street.

It was obvious someone was watching the warehouse. She remembered the snap of the blind earlier and realized that Allister must have been keeping an eye on the street out front.

Then there had been the phone call. As soon as Allister had found out the man's name—Vince Fenton—he'd been anxious to go.

Stevie suddenly knew where they were heading, what Allister intended to do. She reached across and placed her hand on his thigh then, surprised at the way her voice trembled. "You're going to Vince Fenton's place, aren't you?"

Allister's silence was all the answer she needed.

After another minute he stopped the car and turned off the ignition. Stevie heard him switch off the lights and release his seat belt. She didn't remove her hand, and when he placed his own over it, he stroked it thoughtfully.

"Fenton's still back at the studio," he said at last. "My guess is he'll be there for another hour or so before he decides we're going to stay put for the night."

"So you're planning to break into his place?"

"It's the only way, Stevie. Unless I can find something to link Fenton to Bainbridge, we've got nothing."

"But even if you do find something, Allister, you'll be committing a crime. Breaking and entering."

"Yeah, but at least we'll have a bargaining chip when it comes to Bainbridge." Allister undoubtedly recognized her uneasiness. "Stevie, don't worry. I'm just going to go in and take a look around. I'll be ten minutes, tops."

"I don't like this," she said, shaking her head. "You can't just break into this guy's place."

"It's not as if I've got any other choice at this point."

"Have you forgotten who this man is? Have you forgotten what happened to Gary? He was murdered, Allister. Beaten to death. And quite likely by this same man."

"Unfortunately that's the one thing we can't prove."

"Allister! That's not the point! He's dangerous, and you know it. This is too risky. Way too risky."

"Stevie, I'm checking out his apartment. That's all."

"It's too dangerous. What if there's someone else in his apartment? What if he comes back? What are you going to do then?"

He didn't answer.

"I don't like this," she said again, breaking the tense silence.

"Neither do I." He touched her cheek with one finger. "Neither do I."

"So what do you want me to do?" she asked, already knowing his answer.

"Stay here. Listen. If you hear anything—"

She let out a nervous laugh. "Oh, right, I lose my sight and all of a sudden you think I've developed heightened hearing? Dammit, Allister, this isn't right. Let's just go home."

"It'll be fine, Stevie. Trust me. Now give me your watch."

"My watch?"

"Please."

She pulled back her sleeve and undid the clasp. "My mother gave me this, Allister. If anything happens to it, you can bet she'll fly up from Tampa to deal with you personally. And believe me, if you think I'm bad, wait'll you meet Ma."

His laugh momentarily eased the tension for both of them.

"I'll just have to be extra careful then. Here." She heard a series of high-pitched beeps before he put his own watch in her hands.

"What's this for?"

"I've set the alarm to go off in fifteen minutes. If I'm not back by then..." He handed her his cellular phone.

"Oh, right, Allister, and who the hell am I supposed to call? The police? Or maybe you'd prefer I just call Devane at home?"

"No, Stevie, you call Paige. If I'm not back when that watch alarm goes off, I want you to call Paige and lay low. She can come and pick you up in your car."

"And what about you?"

She heard him turn in his seat, and then he grasped her shoulders firmly with both hands. "Stevie, don't worry about me, okay? I'll be fine."

"Right." And if he wasn't back in fifteen minutes, she thought, he'd only be lying facedown in a pool of blood. Just like Gary.

"Stevie, nothing's going to happen."

She heard the soft creak of leather, and in the next instant his lips were on hers, muffling her small cry of dread.

She tried to relax, drinking in the tenderness of his kiss. She tried to convince herself that Allister knew what he was doing. Why, then, did she feel as if this could be their last kiss?

Frantically Stevie slid her fingers back through his silky hair and pulled him closer, kissing him desperately, letting her hunger drive out the fear. She wanted to hold him, to feel his life pulsing against hers, to embrace him and not let him go.

Her hand brushed past the edge of his leather bomber and rested on his chest. Beneath her palm she felt his heart beating as fearfully as her own. But it was when her hand glided downward, following his muscled abdomen to his waist, that she froze.

Tucked into the waistband of his jeans was something cold, hard and metallic. Her hand recoiled as though she had just touched red-hot iron.

"Allister—"

"Stevie, I'm sorry, you weren't supposed to... It's Gary's gun. He'd bought it for protection at the warehouse, and he'd shown me where he'd stashed it. I picked it up when we were there today."

"And you didn't tell me you were carrying it?"

"Stevie, listen, it's just in case..."

"Just in case what? No. No, you can't go through with this. Not this way. God, Allister, you're carrying a gun! Is Bainbridge really worth risking your life for? Let it go, for God's sake."

She pleaded with him, but he'd already made up his mind. She heard him zip up his bomber.

"Please, Allister, just let it go. We've gotten in way over our heads now. We're not trained for this kind of thing. We're not detectives or cops."

"That's right, Stevie. We're *not* cops. We're the good guys."

When he kissed her this time, there was an unsettling severity to it, and when Stevie touched his face, her desire to see it was greater than ever.

"I won't be long. I promise." His soft whisper did little to assure her. "Remember, if the watch alarm goes off, call Paige. Don't do anything else. Just sit tight and call Paige."

She nodded. Her fingers caressed empty space now as he opened the car door to a whirlwind of freezing air and snow.

"And, Stevie?" she heard him say as several flakes melted against her skin.

"What?"

"I love you." And with that, Allister was gone. The car door slammed, and there was only a dark cold silence.

CHAPTER TEN

ALLISTER TUGGED at the sheepskin collar of his bomber jacket, drawing it around his face as he sprinted across the empty one-way street. A block and a half away, Adelle Avenue intersected Dutton, one of the major east-west arteries of the city, but the sounds of the heavy traffic were muffled by the recent snowfall. The only thing Allister could hear above his own hammering heart was a television through the partially open window of one of the apartments.

Pausing on the sidewalk outside 56 Adelle, Allister gazed up at the three-story building. Snow clung to the old redbrick exterior, and a cracked and chipped concrete archway bore the name The Royal. Obviously the residence had seen better days.

The front door seemed appropriate to its derelict setting; its steel frame was battered and the reinforced glass panel was shattered from what appeared to have been a well-aimed kick. Allister pushed the door open.

To his immediate left was a wall of steel mailboxes, some with labels, others with only a tacky residue where previous ones had been. Allister scanned the row until he found 2C. Luckily Fenton's was one of the few that was marked. It wouldn't have been the first time the DMV had gotten an address screwed up, Allister thought as he took the stairs two at a time.

With only four apartments on each level, and with 2C at the back, it was simple enough to locate the apartment's windows from outside. There was no light under the door, and when he put his ear to the dingy veneered surface, Allister heard nothing.

Contrary to Stevie's fears, Vince Fenton appeared to live alone.

Not expecting it to be that easy, Allister tried the door, anyway. It was locked of course, and with two dead bolts. He didn't fool himself that he could do anything with those. No, he'd have to go with his original plan. An outside approach.

Allister welcomed the cold air after the stuffy stairwell. He paused at the side of the building and glanced across the street. He'd deliberately parked Paige's car out of range of any street lamps so that the interior was unlit. From here, if he hadn't known better, he'd have sworn the car was empty. In fact, he had to look twice to be sure Stevie was there, slumped down in the passenger seat.

The back of The Royal looked out onto a row of tall coniferous trees, and beyond those, the parking lot of an auto-repair shop. Pretty much all the cover Allister could have hoped for, he realized as he climbed the rusting fire escape to the second floor and the darkened windows of 2C. Then again, what did he know about cover? It wasn't as if he'd ever done this kind of thing before. He started to pry off the corner of one window screen.

Well, there was the time he and Gary had tried to sneak into Old Man Hooper's house. Word was Hooper had gone upstate to his daughter's for the weekend, and with all the rumors flying around the schoolyard about the old man in that dilapidated house down on Egert, Gary and Allister had gladly taken up the dare. Under cover of darkness, they'd climbed to the second story and popped the torn screen off one of the hall windows. It had been that easy. Until, of course, Old Man Hooper, who *had* been home, found them out and hollered curses at them all the way down the block.

Even now, years later, the look of shock on Gary's wide-eyed freckled face when they'd been caught never failed to bring a smile to Allister's lips. Gary. If Allister had had a brother, he couldn't have loved him more than he had Gary.

The screen loosened at last, and Allister pried it off almost as easily as he had all those years ago. But this was a far cry from any childhood escapade with Gary. Hooper's had been a dare, and they'd been kids. And no matter how vile Hooper's curses were that night, the old man had nothing on a thug like Vince Fenton.

Allister propped the screen on the landing beside him. His heart was pounding even faster as he worked his gloved fingers under the window's frame, and when it finally budged, Allister thought the whole world could hear the wrenching grind.

But, it seemed no one did. And no one saw him shimmy the window up the rest of the way and slip inside the dark apartment.

The heat was stifling, and the place smelled of stale cigarette smoke. Allister switched on his pocket flashlight and scanned his surroundings. The living room. The thin beam passed over a beige sofa and armchair, worn and dotted with burn marks. Newspapers and magazines were strewn throughout the room, from the sofa to a scarred coffee table, and across the pale green stained carpeting.

Where to start? It was hard to know, especially since he had no idea what he was looking for.

The glow of his flashlight caught the table shoved in a corner near the window. More newspapers were stacked there, and balanced on top of this teetering stack was a black rotary-style phone. Maybe Fenton took notes while on the phone. Allister moved to the table.

As he passed the window, he noticed the dirty pools of melted snow and salt he'd left on the sill and the floor. Concealing his presence in the apartment was going to be impossible, not to mention the fact that he'd probably never get the screen back on the window. Then again, what was the sense in being careful? A man like Vince Fenton was not likely to report a break-in.

Allister took Stevie's watch from his pocket—ten minutes left. If he didn't find something before then, the entire undertaking would have been for nothing.

He could feel sweat practically rolling down his back as he started to scan the papers and bills on the table. Clenching the penlight between his teeth, Allister unzipped his jacket. His hand grazed the walnut grip of the Ruger semiautomatic.

Stevie was right about their getting in too deep, but that was precisely why he'd taken Gary's Ruger from the warehouse this morning. That was why he had it with him now.

Vince Fenton was not someone Allister planned to deal with personally. But if he had to, he certainly didn't want to be unarmed.

As he riffled through unpaid bills, receipts and meaningless scraps of paper, Allister thought about the man back at Stevie's studio, sitting in his brown sedan. No doubt, with the temperatures dropping, Fenton would be getting edgy. It could only be a matter of time before he decided that Allister was staying the night at Stevie's. After that, he'd give up his vigil and most likely head home to his dingy apartment.

Allister had to move fast.

VINCE FENTON was chilled to the marrow. He figured he must have gone through a quarter tank of gas just running the car off and on to keep warm tonight. And for what? Quaid wasn't going anywhere. Not now, not this late.

And even if he was, Fenton thought, at this point he didn't give a damn. It was ridiculous, sitting around outside in the middle of bloody January. No one could pay him enough for this.

No, he was definitely beginning to feel the same impatience Bainbridge felt for those damned coins. He had to get this job over with and fast. He needed to get his money and leave this goddamn burg for good.

Maybe his strategy required a slight modification. Maybe it was time for a little force. Not necessarily the kind he'd used on Palmer. No, this would call for a bit more finesse.

From seeing Quaid and the photographer woman together, he had his suspicions about what was really going on between them. And maybe what this assignment needed now was some light pressure applied in just the right spot—namely the woman. Through her he'd be more apt to get somewhere with Quaid. The plan was worth mentioning to Bainbridge. As a backup.

Besides, after two attempts he still hadn't gotten the right film. Taking care of the Falcioni woman could be the one stone he needed to kill both these birds. He'd get the film and he'd get to Quaid.

But for now, the most important thing was getting home to a hot shower. Tonight, even a beer at Mario's wasn't at the top of his agenda, Vince thought as he hit the gas.

STILL NOTHING. Allister cursed under his breath. He'd been fooling himself to think that this scheme could work, that he could actually get somewhere by breaking into Fenton's apartment.

He stood back from the table and surveyed it once again. He'd been through practically everything. Every scrap of paper, every envelope. He'd even leafed through the newspapers and Fenton's collection of survivalist and gun magazines.

But nothing.

The only thing he'd found was an address, scratched in a backhand scrawl across a utility-bill envelope. He'd recognized the address instantly—Edward Bainbridge's. But there was nothing incriminating about an address written on an old envelope.

Allister released a frustrated breath and leaned heavily against the table. Maybe he'd been grasping for straws, rushing out here like this tonight. Desperate to put an end to this whole mess with Fenton and Bainbridge, he hadn't thought the plan through. And leaving Stevie out there in the car...what had he been thinking? Hadn't he put her life in enough danger as it was?

He had to get back to her.

He took out her watch again. Time was up.

Still...this was the last chance he'd have. He wouldn't be able to break into Fenton's a second time. Once Bainbridge's thug discovered that someone had been in his apartment, he'd be on the alert, and there would be no getting past him then.

No, if he was going to get anything on Fenton, it had to be now.

Allister reached for the phone. He'd call Stevie on the cellular. Make sure she was all right. And then he'd tell her to give him another five minutes. There had to be *something* here.

But when he turned the beam of his flashlight onto the old rotary phone and reached for the receiver, Allister's heart froze.

From across the dark room, he heard the metallic rattle of a key in the lock.

STEVIE SLUMPED LOWER in the seat when she'd heard the first car pass by. She checked the locks on both doors, but Allister had already seen to them. Then she opened each window a crack, just far enough so she could hear any sounds from the street or the building.

Eventually a second car passed. She sank even farther in her seat, listening to the sound of the engine fade down the street. Earlier, when she could no longer hear Allister's boots against the snow, she had started to count the seconds and minutes. But when the third car passed the Tercel, Stevie was aware that the sounds were different. There had been a low rumble, as if the car had slowed. She couldn't be certain, but then it sounded as if the car had pulled into a lot across the street. She heard the engine rev once before all was quiet again.

There was the slam of a car door. And immediately Stevie had thought of Vince Fenton. What if he had decided to call it a night? What if that was him returning? There was no way she could warn Allister. Fenton would go to his apartment and—

Stevie heard someone whistling. It took her all of five seconds to play "Name that tune," and when she did, she was certain it was not Fenton. Somehow she couldn't imagine a man like Fenton, a murderer, whistling the chorus from *The Pirates of Penzance*.

Allister should be back, she kept thinking over and over again. Her hands were cold as she held his watch. She rubbed the worn leather band with her thumb as though willing the alarm not to go off. Because if it did and Allister still wasn't back...

No. He'd be back. Any second now she would hear him come across the street.

When the alarm pierced the silence, Stevie almost dropped the watch. She fumbled with it, pressing whatever buttons she could feel until the high-pitched beep died.

"Allister." She whispered his name, each syllable slipping into the hush of the car like a desperate plea. "Where are you?"

She reached for the cellular, and her index finger worried the number pad.

"Please, Allister..."

ALLISTER WAS PROUD of himself for getting out of the apartment and scrambling down the fire escape so quickly. It wasn't until he hit the ice on the last step and rammed his knee agonizingly against the steel railing that his pride deflated. Pausing to rub his bruised bone and gaze up at the window through which he'd escaped, he saw a light come on.

It would be only a matter of minutes, seconds even, before Fenton discovered the disarray of his papers, the puddles on the floor and the missing screen. Allister would have to be long gone by then.

He hobbled the length of the building, staying close to the wall in case Fenton looked out. His jacket flapped open in the wind as he ran across the empty street, and he laid his hand against the butt of the Ruger to make sure it didn't slip.

"Stevie, it's me." He knocked on the window of the Tercel and saw her jump, almost dropping the cellular phone.

She reached across to unlock the door, and when he got in, he could see how on edge she was. She said nothing, and Allister wondered if she somehow sensed how urgent it was that they get out of there immediately. He turned the key in the ignition, half fearing it wouldn't start. When it did, Stevie's sigh of relief echoed his own.

It wasn't until they reached Dutton and turned into the northbound traffic that Stevie finally spoke.

"So did you find anything?"

He eased the Tercel into the right lane and let the flow of traffic carry them along. Then he glanced over at her profile. Her gaze was fixed forward as though she were actually watching the traffic, and her complexion appeared blanched in the pallid glow of each passing street lamp.

"No," he admitted eventually.

"That was Fenton, wasn't it? He came back."

"Yes, it was."

In that moment, Allister realized just how terrified Stevie must have been, sitting out there, alone, vulnerable, powerless to warn him.

"But I got out in time, Stevie," he said, hoping to ease her anxiety. "I heard him coming, and I got out in time. He didn't see me." At least, he didn't *think* Fenton had seen him. Once he'd started the Tercel and veered away from the curb outside 56 Adelle, Allister hadn't looked back. For all he knew, Fenton might have rushed down the stairs and out the front door, only to watch them drive off.

She said nothing. In one hand she still held the cellular phone, but with the other she maintained a relentless grip on the armrest.

He'd gone too far, Allister realized. Stevie was right—the risk had been too great. He'd been lucky for once in his life. Had Fenton caught him, Allister wouldn't have known what to do. He could have been killed, and Stevie would have been out there alone in the car. Maybe she would have called Paige, but more likely, knowing Stevie, she would have tried to come after him—right into Fenton's clutches.

And if she *had* listened to him, if she had called Paige and gone home, what then? Bainbridge and Fenton would have come after her, and Allister wouldn't have been there to protect her. Even if the tables had been turned, if he had used Gary's gun and hurt or, worse, killed Fenton, it would have been only a matter of hours before Devane had Allister behind bars again. Breaking his parole would have been the least of his problems.

Either way, Stevie—on her own—was a prime target for Bainbridge.

Allister knew he had to be more careful. Tonight's attempt had been irrational. And for the first time, Allister realized it wasn't the coins, or even the hope of clearing his name, that had taken him to Fenton's apartment. It had been revenge that had driven him tonight—revenge for Gary's murder, and revenge for the four years Bainbridge had stolen from him.

Yes, he hated Bainbridge, more than he'd ever imagined he could hate anyone. And it was because of that violent hatred that Allister couldn't let this sudden desire for revenge dictate his actions. Because if he did, he'd not only put his own life in jeopardy, but Stevie's, as well.

And the thought of Edward Bainbridge getting ahold of Stevie . . . Allister couldn't live with that possibility.

STEVIE WAS ASLEEP. And in her own bed at last, Allister thought, shifting his jeans-clad legs. He'd felt her body relax by degrees, and now he could hear her low easy breathing. She was curled up beside him in her oversize T-shirt, the covers pulled to her waist and one arm draped across his chest. Her head rested against his shoulder, and when he brushed her hair from forehead, she only nuzzled more tightly against him.

During the rest of the drive home from Fenton's she'd been unnervingly quiet. Even after he'd helped her through the back door of the studio, she'd remained withdrawn. When Paige had come out of the darkroom, she immediately recognized her friend's distress, and once Stevie had left them to take a bath, Paige had demanded answers from Allister.

While she made a pot of herbal tea, he'd told Paige about Vince Fenton. He'd also filled her in on the coins and Bainbridge and briefly mentioned his prison term before Stevie had rejoined them.

She'd been dressed for bed, but insisted she was not ready to sleep yet. So, while Paige had gone down to the darkroom for what she'd promised would be only another hour of work, Allister had proposed they watch one of the movies she had on video. He hadn't known what else to suggest after seeing the strain on Stevie's face, and fortunately she'd agreed.

The TV was in her bedroom, so they'd made themselves comfortable on Stevie's bed, Stevie half-under the covers, Allister on top of them beside her. But half an hour into *Casablanca,* Stevie was asleep. Allister had figured it wouldn't take her long tonight, after everything she'd been through.

Gently he eased her back onto the pillows. She moaned softly and awakened only slightly.

Now, as he lay beside her, he caressed her cheek with his hand and looked at her. Too much was happening too quickly. Their kiss at the hospital this morning—Allister couldn't remember another kiss that had so totally overwhelmed him. He'd surrendered to an almost primal urgency to be with Stevie, to feel her flesh against his, to consume her with his passion. It had been years since he'd been with a woman, and this morning in the hospital room, when he'd given in to that sudden and fierce hunger, Allister knew he'd frightened her. He'd seen it in her eyes. And he swore now that he never wanted to see her fear him like that again.

Yet, beneath that desperate lust, there had been something deeper, something gentle and sincere. And he had little doubt that Stevie, too, had felt the significance of that kiss, knew as well as he did that it would have been much more than a kiss had they not been in a hospital room.

To top off the whole complicated mess, tonight he'd told Stevie he loved her.

He hadn't told her that simply to stifle her objections when he climbed out of the car at Fenton's, Allister knew as he gazed down into her calm face now. He almost wished that had been the case. Yet as insane as it sounded, after all the lies, those three words were the truest ones he'd spoken to Stevie yet.

But the truth didn't matter now. He shouldn't have told her he loved her. And he shouldn't be feeling the constant ache and the raging desires he did every time he looked at her or touched her or so much as heard her voice.

After all, what kind of future could they possibly have together, anyway? If Stevie regained her sight and recognized him, it wouldn't matter if she believed him innocent of Gary's murder or not. She could never forgive him for the lies and the deceit. On the other hand, if she never found out, if her blindness was permanent, how could he possibly live with the guilt of seeing her day in and day out, her blindness a constant reminder of what he'd done to her, and the terrible truth he was hiding.

Still, he couldn't just leave her. Not with Bainbridge still desperate for the coins. Until this whole mess was over—if indeed it ever was—Allister would be by Stevie's side. He would protect her. But that couldn't entail any intimacy with her. A relationship would interfere with his judgment. It already had. If it hadn't been for his feelings for Stevie, he wouldn't have cared so much about what she said or felt tonight. He would never have given in when she'd demanded he take her with him to Fenton's.

Allister gazed again at her sleeping face, at the satiny curve of her neck. Being this close to Stevie, Allister could imagine pressing his lips against that soft skin, could imagine her returning his caress.

He suppressed a sigh of frustration, got off the bed and pulled the covers higher. She'd sleep well tonight, he hoped. And she'd sleep without him.

From the nightstand, he picked up the remote control. When he turned, about to stop the movie and switch off the television, Paige suddenly appeared at the open doorway. She gave him a warm smile and nodded to the TV.

"Don't turn it off. She'll only wake up," she whispered. "Come on. Looks like you could use a drink."

Allister put down the remote and followed her. He glanced back at Stevie's still form once more before pulling the door shut behind him.

"You drink scotch?" Paige asked when he joined her in the living room.

"Sure." But the truth was, anything would do tonight.

"Stevie doesn't drink it," Paige murmured as she poured a shot into an ice-filled tumbler. "She keeps it out of habit really—her father was a scotch drinker."

She handed Allister the glass and there was the rattle of ice when he tipped it to her. "Thanks," he said, savoring the warmth that raced down his throat.

"Sounds like you two had quite a night," Paige said as she sat across from him with a cup of herbal tea.

Allister nodded, swirling the amber liquid in his glass. "Yeah. I'm not sure if Stevie will be so quick to forgive me this time."

"Sure she will."

He caught Paige's reassuring grin.

"She's just worn a bit thin is all. She's been through a lot these past few days, Allister. The break-in, the crash and then tonight. On top of all that, she's trying to deal with the results of her last appointment."

"She wouldn't tell me much about it." Allister took another sip of scotch.

"Of course she wouldn't. And she won't tell me, either. That's just Stevie. She's gotta keep it all in here." Paige made a fist over her heart. "But she's terrified, Allister. Oh, yeah, she puts up a strong front—the flippant jokes, that sarcastic attitude—but inside..." Paige shook her head and sipped her tea. "Best you can do is go along with it. It's the only thing getting her through this mess."

"So, how do you deal with it?" he asked. "I mean, with everything she's going through and her still shutting you out?"

"I'm here for her. Stevie knows that. I'm here when and if she needs me. She's stubborn and she's independent and she'll take a hell of a licking before she turns to anyone. Like I said, she puts up a good front, but trust me, Allister, I don't think Stevie's ever been more terrified in her life."

Paige must have sensed his frustration, because she retrieved the bottle of scotch and poured him another shot.

"You gotta understand, Allister, you've only known Stevie without her cameras and her work. Photography is her life. Always has been. I have yet to meet anyone else in this industry who possesses the passion and the drive she has for it. From the second I met her, I knew Stevie would go places. She has something. I don't know what it is exactly, but it's something only a few people in this business have. I don't even think Stevie realizes it because her passion for photography is so personal.

"And that's what makes this whole situation so hard on her. It's not just a professional loss she's trying to cope with right now."

Paige circled the rim of her cup with a fingertip, then looked at Allister again.

"I guess I saw it most clearly when Stevie's father died. That was shortly after I started working with her. Of all her family, I think his death hit Stevie the hardest. And her way of dealing with that grief was to turn to her photography. She must have worked twenty-hour days then, for weeks on end. That's what she does when things get rough—focuses on her work. And now, probably the worst time in her life, that's the one thing she *can't* do."

Allister had the urge to tell Paige now, to confess that it had been him at the warehouse that night, that he was the man who'd caused Stevie's fall. It wasn't just the scotch, Allister realized. It was the agonizing guilt that had tormented his every thought and every breath since that night. He needed to tell someone. He needed to get it out. And why not Stevie's friend? Paige, of all people, should know how Stevie would react if she found out the truth. Paige would know what to suggest.

He studied her. How hard could it be to tell the truth? How hard could it be to trust again?

As he hesitated, still uncertain, Paige looked up and met his gaze. There was a sadness in her eyes. With an affection in her voice Allister found almost painful, she said, "Stevie's a very different person right now."

"In what way?"

"Without her photography, she's lost. Every once in a while, when she doesn't realize I'm in the room, I see her fear. And I hear her crying in the middle of the night." Paige shook her head. Her voice had lowered to a whisper. "I don't think she's ever been this lost in her life. And there's nothing I can do or say to console her."

So Paige felt helpless, Allister thought. About as helpless as he did whenever he looked at Stevie, whenever he gazed into those dark unfocused eyes of hers.

"If her sight doesn't come back," Paige continued, "I honestly don't know what she'll do. Sure, she's strong. In my whole life I've never met anyone as strong and determined as Stevie, but you've got to understand, her life's just ended, Allister. Everything she ever lived for is gone."

"Surely there must be *something* we can do for her . . ."

"There's nothing we can do. Stevie's going to deal with this on her own until she's good and ready to accept someone else's help. That's just the way she is."

Paige stood up then, and Allister followed her to the kitchen where she rinsed her cup and his glass. When she turned from the sink, there was a renewed resolve in Paige's smile.

"Just be there for her, Allister. I know it seems like the two of you only just met, but somehow, I think Stevie's counting on you more than she lets on. I think she's going to need you, Allister, and . . . and I really hope you can be there for her when she does."

CHAPTER ELEVEN

SOMETIME IN THE NIGHT the furnace had kicked in. Stevie awoke with the covers shoved clear to the end of the bed and Tiny draped across her stomach, a furry hot-water bottle. She pushed the cat to one side, ignoring his plaintive yowl, and rolled over.

The bed was empty.

Whether she'd been dreaming about Allister or remembering how good it had felt snuggling next to him before she'd fallen asleep, Stevie felt a pang of disappointment at his absence.

He must have gone home during the night.

Except for Tiny's heavy-pawed lumbering out the bedroom and no doubt to the kitchen to check his dish, the apartment was quiet. Stevie swung her legs over the edge of the bed and shuffled to the window. Drawing up the blinds, she could feel the sun's warmth on her face. But when she looked toward that warmth, there was only the relentless blackness she had come to know as her reality.

Finding a pair of jeans and a fresh T-shirt, Stevie dressed and headed for the kitchen. She needed a coffee. When she crossed the living room, she tiptoed, moving slowly, touching each piece of furniture and placing it on the map in her mind's eye. And as she passed the couch, she held her breath. She heard breathing.

Good, Stevie thought as she slipped by and made her way to the kitchen. At last Paige was sleeping in.

In spite of Stevie's demands that Paige not overdo it, she'd been working late hours. One by one, the contracts were being filled. Projects were being completed, and soon, there would be only the Armatrading reshoot hanging over their heads. And after that . . . well, after that Images could close, if it had to.

Paige had cited a dozen valid business reasons for Images to continue as usual, taking on small contracts at the very least, and she'd offered to put in the requisite hours. But Stevie had been adamant they not take on any new contracts. When Paige had finally accepted her decision, she knew that Paige at last recognized the personal reasons behind it.

As long as there was no change in her condition, Stevie didn't want the added pressure of new contracts piling up. At least, that was what she'd let Paige believe. But in truth, Stevie felt her own faith dwindling with each passing day. And when she went out—when and if Images was forced to close—Stevie wanted to go out quietly.

Measuring each spoonful of coffee grounds by touch and each cup individually, Stevie had the machine brewing in a matter of minutes. The steamy hiss whispered through the quiet apartment, and as she waited, Stevie wondered about Allister.

Part of her worried he might have left last night to pull another stunt like the one at Fenton's apartment. She prayed that wasn't the case. Last night had been too close.

But why else wouldn't Allister have stayed?

Then again, why should she have *expected* him to? Did it have something to do with what he'd said to her last night before leaving the car to go to Fenton's apartment? *I love you.* At the time, those three words had struck her as profoundly sincere. His voice had sounded so certain, so heartfelt, that for a while, sitting there in the silence of the car, Stevie had actually believed him.

But eventually, she'd realized that Allister had likely anticipated the shock those words would give her and had said them simply to put an end to her argument. Well, it had certainly worked, she thought now, smiling inwardly at her foolish heart. After all, they'd really only just met; what on earth would possess her to believe that Allister had fallen in love with her in such a short time? Just because her emotions had been turned upside down and inside out over the past week didn't mean his had been.

Stevie shook her head and reached for a mug. But when she turned, her elbow struck something on the counter, sending it flying to the floor. A glass, she realized the instant she heard it shatter.

"Damn!" She didn't have to worry about waking Paige now.

She heard the approaching footsteps.

"Sorry, Paige. I didn't mean to wake—"

"It's not Paige."

Stevie was certain she jumped a good foot. The mug she'd been holding dropped to the floor and exploded, as well.

"Dammit, Allister!"

"Stevie, I'm sorry. I didn't mean to scare you." Both hands were on her shoulders then, and she grasped his bare arms to balance herself.

"I thought...I thought that was Paige sleeping on the couch."

"Paige went home last night. Are you all right?"

She nodded, knowing her smile was a shaky one at best. "Yeah. It's just...you scared the hell out of me." She let out a long breath, feeling her heart gradually recover.

"Sorry." He touched a finger to her chin, tilting her face toward him. For a second she thought he was going to kiss her, but then she realized he was staring at her.

"I'm okay, Allister, really," she assured him, reaching a hand to his chest. He wasn't wearing a shirt. But then, with the furnace running on high all night, why should he?

Under her palm, she felt the mat of soft hair and then the shift of muscles beneath before he slipped an arm around her shoulders.

"Come on, let's get you out of here so I can sweep this up." He guided her to one of the stools along the kitchen bar, but Stevie realized how close he had come to kissing her again. He'd been standing so near she'd felt the heat of his body against hers. She'd felt his breath whisper across her cheek, and the air around them come alive with desire. He'd *wanted* to kiss her, but for some reason had refrained.

And now Stevie understood why Allister hadn't shared her bed last night. He knew as well as she did what would have happened if he had, and in spite of the words he'd spoken last night in the car, he was afraid of getting closer to her. That had to be it.

Stevie wished she could see Allister's face, see the expression there, because maybe then she'd have a better understanding of what was happening between them. Then again, was *she* ready for what could have happened last night?

It was probably just as well Allister had stayed on the couch, after all.

He was sweeping the floor, brushing shards of glass and porcelain into the dustpan. Finally she heard him take out two other mugs and pour coffee, and in moments she had a warm cup in her hands.

"How about some breakfast?" he offered.

"That depends. What can you make?" She grinned.

"Well, let's see." She heard the fridge door open and imagined him surveying the contents. "I make a pretty mean slice of toast and jam."

No sooner had she nodded than Allister set about making them breakfast. She listened to him switch on the toaster and take jars of honey and jam from the fridge.

She should ask him about last night, Stevie thought as she sipped her coffee. She should just come right out and confront him about what he'd said and what those words had meant, what was developing between them and what, if anything, he expected.

But she wasn't quick enough.

"Listen, Stevie—" Allister took out two plates and set them on the kitchen bar "—how much do you remember about the day you were shooting at the warehouse?"

"You mean the day Gary was killed?"

Allister hesitated. "Yeah." It was still too painful for him to even say it, Stevie thought.

"Well, the actual afternoon is pretty clear. It's what happened later that's still a bit cloudy. Why?"

"I'm just thinking there might be something we're overlooking."

"I told you before, Allister, Gary didn't give me anything."

"But maybe he said something, Stevie. I don't know. I'm just trying to figure out if he dropped any clues at all about these damned coins. He knew Bainbridge would be after them, and he probably wanted to get them out of the warehouse. There has to be something he said or did that might lead us to them."

Stevie took a sip of coffee. She'd done her best to forget every last detail of that fateful night and the afternoon leading up to it. And now Allister wanted her to remember it all again.

"We got to the warehouse probably around four," she began, "but since it was Friday, the staff had all gone home already."

As Allister made toast, Stevie told him how they had set up in the main area of the warehouse, how Gary had waved at her from the catwalk before turning back to his office. She told him about seeing Fenton and about her camera jamming. Then how, twenty minutes later, Gary had left for a short time.

"Left? For where?" Allister asked as he slid her plate of toast across the kitchen bar and pulled up a stool.

"I don't know where he was going. He didn't say. He just asked me how much longer we'd be, and when I told him another hour or so, he said he'd see me in a while. He was running an errand, he said, and he'd be right back."

"He didn't say anything else? If he was expecting anyone?"

"No, just that he'd be back. He seemed a bit nervous, though. I wanted to go after him then and ask if he was all right, but we were in the middle of the shoot. He kept looking over his shoulder on his way to the side door, and I remember thinking he was going to crush the shipping box he was carrying because he was hanging on to it so tightly."

"A box?"

"Yeah, one of those with the Palmer logo."

"He was carrying a shipping box?"

Stevie nodded.

"Why didn't you say something about that before?"

"About Gary holding a shipping box? Allister, Gary *always* had some sort of package or envelope in his hand. I didn't think anything of it. I figured he was just making a personal delivery. What, you think maybe that was the coins?"

"Could be. If you saw Fenton on the catwalk just before that, it could be that Fenton was leaving. He could have been at the warehouse to get the coins. But maybe Gary wouldn't give them up. If Fenton made a few threats, maybe it was then that Gary figured he'd better get the coins out of the warehouse."

"As if he'd known Fenton would be back," Stevie said slowly.

"Exactly. So did you talk to Gary when he returned?"

"Briefly. We finished the shoot sometime around seven— I don't remember the exact time. Paige and the rest of the crew packed up the equipment while I stayed to thank Gary for letting us use the warehouse."

"And did he say anything out of the ordinary then? Anything that seemed odd?"

Stevie shook her head. "We just chatted, Allister. I suggested he and Barb take a holiday. He looked burned out. But he said he couldn't get away. And that was about it. He'd obviously had things he wanted to take care of—he seemed awfully distracted—so I left him."

"But you went back?"

Stevie rubbed the handle of her mug. She didn't want to remember that part. She didn't want to have to conjure up the images of that horrifying night again. It was over. She wanted to put it behind her.

But Allister's silence was demanding.

"I went to the warehouse again around ten that night. I'd forgotten one of the cameras—the jammed one with the shot of Fenton. Gary had given me a key, so I let myself in. When I got my bag, I noticed that Gary's office lights were still on, so I went up to talk to him."

The memories came back in a flood now, exactly what she'd wanted to avoid—the disarray of the office, Gary's body by the desk and, finally, the man who had attacked her.

"He'd been standing just inside the doorway," she went on, describing for Allister every detail she could recall. "It was the red of the fire extinguisher that caught my eye. As soon as I stepped through the door, he was going to swing it at me."

Allister wanted to stop Stevie now. This part she didn't need to remember for him. He could see it was a strain for her, as well. Her expression had become drawn, and her grip on her coffee mug had tightened so fiercely he wondered if the ceramic could withstand the pressure.

"I didn't get a good look at the man then. But he was tall, with dark hair and almost black eyes. That's about all I saw before I ducked and ran. Allister, what does Fenton look like?"

Up until now, Allister hadn't even considered the comparison. It hadn't crossed his mind that Stevie might want to match the image in her memory to the man only Allister had seen. And in that second, Allister was grateful for both the brevity of Stevie's memory and for the fleeting resemblance between Fenton and himself. He couldn't have handed Stevie yet another lie.

"From what I saw of Fenton in the car," Allister told her, "and then in your proofs, I'd say he's probably around six foot. And he's got dark hair. But listen, Stevie—"

"He came after me, Allister," she went on, in spite of Allister's efforts to stop her. "Gary's killer. He ran after me along the catwalk. I could feel it vibrating under my feet, and I knew he was chasing me. I remember thinking that if I could beat him outside and get into my car, I'd be safe. But then he was right behind me."

Stevie took another sip of coffee and when she did, Allister saw the cup shake in her hand.

"I was going to swing at him with my keys, but he grabbed me. I don't...I don't know if he hit me then or if I struck my head on the railing or something. But I remember falling."

"Stevie, you don't have to—"

"Allister!" She slammed down her cup so forcefully that the black coffee splashed over the rim. "Allister, wait! I remember... When I fell, just before I blacked out, I saw him again. He was leaning over me. It was dark, and his face was in shadow. But I remember him coming closer, and then I saw this scar."

"A scar?" Allister couldn't breathe. He leaned back on his stool, away from Stevie, needing space. This couldn't be happening. A kind of excitement lit her expression now—excitement at her newfound memory.

"On the man's face." She drew a finger along her left temple to show Allister exactly where she'd seen the scar, and as he watched her, it felt as though an invisible icy finger touched his own temple where the ragged scar indelibly marked him.

He slid off the stool and began to pace the small kitchen. He felt like a caged animal, caught in a trap of lies and ill-fated circumstances. But then why should he have expected any different? For the past six years, that was all his life had consisted of.

"I mustn't have remembered it before," Stevie was saying, "because I only saw the scar that once, when he was leaning over me just before I blacked out. Dr. Sterling calls it selective amnesia."

Allister kept pacing. It was all he could do now. Stevie remembered: she remembered his face, she remembered his scar. All along he'd held on to the thin hope that maybe, in her panic, she hadn't seen him very clearly that night, that when her sight returned she wouldn't be able to identify him. But he'd been fooling himself. If Stevie had seen his scar, then for sure she'd gotten a good look at him, and for sure she'd be able to identify him when her sight returned.

"Allister?"

"Hmm?"

"We could take this to the police now. I mean, I know you don't trust Devane, but we could go to someone else, someone higher up. If this Fenton guy has a scar, if I can prove he was the man who attacked me, who killed Gary, well, someone on the force must be able to help us."

"It's not just Devane I'm suspicious of, Stevie. And besides, unless we've got direct evidence against Bainbridge... He can hire other men. No, we've got to get something on Bainbridge himself. Without that, we're still not safe."

She seemed to mull this last point over, and Allister couldn't help thinking that his logic sounded convincing, especially since there was a very real truth to it—with or without Fenton, Bainbridge wasn't likely to stop until he had his coins.

Allister studied Stevie's blank gaze. Maybe it would have been easier just to tell her the truth, tell her that he was the man she'd seen that night in Gary's office, that he was the person responsible for her blindness.

But would Stevie honestly believe he'd had nothing to do with Gary's murder? After all, other than their connection through Gary, they really didn't know each other very well. And how could he expect Stevie to trust a man she'd never even seen?

What made Stevie any different from Michelle? he wondered as the bitterness of those memories rose again. He thought he'd known Michelle. They'd been together for three years. They'd been engaged. As close as Allister felt to Stevie, as much as he thought he loved her, how well did he really know her? And could he honestly expect her to trust or believe him after all the lies?

"Well, it doesn't seem like we've got many avenues open to us," Stevie said. She pushed her stool back and crossed the kitchen to the counter. "I mean, if we can't go to the police, and if there's nothing Gary said or did that can lead us to the coins, what's left?"

But the question was only a rhetorical one, Allister realized as he watched her grope for the coffeepot. She didn't expect him to have the answers.

Allister admired the skill with which she poured her coffee, no doubt using sound to judge the level of the liquid. And when she turned back to the kitchen bar and drew up her stool again, she did so with such finesse that Allister found himself yet again in awe of Stevie's willpower and courage. There was more to it than her saving him from the river in spite of her blindness. It was the fact that Stevie hadn't let her loss stop her.

But Paige had been right last night about Stevie's being secretly terrified. Behind that dark unfocused gaze, he recognized her fear—fear of an unknown future, a fear Allister knew all too well.

Suddenly Stevie was on her feet again. Her stool scraped across the kitchen floor and she was halfway to the stairs before Allister had even stood up.

"Stevie, what is it?"

"I've got it," she called back to him, and started down the stairs.

"Got what?" But he was sure she hadn't heard him. And by the time Allister reached the first floor himself, he could hear Stevie already rummaging in the darkroom.

"What are you looking for?" he asked, reaching for the light switch. As the overhead fluorescents flickered on, he

saw Stevie squatting in front of the storage cabinets, groping in each systematically.

"Stevie, tell me what you're looking for so I can help."

"My bag, Allister. The one I left at the warehouse that
night." She opened another cabinet.

"A camera bag?"

"No. It's a black duffel bag. My gym bag actually. It was
the closest thing around when the camera jammed, so I put
the camera in it with my gym stuff."

Allister started to rummage now, too.

"It's got to be in here," Stevie was saying. "Paige had it
the other day when she gave me the Nikon to salvage the
film. And unless she's taken to washing my gym clothes—"

"Bingo." Allister pulled the black bag out from between
one of the worktables and the wall. It was the bag Stevie had
had with her that night, the bag he'd slung over his shoulder when he'd carried her into the emergency room. The
memory was vivid, yet it seemed like a lifetime ago.

He brought the bag to Stevie, and she immediately sat
next to it on the floor. "When I went back to Gary's that
night, my bag wasn't where I'd left it," she told him as she
pulled out gym clothes and shoes. "I figured maybe my crew
had moved it, but then if they had, they would have packed
it along with the rest of the equipment. So, what if—" she
turned her search to the side pockets now, having found
nothing in the main section "—what if *Gary* moved the
bag? What if he figured I'd come back for it and—" She
stopped abruptly.

"Stevie, did you find something?"

From the side pocket she pulled out a large flat key and
held it up toward Allister.

"I don't know," she said. "You tell me."

"This isn't yours?"

Stevie shook her head as he took the key and turned it over in his hands.

"Looks like it could be for a safe-deposit box or something. You think Gary put this in here?"

"That's my guess. I mean, this bag was in the warehouse after my shoot and before Gary was killed. And if the coins aren't in the warehouse somewhere, maybe they're in a safe-deposit box—one that key opens."

The kiss Allister planted on Stevie's lips took her by surprise. He enjoyed hearing her small gasp, followed quickly by her eager response.

And when he pulled back to look at her, her genuine smile touched his heart.

"So, what was that you were saying last night about us not being detectives?" he asked.

ALLISTER MUST HAVE checked his rearview mirror a dozen times in the past thirty seconds alone, and still he hadn't seen any sign of Vince Fenton's brown sedan. Either Bainbridge's thug had decided to adopt a more discreet tactic, or more likely, he'd guessed who'd broken into his apartment last night and was now maintaining a safe distance.

It couldn't have been difficult for Fenton to figure out the identity of last night's intruder. After Allister had practically run him off the road the day before, Fenton must have known that Allister had gotten a look at his plates. Then, when nothing had been stolen from Fenton's apartment, it should have been obvious that whoever had broken in had been looking for something specific.

Whatever, Fenton was nowhere to be seen today.

Allister glanced over at Stevie in the Volvo's passenger seat. She was holding the key and rubbing it with her thumb. She leaned her head back against the seat and closed her eyes.

"Are you tired?" he asked.

She nodded but her eyes remained shut. "Just a bit."

"We'll be at the bank soon. We'll check the box and then I'll get you home."

It had been a long morning. After finding the key, Allister had tried to reach Barb in Baltimore to find out if she knew anything about a safe-deposit box. But she was out. He'd spoken to her mother, instead, who'd promised him Barb was doing fine and would call him soon.

They'd driven to the warehouse then, and after being cornered to sign forms and return a number of phone calls, Allister had searched Gary's files. Almost two hours later he'd found the document from the bank, indicating the bank's address and a box number that matched the one stamped on the key.

Through all of it, Stevie had been by Allister's side. In fact, she'd been every bit as anxious as he was, and when he'd found the document at last, it was Stevie who'd given him a celebratory kiss.

"There's one thing I don't get, Allister," Stevie said now, and Allister pulled his gaze from the rearview mirror to glance at her again.

"What's that?"

"Gary's putting the key in my bag. Why would he do that? I mean, it's a key. Why wouldn't he have hidden it at the warehouse someplace? Or in his car even?"

"I'm not sure," he answered. "It could be that Gary knew he was being followed and wanted to be sure there was a key he could get at that was outside his usual route from the warehouse to his home. Or maybe he figured that if he got in trouble, with the key in someone else's possession, it would have taken him only a phone call to get the coins."

"You mean, he would have had me drive to the bank and get them? That doesn't sound like Gary. I don't believe he would have intentionally dragged me into this."

"I can't tell you that, Stevie. I don't know what Gary was thinking when he put the key in your bag. I don't know what he was thinking when he got involved with Bainbridge in the first place."

Allister steered the Volvo into the plaza parking lot and parked in a space just outside the bank. He took the key from the ignition and turned to Stevie.

"Are you ready?"

She nodded. "Let's do it."

Allister was sure Stevie had the same feeling he did—that they were being followed, that as soon as they had their hands on the coins, someone would jump them. If indeed they were actually going to find the coins in Gary's safe-deposit box.

Helping Stevie from the car, Allister slid his arm around her waist and guided her across the parking lot. He scanned the area. Still no sign of the brown sedan.

The bank was bustling, and from all appearances, short-staffed. Allister waited with Stevie near the last wicket, as a teller promised for the third time that the assistant manager would be right with them.

When Allister looked at Stevie, he could see that the unfamiliar surroundings made her nervous. Her mouth was a tight line, and she clutched the velvet-covered partition rope as though it was the only thing holding her up. He reached for her free hand, and she seemed to welcome the contact. The tension in her face eased slightly, and her fingers returned his gentle squeeze.

"You don't see Fenton, do you?" she asked, her voice an anxious whisper.

Allister turned to scan the crowded bank. Vince Fenton could have been anywhere. He wasn't in the long lineup waiting for available tellers, but beyond this string of impatient customers, even more people waited for the banking machines at the front. Any one of them could be Fenton, Allister thought. Or he could be just outside, lost in the bustle of people on the sidewalk, bundled against the cold, practically unrecognizable.

"No, I don't think so, Stevie," he told her, turning back to her. "I didn't see his car either. I think we're all right."

"Mr. Quaid?" The short corpulent man who hurried up to them now gave them an apologetic smile and extended one meaty hand. "I'm Mr. Cavanaugh, the assistant manager," he panted, as Allister accepted his handshake. "I understand you're here about a safe-deposit box."

"That's right."

"From our records, I see that you have signing authority on Mr. Palmer's business accounts. And since the box is registered under the company's name, all I need from you, Mr. Quaid, is a couple of signatures." He nodded for them to follow him to the offices at the back. "After that, the box is all yours."

FOR THE SECOND TIME, the woman in the lineup behind him at the bank machine cleared her throat sharply. Vince Fenton wanted to turn and give her a nasty glare or, better yet, tell her what she could do with the bank card she tapped annoyingly against the edge of her wallet in a display of dwindling patience.

But he didn't dare turn around. With the collar of his coat pulled up tight around his chin and a black toque covering his head, he was sure Quaid hadn't spotted him.

After the break-in last night, Vince had guessed Quaid was on to him. No doubt when Quaid had tried to play chicken the other afternoon, he'd done so with the intention of getting the plate numbers off the Plymouth. With that, Quaid could have found out his name and address. Vince had to keep a lower profile.

The second he'd stepped into his apartment last night and kicked off his boots, he'd had a feeling that something was up. It wasn't until he'd spotted the shimmering puddles of melted snow on the windowsill that he'd known for sure. Then he'd seen the missing screen and heard someone on the fire escape.

By the time he'd struggled into his boots again and raced downstairs to the front door of the apartment building, he'd caught only the tail end of the compact heading down Adelle. But he was sure it had been Quaid. Unless Bainbridge was having him followed now, a possibility Vince wasn't ruling out.

The woman behind him coughed again, and he punched a few keys on the number pad to keep up appearances.

In the reflection in the Plexiglas side panel of the money machine, Vince could see most of the bank behind him. And by standing just a little to the right, he had a clear view of Quaid and the Falcioni woman at the far end. They were talking to a suit, whom they then followed to the back.

When finally Vince turned around, he watched Quaid drop his hand to the small of the woman's back and guide her toward the vault. So this was where Palmer had stashed the coins. At last he was getting somewhere.

"Are you finished, sir?" The woman with the tapping card frowned at him, and Vince glared back.

"Relax, will ya, sweetheart?" he said, and shoved his card into his coat pocket.

CHAPTER TWELVE

"THERE YOU GO, Mr. Quaid," Mr. Cavanaugh said. "Number 501."

Stevie heard the metal box glide out of its slot.

"There are some rooms off to the left there if you'd like privacy. And one of our staff will help you out when you're done. Once again, I'm sorry to hear about Mr. Palmer. Very unfortunate."

"Thank you."

There were the departing clicks of the assistant manager's shoes on the floor of the vault before Allister lead Stevie to their left.

He hadn't let go of her hand, and it was only once they'd stopped and she'd heard the door of the small room close behind them that he placed her hand on the corner of the table. She listened as he set down the safe-deposit box and released the catch on the lid.

The room was like a tomb, its silence pounding in her ears as she waited for Allister to open the box. When he did, she reached for him, needing contact, and found the edge of his open jacket. She grasped the soft leather and took a step closer.

"What is it, Allister? What's there?"

She heard him slide something out of the box—the scrape of cardboard against metal.

"It's a shipping box," he said.

Stevie waited, listening to him peel back the flap. Then there was the crinkle of paper and more rustling. And finally, silence.

"Allister." She tugged at his coat, but he didn't respond. "Come on. What is it?"

She placed her hand on his arm and followed its length to where his wrist rested on the corner of a small box. With outstretched fingers, Stevie reached past his hand. Her fingertips fluttered across the crushed velvet lining, and then, her breath catching, she felt the smooth curves that protruded from each slot in the padded casing. As she touched the embossed surface of each coin, Stevie tried to envision the ancient markings and the timeworn impressions.

So this was what Bainbridge was after, she thought. This was what Gary had been killed for—a box of coins.

"What do we do?" she asked, finding Allister's hand again and clasping it in hers.

"I'm not sure yet." He closed the box and she knew he was putting it back.

"Can't we take this to the police now? Just get it over with?"

"No, Stevie."

"Allister, if we give this to the authorities, it'll be out of our hands once and for all. We can be done with this."

"We can't, Stevie. We need something on Bainbridge first."

"But why?" Exasperation sharpened her tone. These were the coins that had gotten Gary killed, and now that they'd found them, she wanted nothing to do with them. "Allister, what does it matter if you get anything on Bainbridge? Why does this have to be about revenge?"

"It's *not* about revenge, Stevie." She almost didn't recognize his voice then; it was so cold and intense, cutting through the small room with an unfamiliar hostility. "It's not," he repeated as though trying to convince himself. "It's about finding evidence against Bainbridge so that there won't be any question as to who was behind the burglary in the first place. Devane already suspects I'm somehow involved. If we go to the police now, I have no way of proving I'm not. Besides which, I can't know for sure if Devane or anyone else on the Danby force is in with Bainbridge. So until I've got hard evidence . . ."

He turned to her, taking her by the shoulders, and she knew he was searching her face for the understanding he seemed to need.

"So what now?" she asked when she could take his silence no longer.

"Now we have exactly what Bainbridge wants," he said finally. "Now *we've* got the upper hand."

VINCE WATCHED the bank's entrance from behind the wheel of Stan Swanson's Skylark. He drummed his fingers against the door panel and cursed Stan for being too cheap to install a tape deck. He'd borrowed the car from his friend this morning, figuring that Quaid would be on the lookout for the Plymouth. But still, Vince had been careful to hang well back when he'd tailed the Volvo through traffic earlier.

When at last Quaid and the photographer came out of the bank, Vince sat up and followed them with his gaze. They weren't carrying anything. He'd hoped they'd come out with a package; he'd hoped they'd found the coins. They'd either come up empty-handed, or Quaid figured the coins were safer in the bank. Either way, there was no sense jumping them. Not if they didn't have the coins.

No, he'd have to talk to Bainbridge first, he thought as he started the car. He'd have to find out how his boss wanted to handle this before he made a move. But something told him he'd be moving soon. Very soon.

FROM THE SECOND they'd left the bank to the moment they pulled up at the studio, Stevie knew there had been only one thing on Allister's mind. Or one person—Edward Bainbridge. For the duration of the drive, she'd given Allister his space, letting the silence grow between them until she thought she could take no more. And when Allister finally turned off the car, Stevie was grateful to be home.

She should have known Paige would be there, working as usual. She could hear the radio playing some big-band tune in the darkroom.

"We're home, Paige," Stevie called as she shrugged off her coat.

"I'll be there in a second," came the muffled reply.

"I know it's a bit late for it, but do you want some lunch?" Stevie asked Allister.

He lingered by the door. Stevie was pretty sure she hadn't even heard him take off his coat.

"Allister?"

"Listen, Stevie, if Paige is going to be here for a while, I really should get back to the warehouse for a couple of hours. There's a lot of paperwork that's falling behind and—"

"Allister." She moved to where she'd heard his voice and reached out for him, finding his arm and taking hold of it. "Allister, you're not . . . you won't do anything about Bainbridge, will you?"

"No, Stevie. No." As reassuring as he tried to sound, she found little comfort in it. "No, I'm just going to the warehouse. I'd take you with me, except that you look tired. Honest, Stevie, I won't be more than a couple of hours."

"Allister, promise me . . ."

"I promise," he said, and gave her a quick kiss just as they heard the darkroom door open.

"So you guys finally decided to come home, huh?"

Paige crossed the studio toward them, and when Stevie turned she could still taste Allister's kiss on her lips.

"Well, it's about time. Another ten minutes and I was going to call out the state troopers," Paige joked, but the relief in her voice made it obvious she'd been worried.

"Sorry, we should have left a note," Stevie said.

"Paige, are you going to be here for a while?" Allister asked. "I have to take care of some business at the warehouse."

"No problem. I'll be here."

"Thanks, Paige. Stevie—" his voice lowered and he pulled her close "—I promise—it's only work. I'll be back before you know it." He caressed her cheek briefly and then was gone.

She stood at the door even after he'd left, even after she'd heard the Volvo start up and back out the drive. And she prayed Allister had told her the truth.

"Hey." Paige moved beside her then, wrapping an arm around her shoulders. "Looks serious. You want to talk about it?"

Stevie let out the breath it seemed she'd been holding for the past half hour and allowed Paige to lead her to the darkroom.

"I'm just worried, Paige," she admitted, pulling herself up onto one of the stools.

"About what?"

"Allister. I'm worried he's going to do something."

"You mean, something about Bainbridge?"

Stevie turned toward her friend's voice. "You know about that?"

"Allister told me last night. After seeing how upset you were when you got home, I made him tell me everything. So, you want to bring me up-to-date? Or do I have to milk Allister again for the details?"

Stevie shook her head, unable to suppress a smile. She should have expected that Paige wouldn't have let anything slip by her. From the moment Stevie had woken up in that hospital room a week and a half ago, Paige had been there for her, had been looking out for her.

As Paige put away bottles of chemicals, Stevie filled her in on the key and the safe-deposit box. And then she told her about the coins.

"I'm just worried that Allister will let his anger drive him, you know, Paige? That he might do something rash." When Paige joined her at the table, she said, "He was so quiet in the car all the way home. I know he's just seething about this Bainbridge guy."

She remembered the fierce bitterness she'd heard in Allister's voice at the bank earlier. It had frightened her then, and it frightened her still.

"I'm so afraid he might do something that...that'll land him back in prison."

"I wouldn't worry about that if I were you, Stevie. I think at this point, Allister has one very strong reason for not wanting to jeopardize his freedom."

"What do you mean?" But Stevie hadn't really needed to ask that question; the tone in Paige's voice had said it all.

"What exactly *did* you and Allister talk about last night?"

"It wasn't so much what he told me as what I saw."

"And what was that?"

"Allister loves you, Stevie. I see the way he looks at you, the way he's always got to be right beside you. And when he talks about you, he gets this kind of light in his eyes. He cares a lot for you, honey. Trust me, I don't think you have to worry about him jeopardizing that for some slime named Bainbridge."

Stevie ran a hand through her hair, wondering if it was just her or if the furnace was running high again.

"What?" Paige said. "You're not going to tell me you don't feel the same about him, are you? I saw how upset you were at the hospital the other day. And I've seen the way your face flushes whenever he gets close to you."

"This is moving way too fast," Stevie admitted, even though she recognized the truth in what Paige was telling her. "I don't know, Paige. When you think about it, really, this is all about Gary. I mean, his death—it was such a shock. I miss him, and Allister misses him. And we're this kind of link for each other, you know?"

"Right, and the next thing you'll be trying to tell me is that you're only with Allister because of everything you're going through and you need someone to comfort you."

"Well, maybe that *is* part of it."

"Rationalize all you want, honey, but there's more behind your feelings for Allister than comfort, and you know it. You just won't admit it yet."

Paige left the table and began rummaging through one of the corner cabinets. She was finished saying what she had to say on the topic, Stevie realized. She'd handed out her nugget of advice for the afternoon.

"So, how about rolling some film?" Paige asked.

Stevie smiled as Paige dragged out the equipment and the canisters of film. "Sure, why not."

She heard Paige turn off the lights, and for at least ten minutes they rolled film in a dark and comfortable silence.

"He really gets a light in his eyes?" she asked Paige at last.

"Uh-huh."

"So are you going to tell me what the rest of him looks like?"

"Nope."

"Why not?"

"Because that would be like telling a kid where his parents hid all the Christmas presents. I'm not going to be the one to ruin your surprise. You'll just have to wait to see him when you see him."

NEEDING TO DO WORK at the warehouse hadn't been a total lie. There was a pile of forms and letters awaiting signatures. And phone calls to return. But what Allister had really needed was to get away. He'd needed time to think, to figure out what he was going to do about Bainbridge. And as long as he was near Stevie, he couldn't keep a clear head. Every time he looked at her, every time he touched her, doubts crept in—he'd start wondering if he should just go to the police with the coins, if he should take the leap of faith Stevie seemed to want him to.

No, he'd needed this time to think, to clear his head. And his heart. Now, finally, he had a pretty good idea of what he had to do. And he knew he would have to do it on his own.

Closing the door to Gary's office, Allister paused on the catwalk. Below in the main loading area, a few drivers were just closing up and clearing out for the day. The building was practically empty.

Like the first time Gary had brought him here, Allister thought. It had been the afternoon of his release, eight months ago. After they'd gone for the beer Gary had been promising him for four years, he'd brought Allister back here to show him what he'd done with the business.

Gary had been proud of the shipping company and of the reputation he'd developed. And he'd seemed happy, or so Allister had thought. Gary hadn't let on that there was anything wrong with his marriage, that Barb was unhappy and wanted to leave him and Danby.

Allister leaned his elbows against the railing and surveyed the warehouse that Gary had poured the last few years of his life into. It didn't make sense. Ten days since Gary's murder, and Allister still couldn't figure out why his friend had dismissed his warnings. Gary had seen what Bainbridge was capable of, and yet he'd ignored Allister and—

Allister stood bolt upright.

That was it! His heart raced and his stomach lurched at the realization. That was exactly why Gary had gotten involved with Bainbridge. He'd seen firsthand what Bainbridge had done to Allister. He'd witnessed the ruin of Allister's life: the collapsed business, the broken engagement, the crumbled reputation, those lost years.

Gary had gone after Bainbridge for Allister.

There was no way to prove it of course. But it made sense. Allister, of all people, knew the way Gary thought—always looking for adventure, always game for a challenge. No doubt, with his marriage on the rocks, Gary saw nothing to lose in taking on a man like Bainbridge, bringing him to justice, clearing his best friend's name. The one thing Gary hadn't counted on was Vince Fenton. How was he to know that his plan could turn so deadly? Even Allister hadn't guessed that Bainbridge would resort to murder.

Allister closed his eyes and rubbed his forehead, trying to ease the headache that throbbed there. It all made sense now. He should have seen it before, instead of doubting Gary's motives. Gary had always been there for him. And now, for the first time, Allister realized that Gary had been there for him right to the end.

"Mr. Quaid, I was hoping I'd find you in."

Allister spun around. Devane. He hadn't heard the detective come in.

"Did I catch you at a bad time?" he asked, and Allister wondered if he looked as startled as he felt.

"Actually, Detective, yes. I was just leaving. We're closing up."

"So I noticed. Well, I won't keep you long." He shifted a large box from under one arm and handed it to Allister. "I only came to return Mr. Palmer's personal things. From his office. We're through with them."

"Thank you." He took the box.

"And while I'm here, I did want to speak to you about another matter, Mr. Quaid," Devane added, brushing aside the edge of his police parka to slide his hand into his pants pocket. The movement revealed the detective's holster and revolver. Allister couldn't decide if the gesture was deliberate. "It concerns Ms. Falcioni."

Allister turned. With the box pinned under his arm, he opened Gary's office. Devane was right behind him.

"Just a word of warning, Mr. Quaid. Nothing more."

"Look, Detective, what I do in my personal life is of no—"

"But you see, Mr. Quaid, it is. Especially when that personal life concerns Ms. Falcioni. In case you don't know, Ms. Falcioni is my only potential eyewitness in a homicide investigation—a homicide, may I remind you, for which you have not been entirely cleared as a suspect. So your involvement with Ms. Falcioni does concern me, Mr. Quaid."

"What exactly are you implying, Detective?"

"I'm not implying anything." Devane zipped up his parka, and Allister hoped he was leaving. "Oh, by the way, how much time's still left on your sentence? Another two years, isn't it—if you break parole, that is?"

"Are you threatening me, Detective?"

"Not at all, Mr. Quaid. I'm merely warning you. You'd better watch your step, because that's exactly what I'm doing."

Devane turned out of the office. Allister listened to his footfalls on the steel grating and finally on the stairs. He couldn't let Devane get to him. That was exactly what the detective wanted.

And he certainly had no intention of staying away from Stevie. They'd been apart for less than two hours, and already Allister missed everything about her. No, he was heading back to the studio right now. Back to Stevie.

It was when he was about to leave as well that Allister glanced into the box Devane had given him. There, amongst the papers and desk paraphernalia, Allister saw Gary's microcassette recorder. He picked it up and turned it over in his palm. The device would come in handy for what he had in mind regarding Edward Bainbridge.

"I DON'T UNDERSTAND, Allister." Stevie heard the shock in her voice as her fingers twisted around the stem of her wineglass. "So you don't believe Gary was trying to blackmail Bainbridge, after all?"

"Not for money. I think he agreed to handle Bainbridge's shipment because he saw it as a chance to clear my name."

"But the risks—"

"He didn't know the risks, Stevie."

"But you warned him."

"I didn't warn him that his life was at stake. Even *I* didn't know Bainbridge was capable of going that far."

She sat cross-legged at one end of the couch, turned toward Allister, close enough to touch him. She did so, placing a hand on his shoulder.

When she'd heard Allister's voice in the front hall two hours ago, Stevie had been surprised at the combination of relief and excitement that had charged through her. But Allister's mood hadn't changed. He'd been quiet throughout the dinner she and Paige had made for the three of them, and afterward, when Paige joined them for a glass of wine before she headed off for the night, Allister seemed withdrawn, troubled.

Now Stevie knew why.

Even if it could never be proved that Gary had died while attempting to clear Allister's name, the fact that Allister believed it was enough. Stevie couldn't begin to fathom what was going through his mind, or his heart. To know that his best friend had lost his life trying to help him—Stevie didn't know if that kind of loss filled you with a sense of injustice or anger, indebtedness or guilt, or more likely a dark combination of all those.

"I'm sorry, Allister." She gave his shoulder a squeeze.

"So am I," he whispered, and reached up to take her hand in his, caressing it thoughtfully.

"So what are we going to do?"

"We? No, Stevie. Not *we*." He released her hand suddenly and got up from the couch. She heard him pacing the living room, from the windows overlooking the street to the plants below the skylight, each time passing the couch. "Look, Stevie, I really don't want to argue, but I can't involve you any further in this. It's too dangerous. I won't do it. Last night was a mistake. I should never have taken you along. You could have been hurt."

"So could you, Allister."

There was a slight pause in his pacing, and when he finally passed the couch again, she could almost feel his tension.

"Stevie, can't you understand that this is something *I* have to handle? There's nothing you can do now."

"Because I'm blind."

When he stopped this time, he stood directly in front of her. She felt his eyes on her, wanted to say something to break the silence, but refused. The ball was in his court.

"All right, fine. If that's what it's going to take to get through that stubborn streak of yours, then yes, because you're blind. Because when I finally have to deal with Bainbridge, I won't be able to watch out for you, too. Because I can't have you along with me, knowing you can't defend yourself. And because I will *not* endanger your life."

"Allister—"

"No, Stevie, listen to me—" he put a hand on her shoulder "—even if you weren't blind, I would not involve you in some deal I try to drum up with Bainbridge. There's nothing you can do. And I'd never, *never* be able to forgive myself if something happened to you, too."

He was right, she knew. There *was* nothing she could do. She felt powerless. And as desperate as she was to see an end to this nightmare, she knew it was between Allister and Bainbridge now. He had to take care of it himself and in his own way, no matter how much she hated the thought of that.

Sure, they needed evidence to link Bainbridge with the theft of the coins and Gary's murder so that Allister would be cleared of suspicion and exonerated of his previous conviction. But just as much as those things, Allister needed to do this for himself—for the years he'd lost—and for Gary.

And suddenly Stevie wondered about the Allister she hadn't known—the man untouched by injustice and prison, the man before Edward Bainbridge. She wondered if the old Allister would have had this much hate in him, this much rage and bitterness. She doubted it.

"So what are you going to do?" she asked eventually.

He hesitated, as though unwilling to involve her even in his plans. When he finally spoke, he was standing across the room.

"I'm going to call Bainbridge and set up a meeting."

"Allister, you can't! Gary tried to do that and—"

"Stevie, I need to meet with the man. I need to get him on tape."

"But, Allister..." Dread crept up from the pit of her stomach.

"It'll work, Stevie. I've got more to bargain with than Gary did. I've got Fenton."

"What do you mean?" But Stevie wasn't certain she wanted to hear an answer to that.

"At this point, Fenton knows someone was in his apartment last night. He's probably already told Bainbridge. All I have to do is indicate to Bainbridge that I have evidence linking Gary's murder to Fenton, and Fenton to Bainbridge."

"And where do the coins come in?"

"Bainbridge already suspects we've got the coins. What I intend to do is propose a payoff. He'll think I'm in it only for the money. And my insurance is the evidence I'll claim to have against Fenton. All I have to do is inform Bainbridge that, should anything happen to me, the evidence will go directly to the police."

The way Allister talked about it now, his manner so calm and detached, the plan sounded almost plausible. But this was his life he was risking! As much as Stevie tried, she couldn't put the image of Gary's body out of her mind. And as short a time as she'd known Allister, she couldn't imagine her life without him now. If anything happened to him...

He must have recognized her fear, because he crossed to the couch, sat down beside her and took both her hands in his.

"It'll be all right, Stevie." He pressed his palm to her cheek. "This will work."

"I just . . . I just keep thinking about Gary, you know?" She was sure he felt her tremble. "I keep seeing him there, Allister, lying on the floor with the blood—"

"Stevie, don't."

His arms wrapped around her, and she welcomed his embrace. She needed to be close to Allister, to hold him and believe that nothing or no one was going to take him away from her.

"Allister," she whispered as he stroked her hair, "I . . . I don't think I could stand losing you."

"Stevie—"

"I love you, Allister."

His hand stopped. She felt his body tense just slightly, and in that second, Stevie wondered if she shouldn't have spoken. But then, why shouldn't she? She wanted Allister to know—so he wouldn't leave her, so he wouldn't do anything that might jeopardize his life. But most of all, she wanted him to know, because it was the truth.

He started to pull back. "Stevie, I'm—"

The shrill ring of the phone stopped him, and Stevie could only wonder what it was Allister had wanted to say. As she grappled for the receiver on the side table, he left the couch and started pacing again.

"Stevie? Brian Armatrading here." The voice across the line was extravagantly mellifluous, as she'd come to expect from the fashion designer.

"Brian, hello." Stevie straightened, pulling herself to the edge of the couch.

"Listen, darling, I know it's late. Just wanted to tell you that I *love* the preliminary proofs."

"Proofs? But I—"

"Paige brought them by this morning. I realize you're having to reshoot, but if these are any indication of what I'll be seeing, well, I want you to know that I'm happy to wait, darling. I'm always patient when it comes to getting the best."

"Well...thank you, Brian. I'm glad you liked them."

Allister stopped pacing and watched Stevie now. Her knuckles were white around the receiver, and her expression had tightened.

"I'm fine, Brian. Really. I'm doing all right.... Yes. Yes, I did get the flowers. Thank you.... Yeah, they did. They smelled great." A smile flitted across her face, but just as quickly was gone. "Uh, no, the doctor doesn't know anything yet. Still waiting.... Of course I'll let you know, Brian. You'll be one of the first. Mm-hmm."

She stood up, her back rigid, her shoulders straight, and when she hung up the phone, Allister saw a muscle twitch along that strong jaw of hers.

"What is it, Stevie?" He felt the need to be near her, but when he touched her arm, she started slightly. "Stevie?"

"It's nothing, Allister." But he knew she was lying. He saw her fingers tremble when she combed them through her hair.

She groped her way around to the back of the couch, as though wanting to put space between the two of them, but this time Allister wouldn't let her.

"Stevie, that was the guy about the shoot, wasn't it? The shoot you have to redo at the warehouse?"

She flashed him an unconvincing smile. "Yeah, but it's nothing. He was just calling to say he liked the prelim proofs and is willing to wait till..." Her voice trailed off.

Allister took her hand in his then and was surprised when she didn't pull away. "That's great, isn't it? That he liked—"

"Allister, I don't want to talk about it." She twisted away from him, but he held fast to her wrist.

"Stevie, talk to me. I'm here." When he turned her around and grasped her shoulders, Allister was certain she was about to open up at last. Like Paige had said, Stevie's shell would crumble, she would need him, and he'd be there for her. Even now, he could see the tears welling up in her dark eyes and small lines creasing her forehead as she struggled to keep her emotions locked deep inside.

"Look, Allister, I . . ." Her voice caught, and she cleared her throat. "Maybe I should be alone for a while, you know? I'm really tired and—"

"No, Stevie. You're not going to block me out, you hear?"

The dam was weakening. She bit her lower lip, and when she took a breath, it was as tremulous as her faltering facade.

"You're scared, aren't you, Stevie? Why can't you just admit that?" He held her shoulders tightly when she tried to turn away a second time. "You're afraid you won't be able to do this guy's shoot or anyone else's, for that matter. You're terrified at the thought of never looking through the lens of a camera again. But most of all you're afraid of being dependent, aren't you? Of needing people, relying on them, and—"

"Yes!" Her explosiveness took him by surprise, and she almost managed to tear herself free of him this time. "Yes, all right? Yes! Dammit, Allister, of course I'm terrified. What do you think? You think this is easy? Stumbling around in the dark like this? I can't see a damned thing!"

She was crying now, or at least the tears were flowing. But still she clung to her seemingly invincible front. Her jaw was set and her chin tilted up in that proud manner, as though defying him to find the chink in her armor.

"I may never see again, Allister. I've got people calling me about photography contracts and reshoots, while I'm groping my way around in some perpetual game of blind man's bluff. And yes! Yes, Allister, I *am* terrified. I'm blind, for God's sake!"

Her eyes, wide and unfocused, shimmered with tears. They seemed to search for him now, search through her darkness. And in that moment, understanding the extent of Stevie's fear, Allister wished that Paige was still there so he could make up some excuse to leave.

For how could he be there for Stevie, as Paige had suggested? How could *he* be Stevie's comfort, her solace, when he was the person who had caused the very darkness that drove her into his arms?

And yet, while all this went through his head, he knew that he loved her. And he couldn't leave her.

"It'll be better, Stevie," he whispered to her, trying to find faith in his words. "You'll get better. And until then, I'm here for you. I'm right here."

He drew her into his embrace, feeling her tension ease and her body shudder gently as she wept.

When eventually her quiet sobs faded, she murmured against his neck, "I'm scared Allister. Really scared. I . . . I don't know what I'm going to do."

He couldn't answer that. All he could do now was hold her.

And he did. For a long time he rocked Stevie in his arms, clasping her body close. Finally he pulled back far enough to see her face in the soft glow of the floor lamp behind him, and he saw she was calm. He wiped at one remaining tear and traced the gentle curve of her lips with his thumb.

Neither of them spoke, because nothing needed to be said. As he lifted her chin, tilting her face to meet his kiss, Stevie's lips trembled beneath his. But there was no hesitancy in her response. Allister could taste her hunger as her lips parted; he could feel her almost desperate yearning, as though she needed his passion to drown her fears.

And when Allister heard the quiet moan that rose from her throat, his heart raced and he felt a pull deep inside of him.

"Allister—" she drew back, but he still felt her lips against his, shaping the words "—I want to be with you, Allister."

As he lifted her easily into his arms and carried her to the bedroom, he couldn't tell if he'd actually murmured her name or if it had been pounding so loudly through his mind that he only thought he had.

The orange-yellow glow of the street lamp just outside the bedroom window slipped through partially opened blinds and touched Stevie's face as he lowered her to the bed. Her hands never lost contact with him, even as he moved onto the bed with her. Her fingers twined into his hair, and she pulled him to her, deeper into their kiss. It was with a certain reluctance that he left her sweet mouth, but he wanted more of her than this. He wanted to know every part of her. He wanted to bridle the rampant longing that raged through him now so that he could taste and experience every last curve and hollow.

He trailed kisses along her arched neck, feeling her pulse quicken against his lips as he moved past her throat and toward the V of her shirt. He felt her hand slide under his sweater and tug his T-shirt free from his jeans. And when her fingers fluttered over his stomach and up his chest, Allister's breath caught in his throat.

Torn between answering his primal urges and savoring each intoxicating second, Allister concentrated on the buttons of her shirt. One at a time, he released them, and all the while Stevie's fingers traced the lines and curves of his chest, as though committing each one to a mental image she was creating of him.

With the last button of her shirt undone, Allister brushed aside the crisp cotton to reveal the luminous warmth of her skin. God, how he wanted her! Every fiber of his being screamed for him to take her right there, to give in to the overwhelming drive that coursed through him like a raging fire.

Instead, he let out a ragged breath and traced the edge of the dainty lace bra with one finger, following the gentle swell of her breasts. And when he undid the front clasp, freeing her breasts, he marveled at the perfect dark nipples. Cupping one breast in his hand, he lowered his mouth to it, enveloping the taut nipple, tasting it, circling it with his tongue several times before moving to the other.

Stevie's hungry moan drew him back. Her hands, still under his shirt, reached for his shoulders as she guided him up again, to her throat, her ear and finally back to her mouth. It was in the urgency of her kiss that Allister realized the extent of Stevie's own longing.

And never had a kiss tasted so exquisite. It ignited every nerve in his body and awakened the savage and long-suppressed need that set his heart racing.

Allister drew back slightly, his lips still only inches from hers, and felt the heat of her breath on his face.

"Stevie." He looked down into her exquisitely dark eyes, getting lost in them. He trailed his thumb along her jaw and then up again to tease a curl of hair around one finger. "There hasn't...I haven't been with anyone since..."

She pressed her palm to his cheek and whispered his name. In it he heard her compassion. And when he kissed her again, there was an unbearable tenderness about her.

With his life the way it had been for the past few years, Allister never believed he would ever find such absolute and open tenderness. He never thought he'd find love after the hell his life had been. But Stevie offered both of these and more. Much more.

When he looked at her now, shafts of light touching her olive-colored skin and flowing over each curve of her body, Allister wished there was a way he could hold on to this moment forever. He wondered if she felt the same way.

"Allister?"

"Mmm?"

Stevie propped herself up on her elbows, and with the play of shadow across her face, he could almost believe she was looking at him. "What's wrong?"

"Nothing." He caressed her cheek. "I was just thinking . . . wondering what it must be like for you."

"You mean, not being able to see you?"

"Yeah."

Stevie reached toward Allister's voice and found his jaw. From there she pressed her fingers against his lips and felt their moist firmness. She was aware of him staring at her, of his admiring gaze sweeping over every inch of her half-naked body, and she was surprised at how comfortable she was with that.

"I was just curious," he said.

She rolled across the bed then and pulled open the drawer of her nightstand. In moments she found the bandanna she knew had been there and moved back to Allister.

Sitting in front of him and hooking her legs around his waist, Stevie slid her fingers up over his chest, drawing his sweater over his head. His T-shirt followed, and her heart skipped a beat when she anticipated the searing touch of his skin against hers.

He helped her then, tying the bandanna over his eyes, and when it was in place, he reached for her—touching her face first, then fanning his fingers along her throat and finally over her shoulders to completely remove her shirt and bra.

When he lowered her back onto the sheets, she felt his fingers trail ever-widening circles along her skin, from her breasts, past her ribs to the hollow of her stomach. With her own hands, she mapped out the contours of his body as well: the ripple of each muscle along his back and torso, the wide shoulders and the narrow but strong waist where her venturing touches were blocked by his belt.

Allister moved above her now, his mouth on hers, their quickened breath mingling as their growing passion urged them on. Time became meaningless as they rocked between insatiable fervor and exploratory caresses, each reveling in the other's body, each craving the other's touch.

When Allister at last unzipped her jeans and slid his hand beneath the barrier, past her hips, Stevie gasped and shifted under him, allowing him to remove her jeans. Within moments, she was tugging at his belt. The buckle slipped once in her eagerness, and then her fingers found his zipper.

Already she could feel him straining against the denim restriction. Breathlessly she tugged the jeans free of his waist. Savoring the anticipation, she trailed her fingers slowly upward along the inside of his thigh. And finally she caressed him, marveling at the intensity of his arousal.

When Allister straddled her, Stevie felt his hardness press urgently against her inner thigh. She reached for him, drawing him to her as though he was her only light in this darkness of hers. His kisses burned along her skin, traveling upward across her stomach, past her breasts and at last to her mouth again. She heard him murmur her name—a gentle but desperate sound—and Stevie realized that if she ever needed anyone in her life, she needed Allister.

Then, slowly, deliciously, he moved into her. She couldn't restrain her cry of pleasure, nor the arch of her body against his. Her legs encircled his waist, drawing him deeper, meeting each avid thrust with one of her own.

This time, when Stevie heard a moan, she knew it was not hers. The low guttural sound sent a shiver of raw emotion coursing through her. And as Allister delivered his final thrust, pushing them both to a new plateau, Stevie clutched him to her, determined now in her love for Allister—in everything he was and everything he would be with her.

CHAPTER THIRTEEN

"I'M GETTING really tired of this, Fenton. Why the hell are you calling me if you don't have any news?"

"Like I said, I think they've got the coins." Vince wedged the receiver under his chin and picked up the phone. He started to pace the length of the phone's cord and cast a tired gaze across his living room. The place was a sty. But so what. He'd be bailing out of Danby soon, anyway.

"Of course they've got the damned coins!" Bainbridge was fuming. "Who the hell did you think had them?"

"I'm pretty sure they've got 'em in a bank."

"Great. More complications."

"And listen, someone broke into my apartment the other night."

"So? I don't give a damn about—"

"I think it was Quaid."

"How do you know?"

"I just know, okay? Look, he's on to me. I think you should get someone else to—"

"Like hell, Fenton. You're in this to the end. You already screwed up with Palmer. If you don't see this through, I'll make you my own personal project, after Quaid and that woman, you hear me?"

Vince snapped the lid off an aspirin bottle and shook three tablets into his palm. He swallowed them dry.

"So what do you want from me?" he asked Bainbridge.

"We'll have to go with our backup plan. You know what to do?"

"Yeah, yeah. As soon as she's alone."

"Good. I'll wait to hear from you. And, Fenton? No screwups, you hear me?"

STEVIE AWOKE by degrees, easing into consciousness of her surroundings. First there was the warmth of Allister's breath on her neck, then the steady rise and fall of his chest against her back, and finally the rest of his strong body as it molded with hers. But this time there was no hospital blanket separating them, Stevie thought, a satisfied smile creeping to her lips. No, now there was nothing between them, and every curve and angle, even the heat of his skin against hers, whispered memories of their intimacy last night.

He was lying on his side, and when she turned in his arms to face him, he stirred and drew her closer.

Stevie opened her eyes. Another morning of darkness.

She propped herself up on one elbow and trailed a hand along Allister's shoulder, feeling the familiar planes of his muscles. She wished she could see him, sleeping next to her. But then, she was certain she'd committed every last inch of Allister's body to memory last night. Once she'd tied the bandanna over his eyes, they'd explored each other with an intimacy that had culminated in a passion that consumed them both. No, she didn't need to see Allister to know he was beautiful, to know she loved him.

As she listened to his quiet breathing, Stevie couldn't help thinking Paige had been right. Allister did love her. Never before had she experienced such a combination of tenderness and desperate hunger as she had from this man in her bed.

And for the first time in years, Stevie's waking thoughts had nothing to do with her photography. She could have blamed it on her blindness, how the involuntary break from her work forced her to focus her energies elsewhere, but that would have been a lie.

No, blind or not, for the moment, Allister was her only thought. He was immediate; he was there. And suddenly she envisioned spending the rest of her life with him. Even blind, as terrifying as that possibility was, Stevie could now see a reason for living; she could imagine going on, with Allister beside her, holding her hand.

She followed the line of his shoulder and neck, and traced the chiseled angle of his cheek. Part of her was bitter though, she realized then. Bitter, because she'd never seen Allister's face, never gazed upon his smile or seen the light in his eyes that Paige spoke of. If only she had, she would be able now to at least conjure up an image of the man with whom she'd fallen so deeply in love.

Beneath her fingertips she felt the thin strip of gauze on his forehead where he'd gashed it on the Explorer's steering wheel. These three days later, the memory of how close she'd come to losing him that afternoon still rammed through her. If she hadn't managed to drag him from the freezing river, she would never have known this happiness.

He stirred again, and Stevie smiled when she guessed that he was awake. She imagined that he gazed up at her through half-lidded eyes, and her smile widened as she wondered if he, too, was remembering last night's intimacy.

But in that same second, as her fingers fluttered across his forehead and over his brow to his temple, Stevie's smile faltered, and she was gripped by an icy chill.

A scar. Beneath her fingertips, the tight ridge of twisted skin curled along Allister's temple to the top of his cheekbone.

Her fingers trembled, and a wave of disbelief and panic surged through her. She tried to convince herself it was not a scar but a fresh wound, from the accident perhaps. But she'd already felt the bandage along his forehead.

No, this was definitely a scar. The ridge felt gnarled, and smoothed by time. Just like the one she'd seen at the warehouse on that face she'd never forget, the face that had leaned over her in her final shred of consciousness. It was the last thing she had ever seen. Her attacker's face. And it was the scar she'd focused on as her vision had faded and then was gone.

She thought she heard her own thin cry, but couldn't be sure. Allister covered her hand with his, and instantly she jerked away from him. Her heart was in her throat as she stumbled from the bed and staggered across the floor. She tripped over something she thought at first was Tiny, but then realized was her robe. She snatched it up and pulled it on, tightening the belt in a hurried knot around her waist.

Her darkness was dizzying now. Her panic made everything spin. She backed away from the bed, away from Allister. It couldn't be true, she prayed over and over. What she'd felt, it couldn't be.

But it was. The scar was there. She hadn't discovered it last night because of the blindfold. But it was there now. It had always been there. It had been there the night of Gary's murder, the night he'd attacked her.

Stevie swallowed her fear. She had to get away.

The floor was cold against her bare feet when she stepped off the main rug and onto the hardwood. She should have remembered the throw rug in the middle of the room, the one with the corner that always curled up. Her toe caught the edge of it, and she sprawled to the floor, twisting to stop her fall.

Pain knifed up her wrist.

And when she stood, she'd lost her bearings.

She didn't know where Allister was in the room. Until she heard his voice.

"Stevie?"

She spun around, trying to locate him. He was coming after her. Even as she backed away farther, she heard him leave the bed. She heard each step of his approach and desperately tried to think of anything in the room she might use for self-defense.

"Stevie, what's the matter?"

His voice. It sounded so genuine, so concerned. And if not for the scar, she would have trusted it.

"Stay away from me, Allister."

"Stevie—"

"Don't come near me or I swear I'll . . ."

She heard him stop then, and she tried to imagine where he was. Had he crossed to the middle of the room? Was he near the door? Still, she backed away until finally she found the wall.

"Just tell me what's wrong, Stevie. What is it?"

She was shaking her head now. Frantically wishing, praying it wasn't true.

"It was you." Her voice rasped with fear. "Your scar..."

"What?"

"It was you, Allister. At the warehouse. I know it. It was *you.*"

Silence.

She strained to hear any movement in the room.

Would he come after her? Again?

"Stevie—" He took another step toward her.

"It was you I saw in Gary's office. It was you who tried to hit me, Allister, who ran after me. You tried to—"

"I took you to the hospital."

But she barely heard his words over the hammering of her heart. Her spine was pressed against the wall. Her shoulders ached and her legs where shaking. She thought she might be sick, as the horror of her realization coursed through her veins like a poison.

"I would never hurt you, Stevie. You have to believe that. I could never hurt you."

"No? But what about Gary, Allister?" The words tore from her throat, edged with disbelief and wavering with tears. "Why? Why Gary?"

"Stevie, for God's sake, Gary was my friend. You can't believe that I—"

"You were there. I saw you." For the rest of her life she would never forget the bloody images of that night. "You had . . . you had blood, Gary's blood, on your gloves."

She couldn't even say his name now. She'd fallen in love with a man named Allister. But this . . . this person was the man she'd seen at the warehouse, the man who'd killed her friend, who'd attacked her, and . . . No, it couldn't be true, she tried to convince herself again.

But the scar . . .

"I saw you," she said one more time. "Oh, my God . . ."

ALLISTER COULD SEE her terror. He watched her lift her hand to her lips, stifling her cry. She was still shaking her head, whimpering over and over, "Oh, my God. Oh, my God." A voice filled with so much fear and mistrust that he wanted to pull her into his arms and comfort her.

But *he* was the one she was terrified of.

He took a step toward her, and when he tried to touch her, she flinched and let out a frightened gasp. Instantly she took a stumbling step to the side, away from him.

"Don't . . . don't touch me."

"Stevie." He heard the plea in his own voice, wrenched straight from his heart. "Stevie, please, listen to me."

Her head was pressed back against the wall, her eyes wide and her face as blanched with fear as when he'd first laid eyes on her.

"Yes," he said at last. "Yes, I was the man you saw, Stevie. But it wasn't the way you think, I *swear*. You've got to trust me, Stevie, please."

She shook her head mutely.

"Surely you know me better than that."

When he took another step toward her, she obviously sensed it and backed farther along the wall. Pretty soon she would reach the corner near the door, and she'd be trapped. But she already felt trapped, he realized, and utterly defenseless, helpless without her sight.

"Stevie, you know me, I would never—"

"No. No, I don't. I don't know you."

"Then listen to me, all right?"

She was still shaking her head, and Allister wondered just how much she was actually hearing. "No, Allister, no—"

"Listen to me!" He wanted to reach out and shake her, make her listen, make her see the truth. But he knew he had to grant her space.

"Gary was already... It had already happened when I got there that night. He died in my arms, Stevie."

Why did it feel as if everything was unraveling now?

"He told me about Bainbridge and the coins. He told me about you. God, Stevie, you *have* to believe me."

But it wasn't his fear of being placed at the scene of the crime or being falsely accused of Gary's murder that churned his desperation for Stevie to believe him. There was much more to it than that now. Seeing the fear in her wide searching eyes—fear of him, terror at the thought of his even touching her when only a few hours ago they'd made love—was what forced him to take another step toward her, closing the gap between them as if by simply being closer to her he could convince her of his innocence.

"I thought . . . When I heard you come up the stairs that night, Stevie, I thought it was Gary's killer returning. So I armed myself. The second I realized it wasn't, that you weren't, I stopped. I called out to you, Stevie. I shouted for you to wait. I wanted to explain. But you ran. I couldn't have you rushing to the police and giving them a description of me as Gary's killer. And I knew that Gary's death had something to do with Bainbridge and the coins. With my past, I knew the police would suspect me first. That they might even be in on it themselves.

"Stevie, I was trying to stop you. Nothing more. I ran after you, and I grabbed you, because I wanted to explain—"

"And what if I'd regained my sight, Allister? What then?" Her lips quivered, lips that only moments ago had been curved into one of her glorious smiles. "What would you have done knowing that I could identify you from that night as the man who attacked me? What would you have done to me then?"

"I didn't attack you, Stevie! You're not listening to me. I would never hurt you."

He closed the gap then, and her fright seemed only to increase. But he needed to touch her, needed to make the contact that would convince her of his love.

Her robe had slipped down over one shoulder, and when he reached out to put his hand on the warm flesh that mere hours before had been so willing and so ardent against his, Stevie recoiled as though he'd held a hot flame to her skin.

She gave a strangled scream and staggered away from him. When she reached the corner, realizing she was trapped, she snatched the lapel of the robe and dragged it back over her shoulder.

"I think you should leave, Allister." He could tell that it took all her energy to maintain what little control there was left in her voice.

"Stevie, please, you have to believe me. I—"

"Now, Allister. Or God help me, I don't know what I'm going to do."

"Stevie—"

"No, Allister. Just go!"

He never would have expected the fierceness that flattened her voice or the anger that darkened her face.

But he'd also heard the desperation in his own voice, and that was when his pride kicked in. Even with Michelle, he hadn't begged the way he had with Stevie just now.

He turned from her, crossing the bedroom to gather his clothes. As he dressed, he watched her, still wedged in the corner, her arms wrapped around herself.

Oh, yes, he'd been here before. Remembered it like it was yesterday. When everyone in his life believed him guilty, he'd turned to Michelle. To her, he'd pleaded his innocence, but in the end even she'd doubted him.

Allister finished dressing and moved to the door. He stopped in front of Stevie. But there was no convincing her now. He could see her distrust, as surely as if she'd lowered the gavel and passed her own verdict.

"You know," he said finally, his words sharpened by a reawakened and savage bitterness, "I actually thought you were different, Stevie. But this is just like before. You're just like everyone else. You've played judge and jury all in one before you've even bothered to hear my side of the story. Before you even heard the truth."

She said nothing for a moment, just clenched her jaw. And Allister didn't doubt, given her dark anger, that if Stevie could see him right now, she would have hit him.

"But you never gave me the truth, Allister," she said at last, her voice a fierce whisper. "You never trusted *me* enough to give *me* the truth."

"STEVIE?"

She'd heard the front door slam, followed by Paige's footsteps on the stairs and through the apartment.

"Stevie?"

She wasn't sure how long she'd been sitting there—ten minutes or ten hours. It was all the same to her. Shortly after she'd heard Allister leave, she'd stumbled, in a haze of disbelief, across the room to the bed.

The sheets had cooled, but still, she could smell him. On the sheets and on her skin. Traces of his intoxicating male scent mingled with his cologne, toying with her emotions until she was torn between clinging to the sweet memories of their lovemaking and showering every last trace of him, every lie, from her body.

"Stevie?" Paige crossed the room, and the bed shifted as she sat next to her. "Stevie, are you all right?"

She couldn't answer. If she tried to speak now, she knew her words would be lost in a flood of tears. Instead, she held her hands in her lap, trying to stop them from shaking.

"What's the matter, honey?" Paige asked again. "Tell me what happened."

Paige's arm circled her shoulder, and she guided Stevie into her embrace. She should be strong, Stevie thought as she welcomed Paige's comfort. She shouldn't give in to her emotions. After all, it was her emotions that had gotten her into this mess.

"Stevie, why don't you tell me?"

Still she couldn't bring herself to speak.

"Honey? Allister told me you were upset, but—"

"You spoke with Allister?" Every muscle in her body stiffened as she drew away from Paige's embrace.

"He called me fifteen minutes ago. I came over here right away."

Stevie got up from the bed. Anger and betrayal were her strength now; in fact, if there had been anything within reach, she was sure she would have thrown it.

"It was him, Paige. At the warehouse that night. The man who attacked me."

"Stevie . . . what are you saying?"

"His scar, Paige. You never told me about his scar."

"Why would I?"

She balled her hands into fists and shifted her weight from one foot to the other, wishing she could pace but knowing she'd only stumble and break things.

Paige caught her hand and tried to calm her.

"Honey, look, are you sure about this?"

"I saw his scar, Paige, that night, on the catwalk, before I blacked out. And then this morning, I felt it."

"But maybe—"

"Paige, it was *him*. He admitted it." She was shaking with rage, and Paige obviously saw it because she stood up, as well. She clasped both of Stevie's hands in her own.

"Listen, honey, why don't you take a shower and get dressed. We can talk about this over coffee."

She gave her hands an encouraging squeeze and at last Stevie nodded. Paige was right. A shower would clear her head.

"I'll go start a pot. I'll be just in the kitchen if you need me."

Stevie heard Paige leave the room, heard the soothing kitchen sounds. She slipped her hands into the pockets of her robe and turned toward the bed. She took a deep shuddering breath. Again there was the smell of Allister, the smell of their lovemaking.

And then, as Stevie felt the first hot tears against her cheeks, she began to rip the sheets from the bed.

"HE LEFT YOU half the business, Al," Barb said across the long-distance line from Baltimore. "He wanted you to run it."

But Allister was only partly aware of what she was telling him. Through his living-room window, he watched a new snowfall sparkle and float along the shaft of light from the lamp across the street. It was late, almost ten, and the street outside his apartment building was quiet. A cab drove by. A man, his face circled by a halo of vapor, walked his schnauzer.

Allister looked again to the falling snow, mesmerized by its peacefulness.

"Allister? Are you still there?"

"Yeah, I'm here."

"Gary's lawyer is handling the paperwork. He should be contacting me soon. So, how's Stevie doing? Have you seen her?"

"Uh, yeah, Barb. Yeah, I've seen her. She's...holding up."

What else could he have told Barb? The truth? That the last time he saw Stevie she'd been scared to death of him, that she would probably never speak to him again, and *Oh yeah, by the way, Barb, did I happen to mention that I was the one who blinded her?*

"So there hasn't been any change at all?"

"No, not yet. The doctor thinks it could still take some time."

"Maybe I should give her a call this weekend."

"She'd probably like to hear from you," he said, but Barb obviously sensed his distractedness.

"Al, are you all right?"

He turned away from the window. "Yeah, I just... have a lot on my mind. I'm sorry. How are you doing?"

There was slight hesitation before she answered. "I'm fine, Allister. I think coming here was the right thing."

"That's good, Barb. I'm glad."

"I've already found a building for my new practice, and my brother and I looked at a couple of houses today." There was another pause, followed by a soft crackle over the line, and then Barb said, "I'm not sure when I'll be back, Al. Packing up the house, Gary's things... I'm not sure I'm ready for that yet."

"No one's expecting you to be."

"I miss him, Allister," she said, and this time her voice was so low he didn't doubt she was holding back tears.

"I know you do, Barb." He wondered if she was standing alone in the dark the way he was now, with only her memories for company.

"Even with our marriage falling apart the way it had been the past few months, I always loved Gary."

"And he loved you, Barb." He wanted to tell her then about Gary's dying words and his love for her in spite of the divorce.

Allister took a deep breath and his grip tightened around the receiver. Yes, he would tell Barb. But not now, not over the phone.

"Did you want me to do anything about the house?" he asked, needing to distract himself.

"No, Al, thanks. You've done so much already—taking care of the business and all the arrangements. No, I have to deal with the house myself. I'll try to come back in a couple of weeks. By then the lawyer should have things in order. You'll be sure to call me if anything comes up, won't you?"

"I will, Barb."

"Well, it's late. I should probably let you go. If you see Stevie, please give her my best. I'll try to reach her this weekend. Take care, Al."

"You, too, Barb."

When he hung up, Allister turned again to the window, watching the shimmer of snow. Gary had left him half the business. He should have figured Gary would do something like that. But with everything going on—Bainbridge, the coins, the police and now Stevie—Allister couldn't help wondering if he really wanted the business, if he even wanted to stay in Danby.

There were too many memories in this city—bad memories. And without Stevie, there was nothing holding him here. At this point, the best thing he could do was go to the bank tomorrow, get the coins and go straight to Bainbridge with them. Stevie would be safe then, and that was the only thing that mattered anymore.

Knowing that Bainbridge would be satisfied with the return of his package and that he wouldn't go after Stevie, Allister could leave Danby for good. He could start over.

Or maybe not. There was Devane's investigation into Gary's murder. Leaving Danby might not be that easy.

And now, Stevie remembered him as her attacker. Still, even though she might never trust him again, Allister doubted she would go to the police. Through her fear this morning, he'd seen a glimmer of uncertainty. She may have heard only half of what he said, she may have been terrified, but Allister was sure that at least a small part of her believed him when he'd told her he hadn't killed Gary. And he could only hope that small part would keep Stevie from turning him in.

Perhaps he should have confessed to Stevie the other day when she first remembered the scar. Before they'd slept together. Maybe then the shock wouldn't have been so devastating. And maybe he wouldn't have hurt her so much.

But even then, she probably would have believed that the only reason he'd gotten involved with her was for the coins and the evidence he needed against Bainbridge. Or worse, that he'd gotten close to her simply to keep her from placing him at Gary's murder that night. In hindsight, he regretted almost every decision he'd made, yet he could not think of one thing he could have done differently.

At least Paige was with Stevie now. He was thankful for that. He'd called Paige this morning on his cellular while sitting in Stevie's Volvo outside the studio. He hadn't told Paige much, just that Stevie was upset and needed her. It had been enough, though—Paige was there in fifteen minutes. She told him to take Stevie's car, that he could return it later.

And when he'd called the studio this afternoon, he'd been somewhat relieved to get Paige on the phone, instead of Stevie. Within seconds she'd launched into whispered questions, and he'd known that Stevie had been in the other room. So once again Allister had attempted to explain what had happened, even though he doubted it would do any good.

Paige might believe him, but then it wasn't Paige he'd hurt. And Stevie, well, she was not about to believe anyone, even Paige, until she was good and ready.

Looking past the street lamp, Allister gazed out across Danby. Somewhere, on the other side of that sea of lights, was Stevie. As he remembered the feel of her body against his, as he remembered the intimacy they'd shared last night, Allister wondered if she would ever come to forgive him. He wondered if time could heal this terrible wound.

Allister held little faith in either possibility.

STEVIE HADN'T FELT like eating, so Paige hadn't pushed dinner on her. What Paige *had* done however, was keep Stevie busy most of the day with odd jobs around the studio, as though this might have kept her mind off of Allister.

It hadn't. Even now, with the stereo pouring out the final act of *La Traviata*, Stevie could hear nothing but Allister's words.

She hadn't heard Paige come into the living room, and when she felt a hand on her arm, she jumped. Paige took the stereo's remote from Stevie's hands and turned down the volume, then joined her on the couch.

"How are you doing?" she asked, giving Stevie's shoulder a light rub.

Stevie shrugged and forced a smile for her friend's benefit.

"You don't believe he did it, do you, Stevie?"

But Stevie didn't answer.

"Stevie, you couldn't be more wrong about Allister. Surely you know him well enough to realize he's not capable of something like that. Gary was his best friend."

Still she didn't answer. She hoped Paige would drop the subject. But she wasn't so lucky.

"Stevie, listen to me, do you think Allister would have driven you to the hospital that night if he—"

"Paige, I know he didn't kill Gary."

All day she'd been remembering Allister's words from this morning. But they were all jumbled in her mind because she hadn't really heard half of them. Panic had overridden reason. She couldn't say that she'd actually feared for her life, but she had been terrified. And it was that terror that had deafened her to his words.

Still, she'd known he hadn't killed Gary. But it wasn't Allister's innocence she questioned now.

"I trusted him, Paige," she said finally. "But everything was one lie after the next. From the very beginning."

"What was he supposed to do, Stevie? Have you thought about that?"

Stevie turned away from Paige as she let out a long breath of frustration. The fact was, she'd thought about nothing else.

"Would you have believed him if he'd told you everything the first time you met?"

Stevie shrugged again.

"Allister did the only thing he could, honey. He stayed with you to protect you, because he knew the potential danger you were in. He stayed because he cares about you."

"No, Paige, he stayed because of the coins. He knew I was the link to them. Gary told him that. Allister needed me to get the coins so he could have his evidence against Bainbridge. He used me, Paige."

"I think you're wrong, Stevie. And I think you know you're wrong. The truth is Allister cares about you."

The truth.

What did Paige know about the truth? What did she herself know about the truth? After all the lies and deceit, how was she to know *what* was truth anymore?

She remembered Allister's parting words—something about her playing judge and jury before hearing the truth, something about her being no different from people in his past. And she recalled the first evening they'd spent together, after the break-in, when he'd taken her to his place. Allister had told her about his past, and she'd heard the bitterness in his voice.

It was the same bitterness she'd heard this morning.

Stevie felt a twinge of guilt for not having let Allister explain everything then. But it didn't really matter what his explanations were; the point was, he'd used her to get the coins. He'd lied to her.

Well, now he had his damned coins. And she wouldn't have to see him again.

"He loves you, Stevie," Paige said now.

Stevie had known it was Allister on the other end of the line earlier today when Paige had spoken in hushed tones, and she wondered just how much he had told Paige.

"No matter what you think and no matter why he got involved with you, honey, Allister loves you."

Stevie shook her head. "Do you hear what you're saying, Paige? You're talking about a man who doesn't even *know* me. All he's known is this . . . this blind person. How can he, all of a sudden, love me?"

"Stevie, you—"

"No, Paige, really, just think about it. I mean, what was going through my head, anyway? Getting involved with some guy I've only just met. I haven't even *seen* him, for crying out loud."

"Come on, Stevie, I think you know in your heart that you don't need to *see* someone to fall in love with them."

"I didn't say I was in love with Allister."

"No, you didn't say it, but you are. You know you are. I think you understood what you were doing from the moment you met him, that what you were feeling for him wasn't wrong. You didn't need to see him."

"Actually—" a defeated smile struggled to Stevie's lips "—that's the irony of it right there, isn't it, Paige? In this case, I *did* need to see him."

For a long time Paige said nothing. Only when Stevie got up from the couch minutes later and fumbled through the CD rack did Paige finally speak again.

"Well, I'm not sure about you, but I'm starving."

Stevie nodded. She pulled a CD from the rack and held it up for Paige to identify for her.

"*Madama Butterfly*," she informed her, and Stevie opened the plastic case. "But you're not going to put that on, are you? Come on, Stevie, I think I've had all the opera I can stand for one night."

"Fine, I'll turn it off as soon as you get back."

"Back? From where?"

"From the Mei King. Didn't you say you were hungry?" She shot Paige a smile.

"Oh, right. Hey, Stevie, would you like Chinese tonight?" Paige was already getting her coat, continuing her own conversation in parody. "Gosh, Paige, what a great idea. And since you're such a wonderful kind caring person, would you mind terribly going out in the cold to pick it up? Not at all, Stevie. For you, anything."

"Thanks, Paige," she called out, as she heard Paige start down the stairs.

"I'll be ten minutes," Paige shouted back. "And whatever you do, don't sing along with Pavarotti or whoever it is this time, okay? I think you're scaring the neighbors."

Stevie hit the play button, and only seconds into the opening act, Paige was at the front door.

She was still standing by the stereo moments later when she heard the door again.

"Did you forget your wallet?" she shouted.

But there was no answer. Stevie turned down the volume and crossed the living room to the landing of the stairs.

"Paige?"

Silence. Stevie felt a wave of dread prickle along her skin. She ran her hand along the wall parallel to the landing, feeling for the security system's control panel. Her fingers fluttered over the keys until she found the activate button.

When she pressed it, she should have been rewarded with a single beep indicating that the system was already activated. But instead, there were two short beeps.

Paige wouldn't have forgotten to turn on the alarm—she'd been fanatical about the security system from the moment it had been installed.

Stevie backed away from the stairs and was about to call Paige's name again when she heard a muffled thud.

CHAPTER FOURTEEN

THROUGH THE POUNDING silence of the studio, Stevie strained to hear something, any noise at all that she might have been able to identify. She hoped it was only Tiny downstairs. But now there was another sound—slow and deliberate, like something being dragged across the floor. It was not Tiny.

Someone was in the studio.

She stumbled toward the kitchen. With her heart hammering in her ears, Stevie couldn't be certain if she'd heard footfalls in the studio or maybe even on the stairs. The apartment seemed to take on a life of its own: breathing around her, whispering its secrets in unfamiliar creaks and bumps.

On the wall next to the fridge, she found the fuse box. In seconds, she flung it open and grappled for the main breaker. There was a satisfying click.

She had to hide.

No, she had to get to the phone. The bedroom was closest.

She'd call the police. They'd get here, just like before, she told herself.

She was about to step out of the kitchen when she stopped. Adrenaline pumped through her as she brushed her hands across the counter. Her fingers were shaking almost uncontrollably, trembling along over the smooth tiles. And then she found the wooden knife block.

Closing her fingers over the largest handle, Stevie drew out the wide-blade butcher's knife. The cool grip against her sweaty palm fed her new determination.

But when at last she did step out of the kitchen, her left hand sweeping the air in front of her, Stevie was struck with a terrifying thought and she froze.

What if the intruder was already upstairs in the apartment? What if he was watching her now? Standing maybe five feet away?

She listened again. But all she could hear were her own shallow, rapid breaths. She could feel her blood coursing through her veins, pounding in her head.

No, she couldn't let her fear paralyze her. She had to keep moving.

The knife handle slipped in her sweaty grip. She switched it to her other hand, wiped her palm against her jeans and clutched it again. This time when she searched the darkness in front of her, she used the knife, as well.

In moments that felt like hours, Stevie reached the bedroom door. Behind her, in the apartment, she thought she heard footsteps, quiet and cautious, but she couldn't be sure if it was only her fear playing tricks on her mind. She crossed the bedroom to the nightstand and lowered herself to the floor. Even as she pulled the phone onto her lap, Stevie wondered if the blinds were drawn, or if the street lamp outside illuminated the room.

Like before the dial tone seemed to shriek its presence. She laid the knife down next to her and covered the earpiece.

But even as her finger trembled over the nine, Stevie smelled the cheap after-shave, sharp and pungent.

There was the quiet brush of slick fabric.

And then a voice that sounded like death itself. "Not this time, you don't," it said.

In an instant Stevie felt a rush of air and the phone was torn from her hands. There was a loud clatter on the other side of the room—the phone smashing against the opposite wall.

A scream started deep down in her chest and clawed its way to the top of her throat. But she swallowed it. She had to be strong. She could not let this man see her fear. Besides, there was no one to hear her.

Yet another part of her wanted to give in then. To let this nightmare run its course. *Don't fight it,* a small voice in her head whispered. *You're blind. You can't possibly win.*

And then Stevie remembered Gary.

No! She was not going to end up like Gary.

Her right hand groped the floor beside her, and with her last remnant of hope, she seized the knife.

He was standing over her. She could hear him breathe. He was just staring at her. She was certain of it. She was also certain it was too dark for him to see the knife.

"So, you gonna make this easy on yourself?" he asked.

The assuredness in his voice alone threatened to immobilize her, and Stevie bit down hard on her bottom lip to stop from crying out. The knife handle burned in her palm.

"Choice is yours, sweetheart," he said.

And then he reached for her. The air churned in his wake, thick with the stench of his after-shave.

It was then that Stevie lunged at him. She swung the big blade through the air, and she heard her own gasp along with his when she felt it strike.

"Son of a..."

He staggered back, cursing.

In an instant Stevie was moving. Still gripping the knife, she scrambled across the floor, away from him.

This time when she felt his hands on her, Stevie did scream. Like vices, his fingers clamped around her ankles, dragging her back. Dragging her toward him. She kicked and thrashed. With her left hand she groped for anything to hang on to, anything to give her a hold.

The throw rug bunched up beneath her, and she floundered against the bare hardwood. And when she'd managed to tear one ankle free, she kicked out. She heard a low grunt. The kick had obviously been well placed. She only regretted that it hadn't been harder.

In seconds he was after her again. He grabbed the waist of her jeans and almost lifted her right off the floor. Savagely he flung her over, but this time he was ready for the knife. When Stevie lashed out at him, he caught her wrist in his iron grip, which Stevie was sure would snap every bone. The knife fell uselessly to the floor, skittering across the boards.

He straddled her then, pinning her arms with his knees. And still Stevie fought him.

It was when he forced the damp cloth over her face, when she breathed in the sickeningly sweet stringent odor, that Stevie at last comprehended her defeat. She tried to hold her breath, gagging against the fumes, but it was impossible. Her throat burned. Desperately she tried to turn her head from the cloying smell, but he held her tighter still, pressing her head back against the floor.

When his knee slipped and her arm was freed, Stevie thought she would tear at his face. But she couldn't even lift her arm. She heard her own cry muffled against the brute force of his hand. And she thought she saw lights—flickering splinters exploding in front of her—and guessed they were the effect of the solution on the cloth.

Then, as she felt her body slacken, as her consciousness gradually bled away, Stevie's last thought was of Allister. His name whispered through her mind in a final desperate prayer.

VINCE FENTON stood over the woman. She was out at last.

He left the cloth draped across her face. He wanted to be sure she inhaled enough ether to keep her unconscious for a while. After the struggle she'd put up, he wasn't going to risk her coming to in the back seat of his car.

He hadn't expected her to put up such a fight, being blind and all. And he cursed her again when he drew off his blood-soaked glove. He turned his hand to catch the light from the street lamp outside. It glistened a dark crimson, and he could see the long gash the tip of the knife had carved through the thin leather and across his skin. He was damned lucky, though. If he hadn't seen the glint of the blade in that split second and pulled back, she might have really got him.

Still, he was bleeding pretty heavily. From his pocket he took out an extra strip of cloth and wound it tightly around his hand.

He looked at the Falcioni woman again. Yeah, she was a feisty one. A real handful. And if her kick hadn't been so well placed, catching him square in the groin and temporarily knocking the wind out of him, he would have almost enjoyed her little struggle. He liked a good fight.

Not like her friend downstairs. The other woman had almost been too easy. Sure, he'd had to time it exactly right, grabbing her before she could activate the alarm system. But that had been the only challenge.

Through the uncovered windows of the studio, Vince had seen the other woman come down the stairs with her coat on and had known he'd have to make his move. He'd waited at the door, and when she opened it, he grabbed her before she could even scream. It had been a while since he'd felt that kind of rush.

In the end, though, she'd been disappointingly easy.

But Falcioni... He squatted next to her, removed the ether-soaked cloth and tucked it into his coat pocket. He had to admit, he admired her spunk. In fact, he almost liked her for it.

And Vince Fenton smiled to himself as he lifted her from the floor.

AT BARELY EIGHT in the morning, Allister steered Stevie's Volvo into the short driveway of the Images studio. He knew it was early, but he hadn't been able to sleep. All night he'd lain awake watching the headlights of cars in the street outside sweep across his ceiling. And he'd thought about Stevie.

He must have come up with a dozen different scripts in his head—things he might say to her to explain his actions, to apologize, to try to make her understand. But none of them would work, he'd decided by six-thirty.

He'd gotten up, showered and phoned the car rental agency to make arrangements for a pickup at Images. He'd call once he got there, he said, and something told him he'd be placing that call very soon after his arrival. He didn't count on receiving any invitations for coffee this time.

Parking beside Paige's Tercel, Allister was comforted by the fact that they'd stayed at Stevie's. He'd half feared that Stevie might have convinced Paige to take her to Paige's apartment downtown, to get away from the studio and the memories of him. But he was glad Stevie hadn't forgone safety for emotions.

With any luck, he thought as he walked up to the front door, Paige would answer. He could give her the keys to the Volvo and avoid Stevie altogether. It would be best for both of them.

Allister knocked.

And if it was Stevie who answered? He wasn't sure what he'd say to her.

He knocked again, a bit louder this time. Maybe they weren't up yet.

The neon Images sign was off, Allister noticed then, and he wondered if the power was down, if something was wrong, but then he heard movement on the other side of the door.

Someone was coming into the front hall, and then he heard a muffled crash. It had to be Stevie.

Just like that first time he'd come to see her, Allister recalled. He felt a tug in his chest when he remembered the way Stevie had greeted him at the door, her sense of humor, her laughter, the smile that had lit her face.

There wouldn't be a smile greeting him today, he could be sure of that.

But when the door opened at last, it wasn't Stevie.

"Paige?" He must have sounded disappointed, Allister thought. She didn't smile.

"Allister." Her voice was barely a whisper. She looked at him, squinting against the morning light, and held a hand to her forehead. Her face was pale and drawn.

He brushed past her through the door, and when he turned to look at Paige again, she sagged against the wall, one hand clutching her stomach.

"Rough night?" he asked, wondering what the two of them could possibly have been drinking to make Paige look so ill.

And then her knees buckled. Allister rushed to her side, catching her halfway down the wall.

"Whoa, Paige." He helped her up, holding her for a moment as she swayed slightly. She seemed to gather herself, but still she maintained a grip on Allister's arm. "Paige, what's the matter?"

"I . . . I think I'm going to be sick."

No more words were needed. As quickly as he could, Allister helped her to the studio washroom. But once there, she barely had the strength to throw up. When eventually she staggered to her feet, he handed her a towel and put an arm around her shoulders to steady her.

"Feel any better?"

She nodded weakly, but he could see she was still woozy and disoriented.

"Are you sure, Paige?"

"I don't . . . I don't know, Allister."

Allister couldn't tell what it was about Paige that was so unsettling. Maybe it was her expression, but he knew something was wrong. Terribly wrong. This wasn't a hangover from too much alcohol. Paige had been drugged.

Panic coursed through him.

"Paige, where's Stevie?"

She shook her head, a feeble motion he feared might make her sick again.

"Paige—" he took her by the shoulders "—where's Stevie?"

But he didn't wait for an answer.

"Stevie!" His voice exploded through the hollow studio as he barreled up the stairs, his boots hammering on every second step. "Stevie!"

Terror seized him. It snatched his breath, pounded in his head.

"Stevie!"

He charged through the living room, the kitchen and then into the hallway, dread clutching at his heart as each stride took him closer to something he did not want to know.

And when he rushed to the bedroom, stopping at last in the doorway, a tormented cry twisted up from his gut.

The throw rug was crumpled in the middle of the room. The phone had been ripped from the wall and hurled against the far wall. It had hit a table lamp; the porcelain base lay in shards on the floor along with the phone. And there was a knife, its blade gleaming against the hardwood floor.

But what horrified him most was the blood.

It wasn't a lot, but it was enough, its dark crimson trail a vivid blueprint of the violent struggle that had taken place.

She'd been utterly defenseless, Allister kept thinking over and over as he stood transfixed in the doorway. She couldn't see her attacker. She couldn't even protect herself. She'd been all alone. The terror she must have gone through...

Paige was behind him all of a sudden, pushing past Allister.

"Oh, my God," she cried, teetering slightly. "Oh, my God! She's gone, isn't she? Stevie's gone?"

Paige turned to him then, her face a visage of shock, as she crumpled into his arms with a sob. And Allister held her. He held her because she needed to be held, but mostly he held her because he didn't know what else to do.

STEVIE AWOKE to pain, a heavy, persistent pounding in her head that made her think of the hospital. And for a moment that was where she imagined she was. But it wasn't the sterile odor of starched sheets and antiseptic that reached her nostrils. Instead, it was a peculiar stale mustiness, and the wool blanket that scratched her cheek smelled of dust and mothballs.

This wasn't the hospital.

And then she remembered.

Stevie lay still, afraid to move, afraid he was next to her, watching, waiting for her to wake. She kept her eyes shut, listening to the noises around her, hoping for any sound that might give a clue as to where she was.

She could hear birds—pigeons, she was certain—a flurry of wings outside a window and then a soft cooing. Beyond that, there was the wail of a train whistle. It didn't sound too far-off, and Stevie thought about the abandoned factories and storehouses along the tracks at the south end of Danby.

More immediate than the pigeons and the train, however, was a low constant thumping and a high-pitched whine like metal on metal—old and rusted. She imagined an exhaust vent, one of those big-bladed fans, turning lazily in a draft.

But there was nothing else.

Stevie risked moving then, surprised she wasn't tied or restrained. She was stiff, though. Every muscle screamed in protest as she shifted on the hard mattress.

She remembered the struggle. Pain rippled through her joints, and she felt as if she had a million bruises. Her hip throbbed when she rolled her weight onto it. With a major effort, she sat up. She drew her knees into the circle of her arms, feeling still more aches and pains, and when she brushed a hand across her face, she was sure one cheek bore a nasty bruise.

But most of all, her head hurt. And then her stomach lurched with nausea.

The cloth. He'd held it to her face, and there had been fumes. Whatever it had been, it made her sick now. She swallowed, containing it. She wanted water.

The room was hot and the air stale. The cotton T-shirt she wore under her sweater was damp against her back, and wet strands of hair clung to her neck and forehead. She brushed them away, the simple movement making her dizzy.

Stevie rubbed her forehead and opened her eyes. A blurred square of light flashed before her. It was the after-effects, she tried to reason, from the fumes on the cloth he'd held over her face. Whatever he'd used was causing these flickers of light. Just like the ones she'd seen before she'd blacked out last night.

She blinked. The light was still there. She turned her head from side to side, fighting down the nausea, but the dim square remained, fixed in space. She looked directly at it and blinked again.

She lifted a hand and passed it before her eyes. A blurred shadow moved across the square of light. Her hand. She could *see* the shadow of her hand.

A thin whimper of excitement escaped her lips.

Dr. Sterling had said it would happen like this. He'd told her that when her vision returned she would distinguish light and shadow first, then movement. And gradually, he'd promised, she would regain more focus. The process could take a matter of hours—ten to twelve, he'd said.

And then, as Stevie stared at the light she guessed to be a window, the bittersweetness of this sudden breakthrough hit home. Yes, she was regaining her sight, but did that even matter now? Would she live to appreciate it?

She had little doubt that it was Vince Fenton who had broken into her apartment last night, who had savagely attacked her and then dragged her off to this airless hideaway. And she had no doubt he was here now.

Since she wasn't bound, Stevie could only guess she was locked in a sort of storage room. Fenton had to be just outside, or at least within earshot.

Memories of her violent struggle with him last night churned in her mind. And with a jolt of sickening realization, Stevie thought of Paige.

Paige would not have neglected to activate the security system. Fenton must have gotten into the studio just as Paige was leaving.

A hot terror gripped Stevie. Fenton must have jumped Paige. It was the only way he could have bypassed the alarm. He must have attacked her at the door.

What had he done to her?

Fear sent another shudder of nausea through Stevie. She'd seen the violence Fenton was capable of. What if Paige was injured? What if she was back at the studio and no one knew she was hurt?

Or maybe it was even worse than that. Maybe—

No, she would not consider that possibility.

She swung her legs over the side of the mattress. She had to do something. She wasn't sure what, but she couldn't just sit here.

She swept her hands across the black shadows around her until her wrist struck something hard and sharp. Pain shot up her arm, and there was a resounding crash.

Within moments there were footsteps—boots heavy against creaking floorboards. Stevie's heart stopped. There was the slide of a metal bolt and the unmistakable squeal of hinges.

And then his voice, cold and rough, the same as last night, sent a chill through her.

"So, you're awake," he said, and she heard him take a step toward her.

"THINK, PAIGE. You've got to try and remember everything that happened last night," Allister urged. He'd had to physically drag her, drag himself, out of the bedroom, away from the horror of what had taken place there only hours ago.

"I don't remember, Allister." Her voice trembled. She was on the verge of tears. He handed her a cup of instant coffee, hoping to snap her out of her grogginess.

"Come on, Paige."

She drew a long shaky breath. "Uh ... I was going out to get some dinner. We were hungry and—"

"What time?"

She shrugged. "I'm...not sure. It was late. Ten, I guess. Maybe later. Stevie wanted Chinese, so I agreed to go to the takeout place around the corner. I was going to be fifteen minutes, Allister. Fifteen minutes. I didn't think anything of leaving her, because of the alarm system."

She shook her head. He had guided her to one of the stools, and she sat there now, wringing her hands on top of the kitchen bar.

"I should have taken her with me," she said. "I wanted to, you know? But Stevie...she looked so tired. Still, I should have forced her. I should have made her come along."

He placed a hand over hers. "It wouldn't have made any difference, Paige."

Even here in the kitchen, away from the dreadful evidence of Stevie's struggle in the other room, Allister could not let go of the images that lay back there. Every time he blinked, he saw the blood.

"Paige, do you remember seeing him? Did you get a look at his face?"

She glanced at Allister and then back at her hands again. "No. I didn't see anything. He came out of nowhere. He was there the second I opened the door. Like he'd been waiting for me."

It had to have been Fenton, Allister thought. And that was what frightened him the most. He'd seen Fenton's handiwork in Gary's office. He'd seen Gary. Allister's throat tightened at the thought of those same hands on Stevie.

"I...I tried to warn her," Paige was saying. "To call out. But he clamped a hand over my mouth. A cloth. It was a cloth soaked in something. And the fumes—that's the last thing I remember before I woke up on the floor downstairs."

He'd used chloroform, Allister figured, or maybe ether. And he must have used the same on Stevie. But why the blood then? Why the knife?

Fenton could have walked right up to Stevie, overpowered her the same way he had done with Paige. Easier even. Unless... unless Stevie had struggled.

And of course she would have. Allister didn't doubt that. She must have put up a damned good fight, considering the state of the room. And Allister had to wrestle down a hot rage as he imagined the attack, as he wondered what must have been going through her mind in those last frantic moments.

He looked across at Paige. A trace of color had returned to her face, but her expression was still drawn with fear and dread. Even though there was nothing Paige could have done, she blamed herself.

But if anyone, he was to blame. It was his fault Stevie was gone. He should have stayed. He should have parked outside all night, knowing that Bainbridge would make his move as soon as Stevie was alone.

"I'm phoning the police." Paige dropped from her stool. "I'm going to call Devane and—"

"No, Paige. You can't."

"What are you talking about, Allister?" she shrieked, her grogginess vanished. "Stevie's gone!"

"Paige, listen, you can't call Devane. It's Bainbridge who's got Stevie. He wants the coins, Paige. He's—"

"I don't give a shit about your damned coins! Or whatever vendetta you've got against Bainbridge. Stevie's gone, Allister! That's her blood all over the floor in the other room there, and if you think I'm just going to—"

"Paige." He reached out and caught her arm. She was on the verge of tears. "Listen to me."

"No, Allister!" She tore free from his grasp and started for the phone. "That's my best friend out there!"

He was after her like a shot. "Paige!"

But she wasn't listening. She stormed through the room. And when he tried to grab her arm again, she jerked away from him, snatching the phone.

"Paige, please!"

She ignored him. Only when Allister yanked the receiver from her hands did she turn on him, a combination of desperation and fury in her eyes.

"Paige—" he glared back at her, the phone clutched to his chest "—she may be your best friend, but she's the woman I love."

Fresh tears trailed down her face.

"And I'm not letting some two-bit dick like Devane jeopardize her life," he continued. "Now listen to me. We have to think this through, okay? We have to deal with Bainbridge *his* way. As long as he has Stevie, we have to play by his rules, not Devane's."

Allister returned the phone to the side table, his eyes never leaving Paige's. He wasn't sure if he should hold her now or give her space.

Finally she broke the silence. "So what do you propose we do?"

"First off, I have to contact Bainbridge. I'm sure he's expecting my call. And *then* we decide whether we can afford to go the police. All right?"

Her nod was barely perceptible, and he felt compelled to give her hand an encouraging squeeze, even though he himself felt the same anxious fear Paige so obviously did.

As he looked up Bainbridge's number in the Danby directory, he thought about Gary's recording equipment he'd left back in the warehouse. The phone call he was about to place to Bainbridge would be the perfect opportunity to get the evidence he needed against the man. But that wasn't important now, Allister realized as his finger trailed down the *B*'s.

Stevie was all that mattered. He had to get Stevie away from Bainbridge. At whatever cost.

CHAPTER FIFTEEN

BAINBRIDGE PICKED UP on the sixth ring. Allister couldn't help wondering if the man had let it ring just to toy with him, knowing it would be him calling.

He recognized the collector's pompous tone instantly.

"What the hell have you done with her, Bainbridge?"

"Ah, Mr. Quaid. It's been a *long* time. Have you been well?"

"Where is she?"

There was an extended sigh over the line. "Still as hotheaded as I remember you. I guess *time* hasn't changed that, hmm?"

Allister caught the double meaning and bit down his rage. Paige was beside him. She placed a hand on his shoulder as though sensing the need for calm.

"Well, I've been expecting your call, Mr. Quaid."

"I'm sure you have."

"Seems to me we've got some merchandise to exchange. Do I need to be more specific?"

"Just tell me where."

"You remember my estate?"

"Sure, I remember. But if you think I'm coming out there, you must really take me for stupid."

There was a pause. "All right then. Where would you suggest we meet?"

"The warehouse," Allister proposed, mainly because he couldn't think of anyplace else offhand.

"I don't think that would be a good idea. I tell you what, Mr. Quaid, why don't we just say that I'll call you at seven tonight and let you know then, hmm? I trust you won't have any trouble putting your hands on the merchandise by that time?"

"Why wait, Bainbridge? I can have your 'merchandise' within the hour. Let's get this over with." The thought of Stevie's being in Bainbridge's clutches a moment longer sent a shudder of rage through him. He could hear the desperation in his voice and knew he was playing right into Bainbridge's hands.

"No, Mr. Quaid, I think this evening would suit me much better."

"Then let me talk to her. I want to know she's all right."

"That isn't possible at the moment."

"Look, you son of a bitch, if you don't let me talk to Stevie right now—"

"I'm sorry, Mr. Quaid, but you'll just have to take my word for it that... your merchandise is in good condition."

"Your *word?* You think your word means anything to me, Bainbridge?"

Paige squeezed his shoulder, harder this time, and Allister clenched his fist.

"Well, I'm afraid my word is about all you're going to get for now, Mr. Quaid. Besides, you don't actually think I'd be foolish enough to have the goods here, do you?"

Allister didn't respond.

"Fine. I'm glad we finally understand each other. So where is it I should call you this evening? At your girlfriend's studio?"

Allister remained silent, and Bainbridge must have taken it as a yes.

"Fine," he said again. "And another thing, Mr. Quaid, I don't expect company, if you know what I mean. If there are any uninvited visitors...well, I don't think I have to spell it out for you, do I? I'm sure I've made myself clear."

BAINBRIDGE HUNG UP and looked out the window, squinting into the glare of sun-drenched snow. It shouldn't have come to this, he kept thinking. This whole situation was rapidly getting out of hand. If it wasn't for the fact that he had everything riding on those damned coins, he'd almost consider cutting his losses and letting it go.

But he needed this deal. He needed the coins. Once he delivered them to his buyer, maybe he'd even sell the estate. Get out of Danby. The Riviera had always had a certain appeal to him. Besides, he was getting too old for these New England winters.

Yes, the south of France would be good. As soon as he got the coins from Quaid, he'd start to make the arrangements. In fact, he'd start today. He'd probably have to move quickly after tonight's rendezvous.

Well, at least he wouldn't have to worry about Quaid's going to the police, Bainbridge thought as he lifted the receiver again and dialed the number to his antiques storehouse. If Quaid had any kind of faith in the authorities, he would have gone to them long ago. Even so, Bainbridge would rest a lot easier if he'd still had his contact on the force.

The lieutenant had been essential six years ago when he'd needed the gems planted in Quaid's car. But the man had taken an early retirement and moved to Florida on the money Bainbridge had paid him over the years. Damn. He could have used the old man right now.

The line was still ringing, and Bainbridge was ready to give up when at last it was answered.

"Fenton. What the hell's going on over there?"

"Nothing."

"You need a hand? You want me to send one of the boys over?"

"No, I've got it under control."

"How's our guest?"

"She's awake."

"And you're sure you can manage her?"

"She's blind. Whaddaya think?"

"I just want to be sure there aren't any screwups, that's all."

"Relax, will ya? Everything's under control."

"Fine then. I want her ready to go by seven tonight. That won't be a problem, I trust?"

"No problem. She'll be ready."

ALLISTER PACED the length of the corridor for what had to be the hundredth time. The gray walls and grimy glass barriers, the reek of burned coffee and pine-scented floor cleaners, all hammered home too many unsettling memories. Danby's main precinct. How had he let Paige talk him into this? How could he have come back here?

He wanted out. He needed air.

He needed to think.

But then, they'd done all the thinking they could, he and Paige. It didn't matter how many times they went over the situation, or how many different ways they looked at it, the fact remained Allister couldn't handle Bainbridge. Not alone.

Things had gotten beyond his control as soon as Stevie had become involved.

Stevie.

Allister closed his eyes, but all he could see was her face. He opened them again and stared at the gray walls. Stevie was the only reason he was here at the precinct—the last place on earth he ever dreamed he'd go voluntarily.

He glanced at Paige, sitting on one of the hard-backed vinyl chairs along the side corridor where they'd been instructed to wait. Except for the anxiety that seemed permanently etched on her face, she looked marginally better. He'd even managed to talk her into eating some dry toast before they'd headed out.

She'd been tensely silent during the drive to the precinct, which had been just as well. Allister wouldn't have known what to say. Instead, he'd kept his attention on the rearview mirror. They hadn't been followed.

Paige caught his glance and smiled weakly. "It'll be okay, Allister," she murmured. "I promise you. You're doing the right thing. We'll make them understand."

He gave her a noncommittal nod and continued to pace. He felt trapped.

It wasn't just the memories of his four years behind bars. It was because as long as he was here, Stevie was out there. With Bainbridge. With Fenton. And if Devane didn't believe him today, if Allister didn't walk out of here with the detective's support and ended up behind bars, instead, Stevie's life would be in Devane's hands. Allister couldn't live with that thought.

But he'd had no other choice. From the moment he'd heard Bainbridge's voice on the phone, he'd been haunted by one numbing fear. He couldn't pinpoint whether it was something in Bainbridge's voice, or if was some kind of sixth sense, but Allister knew tonight's meeting was *not* going to be a straightforward transaction.

Bainbridge was not about to leave loose ends. And that was exactly what Allister and Stevie were to him. Bainbridge would take his coins and leave Fenton to do his cleanup work. Allister was sure of it.

If it had been just him, if Stevie hadn't been involved, he would never have come here. He would have taken care of Bainbridge himself. But Stevie's life came before everything else now, even the possibility of prison. If anything happened to her . . .

One of the doors along the corridor opened suddenly, and Allister stopped pacing. Paige was already out of her chair.

"Ms. Carpenter, Mr. Quaid," Devane greeted them with a thin smile. "You said this was urgent?"

Paige nodded. She shot a nervous glance from Allister to Devane. "It's Stevie."

The accusatory look Devane gave Allister might have deflated a lesser man on the spot, Allister knew, but he refused to bend under the detective's intimidation. He was here for Stevie. If ever there was a time to swallow his pride, this was it.

Devane led them to one of the interview rooms, barren except for a battered table and four chairs. It was every bit as bleak as Allister remembered it from that day six years ago. The blinds on the window overlooking the detective's wing were open, and Allister recognized Devane's partner behind one of the desks.

Devane pulled out a chair for Paige, offering her a coffee. She declined, and as Allister lowered himself into a chair, he was grateful she was here with him. Without her, he doubted he'd stand much chance of getting through to Devane.

The detective took a seat, as well. Allister studied him for a moment, hoping to see something there that would convince him he hadn't made a mistake in coming to Devane, in trusting him with Stevie's life. After all, how could Allister be certain that Devane wasn't working for Bainbridge?

"So, you wanna tell me what's going on?" Devane held his gaze.

Allister glanced over Devane's shoulder through the glass barrier and nodded at Detective Jackson.

"Not without your partner, Detective. I want someone else in here."

Devane let out a short grunt of a laugh. "What's the matter? You don't trust me, Quaid?"

Allister didn't have to answer the question. Devane's chair scraped back against the floor, and he opened the door.

"Jackson," he bellowed across the wing, "get in here, will ya? And bring me a coffee." When he returned to his chair, he stared at Allister. "Something tells me this is gonna to take a while."

THE BLURRED SQUARE of light had faded some time ago. Stevie prayed that evening had fallen beyond the window, and that the light she'd seen earlier hadn't been some cruel trick her vision had played on her.

She was sure Dr. Sterling had said ten to twelve hours. He'd also said something about regaining more perception once she was able to distinguish light. Yet, there had been nothing beyond that dim white square. Maybe he'd been wrong. Or maybe this was all she could expect.

Around her were nothing but shadows—blacks and grays—and dark ambiguous forms. She wanted out of this place. Out of this dusty prison.

She had been out earlier, though, briefly. Twice, Fenton had led her to a washroom down the hall. The first time he'd come in to get her, he'd gripped her arm savagely and dragged her from the bed. At the time she had no idea where he was taking her or what he planned to do. She'd balked, refusing to go anywhere until he told her where they were going.

And once she'd finished with the washroom and they were heading back to the room, Stevie had stopped him, demanding to know about Paige.

She'd heard a sick grin in his voice. "Oh, don't worry that pretty head of yours about her," he'd said.

But Stevie had stood her ground, determined not to budge until he told her. "I want to know what you did to Paige."

Finally, his hand still clamped fiercely on Stevie's arm, he'd said, "Well, lucky for your friend she didn't get a look at me. Otherwise I might have had to take care of her."

That was all Stevie had been able to get out of him. He'd shoved her down the narrow hallway and back into the room. He'd slid the bolt into place, and it was then that Stevie decided she would have to be careful not to reveal her returning vision, minimal though it was. If Fenton had even a shred of suspicion that Stevie could see him, he'd no doubt "take care" of *her.*

The second time Fenton had come to get her, hours later, Stevie could have sworn she'd been able to see more. And she'd considered her chances at making a run for it. But Fenton would have had her in a second.

Other than those two brief ventures, the rest of the day had been spent locked in the room, with nothing but the monotonous cooing of pigeons outside on the sill and the constant dull thumping of the fan blades.

She'd attempted to walk around, to stretch her stiff muscles. But when she tried to maneuver through the clutter of dusty boxes and cobwebbed furniture, each effort had resulted in another thunderous crash, and Fenton would barrel in. By the third time, he'd let out a vicious string of expletives, taken her by the shoulders and shoved her roughly onto the old mattress, warning her to stay put.

"If you don't," he'd snarled, "I'll make damned sure you do."

So Stevie had given up. She'd sat on the bed, her legs drawn up into the circle of her arms, her back against the wall. She hadn't moved. She'd wanted to cry, but didn't have the energy. She'd dozed once or twice in the same position and woken up with a stiff neck. And then she'd just sat, watching the square of light slowly fade.

The minutes had stretched into hours, the hours into a lifetime. The only hope she clung to now was Allister.

She clung to the memories of the brief happiness she'd found in his arms. But she'd thrown all that away. She'd finally found love, and now she wasn't sure it could ever be regained.

She should have listened to Allister. She should have trusted him. Now, more than ever, Stevie regretted her harsh words. She regretted fearing him as much as she had yesterday morning when she'd thrown him out of her apartment and out of her life. And she wouldn't blame him if he never forgave her for that.

Paige was right. Everything she'd said—that Allister loved her, that he'd wanted to protect her, that he couldn't have done anything else—was all true.

Twelve nights ago at the warehouse, Gary had died in Allister's arms. Stevie couldn't imagine the rage that must have seized him then. And when she'd arrived Allister had believed her to be Gary's killer returning. She would have done the same thing. She would have attacked, too. Out of defense, and out of anger.

But then Allister had taken her to the hospital. To bring her to safety, he'd risked being placed at the warehouse that night, of being linked to Gary's murder. He had understood the chance he was taking, yet he didn't just leave her there at the warehouse.

And if she hadn't been blind, Stevie realized, she would have identified him as the man she'd seen, the man she'd believed was Gary's killer. Allister would have been falsely accused once again. She would never have gotten to know him, never have learned the truth.

And she would never have grown to love him.

Stevie wished for sleep, but her thoughts wouldn't allow it.

She should have convinced Allister to go to the police, to get help long ago. She shouldn't have let him try to deal with Bainbridge on his own.

True, one of the things she loved about Allister was his fortitude—the courage it had taken for him to go on with his life after everything he'd been put through. But it was that same admirable courage that made Allister believe he could take on the world, Bainbridge and Fenton included.

No, if nothing else, Stevie should have convinced him to go to the police.

The sudden metallic thump of the door's slide bolt brought Stevie's head up with a start. Every muscle in her body stiffened, and when she heard the familiar squeal of hinges, she hugged her legs to her chest even tighter.

She turned her head in the direction of the door, and almost gasped when she saw the bright rectangle of light and the dark hulking shape that filled it.

Fenton.

Stevie struggled not to squint against the sudden brightness. She couldn't let Fenton know she could see him.

He came into the room, his boots making a hollow sound against the floorboards. She could just discern the hazy line of his massive shoulders, and as he came closer to her, the light from the corridor caught his face. It was little more than a blurred outline—black hair, pale skin, a slash of a mouth, and dark holes where his eyes looked down at her.

Stevie's breath was gone.

When he reached for her, she cringed at his touch and choked on a scream.

"Come on, let's go." His fingers hooked around her arm, bruising the soft flesh as he yanked her up off the mattress.

And then, suddenly, Stevie didn't want to leave her prison. She felt safer here than beyond that doorway, in the unknown. At least she knew this room. Once outside, God only knew what Fenton intended to do with her.

"Come on," he said again, his voice grating with impatience as he hauled her to her feet.

Stevie almost lost her balance, and when she reached out to block her fall, it was Fenton's arm she grabbed. She pulled back immediately.

"Where are we going?"

"For a drive," was his only answer apart from a forceful shove toward the door.

But Stevie had had just about all the manhandling she could take in one day, and she wrenched her arm from his grasp.

"Where?" she demanded more firmly this time, and spun around to face him. She looked up into those dark holes of eyes for a fleeting moment and couldn't help thinking that he looked like a caricature of Death.

"Where?" There was amusement in his voice, as though he took a certain delight in her brashness. "To meet your boyfriend is where."

Allister. So, Bainbridge was going to make a trade. Her for the coins.

"Now come on." Fenton turned her around. "Either you walk on your own, or I carry you outta here. Your choice."

Stevie started towards the light. Allister, Allister. They were going to Allister. Everything was going to be all right, she tried to convince herself. Allister would give Bainbridge the coins and—

"For your sake," Fenton added, as he guided her along the dim corridor, "I hope your boyfriend hasn't decided to keep those coins for himself. Hey, he might have skipped town already. What do you think, sweetheart? You worth a few million bucks to him?"

As repulsive as Fenton was, he had a point, Stevie thought as she groped her way along the banister and to the top of a rickety set of wooden steps. What *was* to stop Allister from taking the coins and running? After everything she'd said to him, after she'd kicked him out of her life and refused to trust him, she couldn't really blame him if he had left Danby hours ago—with or without the coins.

CHAPTER SIXTEEN

THE VOLVO'S ENGINE idled dangerously low, and Allister gave it more gas. He removed his gloves and switched off the heater. But the light sweat that beaded his brow and dampened his shirt beneath his jacket had nothing to do with the car's interior.

It was snowing again. In short bursts of wind, fat flakes tumbled down and melted instantly on the windshield. Allister looked through the blur to the steel girders of the bridge. In the Volvo's headlights, they glistened with a thin shellac of ice.

Tugging his wrist free of his leather cuff, Allister tilted his watch to catch the light of the single lamp at this end of the bridge. Seven-fifteen. He was early.

As promised, Bainbridge had called at seven on the dot. Paige and Allister had been waiting for the call, along with Devane, who had parked his car behind the studio in case anyone was watching. And the second Allister had hung up the phone, they had been ready to move. Bainbridge hadn't given him a lot of time to get out here, but Allister had broken every speed limit along the way. As he drummed his fingers against the steering wheel now, he hoped Devane would be able to assemble his men and get out here just as quickly.

It was obvious why Bainbridge had chosen this spot. The bridge experienced some traffic during the day, being on a primarily industrial street at the northwest end. But after six, when the factories shut down, the bridge would be deserted.

Allister had seen one car, though, a green Impala parked fifty yards from the east end of the bridge. Bainbridge's advance scout, Allister was certain, to ensure he'd arrived alone.

In the glow of the lamp, Allister glanced over at the shipping box on the passenger seat. Luckily Devane had agreed with him about the coins—using anything but the real goods would have been too risky.

At the precinct, he'd told Devane and Jackson everything, starting with the night of Gary's murder, how he'd taken Stevie to the hospital, how he'd tracked down Vince Fenton and had broken into the man's apartment. Finally he told them about the coins in the safe-deposit box. Through it all Devane had sipped his coffee. And when the cup was empty, the detective had methodically crushed it in his fist.

When Allister had finished, he could tell that Devane worked at keeping his voice calm, no doubt for Paige's sake. But gradually his tone had risen until he was ranting about withholding evidence and threatening Allister with the remainder of his sentence as he outlined the many ways Allister had broken his parole.

Even so, Devane recognized the fact that Stevie's life was at stake. He'd agreed with Allister that they couldn't storm Bainbridge's estate without knowing where Stevie was being held. And at last, making it clear that he didn't like the idea, Devane consented to the trade.

But the plan was far from foolproof, Allister thought. There was no way of knowing if Devane and his men would arrive on time. And he had little doubt now, given the isolated location Bainbridge had chosen, that the collector had any intention of letting either Stevie or Allister walk away from this tonight.

Allister shifted in the driver's seat. Gary's Ruger jabbed into the small of his back. He hadn't told Devane about the gun. If the detective had known, he never would have let Allister come out here. But there was no way he would have come unarmed.

Edward Bainbridge had taken everything Allister had ever worked for, everything he'd ever loved. And now the man was doing the same thing all over again. But this time it was Stevie.

And *this* time, Allister vowed silently, Bainbridge was *not* going to win. No one was going to take Stevie away from him. Not Bainbridge. Not Vince Fenton. Not even Devane.

Allister didn't care about the coins. He didn't care about the cops. He didn't even give a damn about getting Bainbridge or clearing his name anymore.

He just wanted Stevie back.

He wanted her safe.

And then he saw the headlights.

STEVIE ROCKED with the gentle lilt of the big luxury car. It smelled of leather and cigars, and faintly of liquor. All that, and she could still smell Fenton's after-shave.

He sat next to her in the back seat. As tightly as she held her body, she could not avoid touching him. His leg was hot against hers, and his broad shoulder pinned her back into the soft upholstery.

On her right was Bainbridge. He'd had at least one drink, she was sure of that. She could smell it on his breath between each quiet wheeze.

Up front, beside the driver, was another man. A big man, Stevie figured, judging by the vague shadowy bulk she could make out through her darkness.

She wasn't certain of the location where they'd linked up with Bainbridge and his other thugs. After Fenton had led her down the rickety stairs, he'd tied her hands and pushed her into the back seat of his car. It had been dark outside when he'd driven the sedan out of what she guessed was a warehouse, and Stevie had tried to catch glimpses of illuminated signs to get a sense of where he was taking her. But the lights only hurt her eyes, and the letters were meaningless blurs.

Once Fenton had pulled the sedan over, he'd guided her to Bainbridge's car, where Bainbridge himself had suggested Fenton untie her. She'd been shivering then, and not only from the cold, although she wore no coat or shoes and her heavy wool socks were wet from the hasty vehicle switch.

Now, as she clenched her hands in her lap, willing herself to stop shaking, Stevie blinked against the glare of light. After all the darkness, after praying for light all these days, she'd thought she would have welcomed it. But it only hurt her head. And the glare in her eyes had been constant from the moment she'd been in Bainbridge's car.

At first she'd thought it was the headlights of oncoming traffic, until she realized that she hadn't heard any passing cars in some time. Yet the glare was still there. And then she understood. It was the rearview mirror. Headlights from a tailing car reflected off the mirror directly into her eyes. She didn't dare squint for fear of tipping off Fenton. Instead, Stevie cast her gaze downward.

But why did Bainbridge need a second car? With Fenton, the driver, and the extra man in the front seat, what could he possibly be expecting of Allister?

"Give Smitty a call and tell him to hang back." Bainbridge's voice came from within inches of her ear, and Stevie cringed at the sound of it. "I want him to wait at the end of the bridge."

When she looked up again, the glare in the mirror was gone. Past the crest of the front seat and through the windshield, two points of light radiated out toward them through the darkness. The car slowed.

"Okay, stop here. That's him."

Stevie felt her heart skip. Allister was here close by. Her gaze fixed on the tunnel of light, and she was certain she saw a shadow pass before it.

Bainbridge turned beside her, but her gaze was riveted on that shadow in the light.

Even when Bainbridge touched a fleshy finger to her cheek, Stevie sat stock-still, focusing on the shadow she knew must be Allister. She'd come this far, she kept thinking. She could deal with anything now. All she had to do was concentrate on Allister. He was here for her.

"Well, we'll see if this boyfriend of yours is as good as his word, won't we?" Bainbridge said to her, his voice sounding as thick and ugly as the finger that crawled over her skin.

"Vince—" his tone became caustic, as though it angered him that he hadn't gotten the reaction he'd hoped for from Stevie "—get out of the car. And if he makes any moves, shoot him."

Stevie's breath caught in her throat. Fenton opened the door, and frigid air rushed in, bringing with it a new level of consciousness. In her limited peripheral vision, she caught a movement, and when she turned, the car's interior light glinted on what she guessed was Fenton's gun.

"No!" she screamed. But it didn't sound like her own voice. It was so thin, so desperate. "No!" she tried again and reached for Fenton.

She wrestled with him, grappling with his massive hands, tearing at his coat, trying to pull him back into the car. Twice she felt the hard sharp edges of the gun against her fingers.

And then someone grabbed her sweater. The collar dug into her throat, cutting off her wind, and she was yanked back into the seat.

ALLISTER CLUTCHED the small box in his left hand. The edges of his bomber jacket blew open in the cold wind as he walked toward the other car. With each stride, he felt the reassuring pressure of the Ruger against the small of his back, tucked into the waist of his jeans. But if the situation did come down to any kind of a shootout, he'd have to be damned fast. And even if he managed to draw the semiautomatic, he wouldn't stand much of a chance against a thug like Fenton.

Bainbridge's car had stopped about forty yards away, its big engine idling. In the vehicle's low beams, swirls of snow danced along the bridge's surface.

Allister never took his eyes off the car as he steadily closed the distance. He prayed that Stevie was all right. And then he prayed that she was in the car. If she wasn't, if Bainbridge had decided to keep her until he had the coins, or worse, if he had already decided she was a loose end and—

God! He couldn't think that. Not now.

The cardboard box threatened to collapse under the pressure of his grip. Another cold wind swept along the bridge and whipped at his hair, blasting snow into his face. Allister blinked and kept walking.

Thirty yards.

Twenty-five.

One of the back doors opened, and Allister stopped.

The car's interior light flickered on. There was a sudden flurry of movement, and seconds later a man got out. It was Fenton. He was holding a gun.

Allister looked back at the car, struggling to see past the low beams into the interior. There were several figures inside, lit up by the dim overhead bulb. One of them, smaller than the others, he was sure was Stevie.

His hand tightened around the box as he fought the urge to race across the bridge toward the other car. He wanted to hurl Fenton to the ground and snatch Stevie away from Bainbridge. He wanted to hold her in his arms, to feel her body safe against his. He would tell her loved he over and over; he would do whatever he needed to convince her of that.

But he had to get her out of this first.

Allister wouldn't have believed it possible, but his heart actually hurt when he thought of Stevie in that car with Bainbridge. A pain twitched deep in his chest when he imagined the terror she must be going through.

"What are you waiting for?" Fenton shouted, his voice almost lost in another gust of wind.

Allister fought the urge to look over his shoulder, to see if there was any sign of Devane and his men. But any gesture of that kind would only tip Fenton and Bainbridge off. Besides, he shouldn't be able to see the police, even if they *were* there.

"Where's Stevie?" Allister shouted, holding his position.

"She's in the car. Just bring the coins."

"No. I want to see her first. Let her out."

Fenton stared at him for a breathless moment and then leaned into the car. Allister heard someone cursing, and finally Fenton reappeared.

And then, at last, Allister saw Stevie. A helplessness churned in his gut. She was utterly dwarfed by Fenton's bulk as he dragged her out from the back seat. She stumbled in his grasp, but even at this distance, Allister recognized her steadfast determination.

It was when Fenton brought his gun up and thrust the muzzle into Stevie's ribs that Allister started to walk again. He knew he should stall the process. The more time he took, the more chance Devane had of getting here with his men. But reason stood no chance against seeing Stevie, helpless, in Fenton's ruthless grasp. And Allister couldn't cross the bridge fast enough.

When he was within ten paces of them, the other door of the car opened and Bainbridge himself stepped out.

Long years had passed since he'd seen that smug bastard's arrogant sneer, Allister thought, yet it seemed like only yesterday.

Allister stopped dead in his tracks. He hadn't imagined it could be this overpowering—the bitter animosity, the vengeful fury. He'd thought that the years would have softened those feelings. Maybe it had to do with Stevie. Maybe seeing her in Bainbridge's clutches was the final straw, but it took every last ounce of humanity left in Allister's soul to stop from screaming and lunging for Bainbridge's throat with his bare hands.

Instead, Allister made a tight fist with his right hand and crushed the box in his other. In the beams of the headlights, Bainbridge stepped to the front of the car. His full-length leather coat flapped in the wind, and with gloved fingers he flipped up the collar.

"Mr. Quaid." He raised his voice above the low rumble of the car engine, and a halo of vapor circled his head. "It's good to see you again after all these years."

"I'm sorry I can't say the same, Bainbridge."

"I'm disappointed. Here I thought you'd be happy to see an old friend."

Allister shot a glance at Stevie. Even with Fenton's arm pinning her to him, she shivered from the cold. And beneath that quiet determination, Allister recognized her fear.

"Let's get this done, Bainbridge."

"Hand over the coins."

Allister shook his head and then nodded toward Stevie. "Not until your hired ape releases her. You let her go, and when she reaches the other end of this bridge, I'll give you your coins."

Bainbridge barked out a laugh. "I don't think so, Mr. Quaid," he said finally. "Besides, she's blind. Wouldn't you rather help her to the car yourself? Now come on, let me have the package. I'd like to examine my goods first." Bainbridge did little more than raise a finger, and another man, even bulkier than Vince Fenton, stepped out of the car to stand next to his boss. "Let's not dally, Quaid. I'm not sure how much longer Vince over there can restrain himself. He's an impatient man, you know."

Allister caught the movement in his peripheral vision, and when he looked over toward Stevie, Fenton had pulled her so tightly to his chest that her feet had almost completely left the ground. A vicious grin cut the man's face in two.

Allister had no choice. He closed the gap between him and Bainbridge, and handed over the box.

It seemed an eternity as Bainbridge opened it and slid out the narrow wooden case. It took even longer for him to unclasp the lid. Allister didn't move. As Bainbridge examined the coins tucked in the velvet lining, Allister snatched glimpses of Stevie.

And when Allister thought he could wait no longer, Bainbridge finally closed the box. He slid it into his coat and looked at Allister, a cold grin sliding across his moist lips.

"It's been a pleasure doing business with you again, Mr. Quaid."

"Call off your goon, Bainbridge. Let her go."

Bainbridge nodded to Fenton, and instantly Fenton shoved Stevie forward. She stumbled onto the snowy ground.

But when Allister was about to rush to her side, he was stopped by Fenton's gun. The muzzle of the short-barreled semiautomatic was trained directly on him.

"You do realize, Mr. Quaid," Bainbridge whispered close to Allister's ear before backing off, "that I can't let the two of you go?"

Stevie's world tilted in a whirl of light and shadows. In it she searched for Allister. But there was only Fenton, standing above her. She heard snow crunch beneath someone's boots, and then she heard Bainbridge's icy voice.

"Kill them," she heard him snarl. "Kill them both."

Blurred shadows spun in slow motion.

In an instant Stevie saw Fenton's arm come up. Headlights gleamed like liquid silver against his gun. Allister's name screamed in her heart. And in a breath of frigid air, she lunged.

Pain jarred through her shoulder when she collided with Fenton's broad chest. She heard his surprised grunt as he staggered back. And then Allister yelled her name seconds before an ear-shattering explosion split the night.

When Fenton threw her to the ground this second time, Stevie thought for a moment she'd been shot. But other than the dull throb in her shoulder, there was no pain. She gathered herself again and was about to go after Fenton once more when Allister's voice stopped her—sure and clear through her dim haze.

"Don't, Fenton." His warning was followed by the metallic click of a gun being cocked.

Stevie squinted as lights suddenly flooded the bridge, and in moments there was a voice amplified over a bullhorn.

"Hold it," the voice demanded. "This is the police. Everyone put down your weapons."

Stevie looked at the vague outline of the figure she knew was Fenton. He didn't move. He stood only a few feet away from her. It was then that she realized his gun was pointed at her.

"I mean it." The voice on the bullhorn blared again, and this time Stevie recognized it as Devane's. "I got twenty men out here on this bridge, and I don't think you wanna find out if I'm bluffing. Now put the gun down and step away from the woman. Now!"

Still Fenton didn't move.

It was Allister's voice that gave Stevie hope. She saw a shadow shift to her right and knew it had to be him.

"Fenton, if you don't believe him," Allister warned, "then at least believe me."

Whether it was a look Allister had given him then, or whether Fenton had finally grasped the futility of his situation, his arm lowered. Stevie saw him drop his weapon, and then his hands came up as he backed off. There were even more lights now, and shadowy figures stormed the bridge, running across the packed snow, shouting orders.

Stevie turned to where she'd heard Allister's voice last. Backlit by the glare of headlamps, she saw a silhouette. Light turned to liquid, seeming to melt around the approaching figure. And when strong arms reached for her, lifting her from the snowy ground, Stevie knew it was Allister.

Allister heard Stevie's whimper of relief and pulled her to him. Her body shivered once against his before she seemed to take strength from his embrace. Her arms tightened around his neck.

She murmured his name, almost chanting it as he held her close. And only when he lowered her to the ground again did she stop. Taking her by the shoulders, Allister held her at arm's length.

Nothing had ever looked so good in his life.

"Stevie, are you all right? Did they hurt you?"

She shook her head. Her face glistened with tears, but her smile shone through.

"Are you sure?"

She nodded, and then Allister noticed her eyes. It could have been the play of the lights coupled with his own exhaustion, but as her face tilted toward him, it seemed as though she was looking at him.

Allister touched her cheek with one cold finger and wiped away a tear. Her eyes never left his.

"Stevie, can you . . ."

But he didn't need to finish. She was already nodding.

"Allister," she whispered, the last syllable curving her lips into a heartrending smile. She reached for him, her fingers trembling as they caressed his face.

When he swept her up into his arms, Allister felt his own darkness slip away. As the police stormed the bridge, he was only vaguely aware of the arrests being made. It was Stevie who was the center of his world now. And if she could ever find it in her heart to forgive him, Allister swore he would never let her go.

CHAPTER SEVENTEEN

STEVIE PULLED her robe around herself and stepped closer to the window. Her breath cast a thin fog against the cold pane, and when it cleared, she watched snow sparkle down in the pale shaft of lamplight. It scurried in fleeting tunnels of wind, and then disappeared into the early-morning shadows.

Behind her, the bedroom lay in darkness, and she could hear Allister's low breathing, a familiar and comforting sound.

With the nightmare of Bainbridge behind them, remembering last night's events was not so terrifying. It wasn't until Devane had found them in the midst of the commotion, assuring them that they had Bainbridge, Fenton and his other thugs in custody, that Stevie realized what Allister had done. By going to the police for help, he had taken a gamble with his freedom. He'd had to set aside his mistrust and his personal fears, and then he'd risked his own life for hers. If there had been any lingering doubt whatsoever in Stevie's mind about Allister's love, it was gone in that instant.

As Allister had guided her to the car, Devane had followed. She remembered the detective commending Allister. And when he'd told her she was lucky, she hadn't known if the detective was referring to her ordeal with Bainbridge or to her reunion with Allister.

Devane had agreed to let them go, provided they file statements in the morning. But when he suggested that Allister take Stevie to the hospital, Stevie was adamant. She'd had more than her share of hospitals, she argued, and so Allister had driven her home.

Paige had been absolutely frantic with worry by the time they came through the front door. She'd thrown her arms around Stevie, and when she realized that Stevie could actually see her, Paige had hugged her again. By the time Paige left the studio a little later, she was already bubbling over with plans for the Armatrading reshoot.

Still, Stevie's vision had been very distorted. Dr. Sterling had been wrong about the recovery time, but he'd been right about one thing. The best place to be during that disorienting period of blurred vision and wavering peripheral was in bed.

Stevie couldn't resist a smile now as she remembered how Allister had carried her to her bed, and the tender and passionate lovemaking they'd shared. No, she couldn't think of anyplace she'd have rather been.

She was still smiling when she heard Allister move through the dark room and come up behind her. He wrapped his arms around her waist and drew her back against his strong solid body.

"What are you doing up so early?" His question was a hoarse whisper in her ear.

"Watching the snow." She swayed in the solace of his embrace. "I never thought snow could look so good."

And she never thought she could feel so good, Stevie mused as she leaned her head back against Allister's chest. She never dreamed that the kind of love she had for Allister was possible. For all these years, she'd always been too wrapped up in her work.

It had taken the blindness, a forced break from her photography, to make her realize what she'd been missing in her life. And now that her sight had returned, she understood that its temporary loss had actually been a blessing. Without her blindness, she might never have found Allister. And he was the one and only thing she *had* seen in that darkness.

Turning in his embrace, Stevie pulled away far enough so she could look at him. Dark hair framed his handsome face—a face more beautiful than anything she could have possibly imagined. She traced her fingers along the lines of his face as she had before, but this time her eyes followed: caressing the high, chiseled cheekbones, roving along his square jaw to his almost defiant chin, and finally trailing down and across his broad chest. And when she looked up again and caught his dark gaze, she saw the smile in his eyes as his lips curved beneath her fingertips.

Seeing him in the delicate glow of the street lamp, feeling the heat of his body against hers, Stevie felt a shiver of familiar desire sweep through her.

"What?" Allister asked, amusement turning up the corners of his mouth.

Stevie shook her head. "Nothing," she said, and traced the softness of his lips. "It's just... you're a real sight for sore eyes, you know that?"

She couldn't see his smile as he drew her to him, but she felt its curve against her mouth. And as he kissed her, as he pressed his body to hers, Stevie felt utter peace. In Allister's arms, she'd found a profound sense of belonging, and she couldn't imagine ever being anywhere else.

Allister pulled back from their kiss and stared down at her. She met his admiring gaze, and he hoped she could see the love there.

"So, do you think it's a sight you could get used to?" he asked.

"And what exactly do you mean by that?"

But Stevie knew what he meant. He could see her understanding in the way her eyes sparkled and her lips parted into one of those breathtaking smiles of hers.

"What I mean is, do you think it's a sight you could spend the rest of your life with?"

She studied him then, as though thinking about it, but her answer was already there, lighting up her eyes.

"Yes," Stevie said at last. "Yes, Allister, I think I could—quite easily."

When he drew her into his embrace, Allister wondered if he should pinch himself to be sure he wasn't dreaming.

Get on with your life, Gary had advised him. But never in his wildest dreams had Allister imagined that getting on with his life could be this glorious, that he could find such love and passion. Yes, he'd get on with his life now—his new life with Stevie.

Allister felt her tense slightly and pull away, and in a glimmer of panic, he followed her gaze out the window. But the street was empty, only the pale glow of the lamp and the drifting snow.

"What is it, Stevie?"

She gave him a quick smile and stepped back.

"Where are you going?"

"To get my camera, Allister. I don't want to ever forget this moment."

But he caught her wrist then and tugged her back, wrapping his arms around her.

"I'll give you something to remember this moment," he murmured seconds before he claimed her lips.

They were breathless when at last they parted, and he searched Stevie's dark eyes. "So, do you still want your camera?"

"Camera?" she asked, sharing his smile. "What camera?"

Heartbreak RANCH

Four generations of independent women…
Four heartwarming, romantic stories of the West…
Four incredible authors…

Fern Michaels
Jill Marie Landis
Dorsey Kelley
Chelley Kitzmiller

Saddle up with Heartbreak Ranch, an outstanding
Western collection that will take you on a whirlwind
trip through four generations and the exciting,
romantic adventures of four strong women who
have inherited the ranch from Bella Duprey,
famed Barbary Coast madam.

Available in March,
wherever Harlequin books are sold.

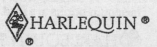

HARLEQUIN ®

FREE VALENTINE'S BROOCH!
$9.95 U.S.
retail value

This Valentine's Day Harlequin brings you
all the essentials—romance, chocolate
and jewelry—in:

VALENTINE *Delights*

Matchmaking chocolate-shop owner Papa Valentine
dispenses sinful desserts, mouth-watering
chocolates…and advice to the lovelorn, in this
collection of three delightfully romantic stories
by Meryl Sawyer, Kate Hoffmann and Gina Wilkins.

As our special Valentine's Day gift to you, each copy
of *Valentine Delights* will have a beautiful, filigreed,
heart-shaped brooch attached to the cover.

Make this your most delicious Valentine's Day
ever with *Valentine Delights!*

Available in February wherever
Harlequin books are sold.

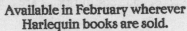

HARLEQUIN ®
®

Look us up on-line at: http://www.romance.net

VAL97

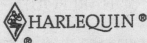

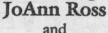

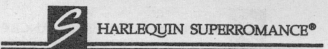

HARLEQUIN SUPERROMANCE®

ANOTHER MAN'S CHILD
by
Tara Taylor Quinn

Marcus Cartwright is rich and handsome. What's more, he's in love with his wife. And Lisa Cartwright adores her husband. *Their marriage, however, is falling apart.*

That's because Marcus can't give Lisa the baby they've always longed for.

So he's decided to give Lisa her freedom—to find and marry someone else. To have her *own* child.

It's a freedom Lisa doesn't want. But she can't convince Marcus of that.

So Lisa decides to take matters into her own hands. She decides to have a baby. And she's not going to tell Marcus until the artificial-insemination procedure is over....

But will Marcus be able to accept Another Man's Child?

Watch for *Another Man's Child* by Tara Taylor Quinn
Available in February 1997
wherever Harlequin books are sold.

Look us up on-line at: http://www.romance.net

9ML-2/97